美语从头学

赖世雄初级美语 上

赖世雄 著

外文出版社
FOREIGN LANGUAGES PRESS

图书在版编目(CIP)数据

初级美语. 上 / 赖世雄著. — 北京 : 外文出版社, 2014 (2018年重印)
（美语从头学）
ISBN 978-7-119-08682-8

Ⅰ. ①初… Ⅱ. ①赖… Ⅲ. ①英语－美国－教材 Ⅳ. ①H310.1

中国版本图书馆CIP数据核字(2014)第024159号

选题策划：知语文化
特约编辑：贾志敏
责任编辑：李春英
装帧设计：郭海亭
印刷监制：冯　浩

初级美语. 上

作　　者：赖世雄

出版发行：外文出版社有限责任公司
地　　址：北京市西城区百万庄大街24号　邮政编码：100037
网　　址：http://www.flp.com.cn　电子邮箱：flp@cipg.org.cn
电　　话：008610-68320579（总编室）　008610-68995964/68995883（编辑部）
008610-68995852（发行部）　008610-68996183（投稿电话）
印　　制：北京华创印务有限公司
经　　销：新华书店 / 外文书店
开　　本：880 mm×1230 mm　1/32
印　　张：10.625　字　　数：300千字
版　　次：2018 年 6 月第 1 版第 17 次印刷
书　　号：ISBN 978-7-119-08682-8
定　　价：34.00元（平装）

　如有印装问题本社负责调换（电话：68995852）
如有光盘质量问题，请致电 60555932

序

这套《赖世雄美语从头学》系列丛书是专为英语初学者以及想重新学好英文的人士所编写的。

本系列丛书其实是我一生学习英文的缩影。1961 年,我在台北念初一起就接触英文,6 年的中学生涯中,由于语法的艰涩用语不易了解,背单词又太累,懒散的我索性放弃了学习,结果在大学联考中名落孙山,英文竟只得了 7 分(满分是 100 分)! 和很多联考失利的年轻人一样,我选择了当兵,我的英文就是在当兵期间重新学习的。这段期间我扭转了学习态度,按照自行摸索的方法,竟然让我全凭自修学好英文,后来也考上了公费赴美留学,在美国明尼苏达大学攻读大众传播及英语教学的硕士学位。可惜在念博士课程时内人罹患尿毒症,不得不中断学业,赶返台北照顾内人迄今。

从一个原本对英文一窍不通的我,到今日热爱英文并以英语教学为终身职业的我,这个转变全在于我在学习英文的路途上一路坚持。1990 年,时任中央人民广播电台科教部主任的张力先生请我在该台向全中国推广英文听、说、读、写的全向式教学。面对这项既光荣又艰巨的挑战,我随即召集台北常春藤出版社所有的中外编辑,按照我学习英文的切身经验,历经数年辛苦编写以及反复斟酌修改,这套《赖世雄美语从头学》终于问世。

为了让读者真正学懂学透这套丛书,我特别邀请发音纯正的 Jennifer 以及在台湾大学外文系任教的美籍老师 Bruce 一起逐课录制讲解。这些内容早年在中央人民广播电台播出以来就一直深受好评。阅读本套丛书时若能配合这些有声课程的使用,学习效果会远超出读者的想象。

这套丛书自从上市以来就一版再版,由此可见广大读者对这套书的信任和喜爱。这些年我们在全中国不知培养了多少因为学习本套丛书而成功的人士。例如知名的李阳老师。有一年李老师邀请我去他的广州集团总部访问时,就当面跟我说:“我就是看了您的书才有今天!” 这套书上市以来,无数读者纷纷感慨相见恨晚。他们直言这套书充满了 “正能量”,帮助他们少走了很多弯路。一位读者通过微博告诉我们他大学四级没过,很是沮丧,经同学推荐开始学习这套书,结果一发而不可收拾,半年苦读后在研究生考试中英语取得出人意料的高分,顺利考上了研究生。还有一位同学在跟着这套教材学习之后,凭借优秀的英语能力获得了在联合国机构工作的机会。他们虽然都是普通的学子,但他们的这些进步让我们倍感欣慰。如果这套丛书能够帮助海峡两岸超过四亿的英语学习者重拾丢掉的英语,让流利的英语成为大家自信的资本,点亮以后的人生,那是一件多么荣幸的事！我本人愿以此为终身职志。

随着时代的进步,大家对英语学习资料的要求也更加多元化。我们编辑团队也在不断努力为大家提供更加便捷的学习途径,我们也在手机、网络等方面做着全新的尝试。对于本套丛书我们也一直努力改版升级。此次改版除了让版面更加赏心悦目外,重点在于我们又增加了辅助大家学习的新内容。

1. 增加了朗读音频。除了详解的讲解音频外，我们力邀美籍专业老师录制了纯正的美语朗读音频。标准的语音一定能够让你更加自信地讲英文，迅速在人群中脱颖而出。

2. 随书附赠学习手册。每册书我们都附赠一本实用手册。内含本册书的单词表、短语表以及根据读者学习程度精心设计的“对症”学习锦囊，包括生活口语、职场口语、实用写作、成语妙解等。我们希望这些锦上添花的学习资料能够将读者打造成为真正的英语全能王。

本人在人生最黄金阶段编写及讲授本套丛书,愿将它献给所有想学好英文的朋友!

赖世雄

于台北常春藤

学英语，其实有方法

由于我学英文时，听、说、读、写并重，使我多次在国际性会议中担任同声传译及在大学教学时，皆能游刃有余。我是怎么学好英语的呢？我天赋平平，起步也就是当年的英语七分，只不过在后来的英语学习中秉持了以下三个学习态度，经历了三个学习阶段而已。

三个学习态度：

1. 善用零星时间：我在走路、等车、坐车、休息的时间都在说英语或看英文书籍。
2. 少就是多、慢就是快：我英文程度差，所以每天只看一两句英文，勤查字典，了解句意后，就利用零星时间慢慢地念，一遍遍地重复念，我最后竟然能够凭声音记住单词、短语或句子，不知不觉中说英语的速度也愈来愈快了。
3. 持之以恒、永不放弃：学习语言贵在勤加复习，每日不间断地练习，终有成功的一天。

三个学习阶段：

第一阶段：学习音标

我善用零星时间，每天只学三至四个音标，配合胶质唱片随着外籍老师灌制的录音跟着念，一遍一遍重复地念。元音学完后，再学辅音，约两个星期为一周期，如此反复练习三个月后，我打开字典就可以凭音标念出每一个英文单词的正确发音。

第二阶段：学习入门会话

我的做法是：先查字典以了解每一课会话的字词内容，再慢速将会话内容利用零星时间反复念出来。到了下午我会找个无人的地方，以一人分饰两角的方式把会话反复表演出来，并不时加入自己曾学过的词汇以扩大会话内容，如此才能活学活用。经过三个月后，我在路上见到外国人时竟然敢开口，更因为自己对发音的挑剔及自信心，常获得老外的称许。

第三阶段：大量“阅读”

我深知仅从会话学英语，所学得的词汇及常识是有限的，于是我在自修学会基础会话的能力后，便转而注重英文阅读能力的培养。

我的做法是看到文章就念出来，这才是真正的“阅读”：我选择内容生动、文字浅显的文章入门。一旦选定文章后，我本着“少就是多”的学习态度，每天只精读一小段。我会先以慢速朗读这一小段（愈慢愈好），以粗略了解这一小段的内容。再以字典勤查每一个单词，并将字典内的相关短语或例句一一抄写在笔记本上。最后，我再将该小段的英文译成中文，然后将此中文以口译的方式翻成英文。之后，就以自己的英文叙述该小段的内容，直至我当天深夜上床睡觉为止。这个做法有助于我对字词运用的了解及口译能力的培养。时至今日，我可以在阅读英文报纸或杂志之后，随即用英文说出报章杂志的内容！

读者不难发现，《赖世雄美语从头学》就是我学习英文的过程。读者购买这套丛书时，马上会发现不论哪一本书，我们都本着“完全解析”的态度将读者学习英文可能遇到的疑难杂症全都以系统而又完整的方式解说，读者在看这些书时会觉得我就在您身旁一样，不时鼓励您向前迈进。

我们都想把英文学好，我做到了，你当然也可以做到！如果你现在的程度比“七分”好，那你就可能比我做的更好。

赖世雄

于台北常春藤

目 录
CONTENTS

Lesson 1 Self Introduction
自我介绍 …… 1

Lesson 2 Nice to Meet You
幸会 …… 5

Lesson 3 My Family
我的家人 …… 7

Lesson 4 What Do You Do?
你是做什么的？ …… 12

Lesson 5 Tony and His Family
托尼和他的家人 …… 14

Lesson 6 Is This Your Dog?
这是你的狗吗？ …… 19

Lesson 7 Tony and Tina
托尼和蒂娜 …… 21

Lesson 8 Do You Speak Spanish?
你会说西班牙语吗？ …… 26

Lesson 9 A Busy Family
忙碌的家庭 …… 28

Lesson 10 What Are You Doing?
你在做什么？ …… 33

Lesson 11 My Foreign Classmates
我的外籍同学 …… 35

Lesson 12 Where's Chen from?
小陈是哪一国人？ …… 40

Lesson 13 Nobody Is at Home
没人在家 ······ 42
Lesson 14 Why Are You Smiling?
你为什么在微笑? ······ 48
Lesson 15 Mrs. Lee's Kitchen
李太太的厨房 ······ 50
Lesson 16 Where Are My Keys?
我的钥匙在哪里? ······ 56
Lesson 17 My Hometown
我的家乡 ······ 58
Lesson 18 Is It near the Post Office?
就在邮局附近吗? ······ 63
♫ 怀念老歌园地 ♫
Dreamin'
梦想 ······ 65
Lesson 19 I Have Two Friends
我有两个朋友 ······ 71
Lesson 20 She Is Beautiful
她很漂亮 ······ 76
Lesson 21 I Don't Know Anyone
我谁都不认识 ······ 79
Lesson 22 Do You Want to Dance?
你想跳舞吗? ······ 85
Lesson 23 The Book Is Mine
这本书是我的 ······ 87
Lesson 24 It's Mine
它是我的 ······ 93

Lesson 25 My Father
我的父亲 …… 96
Lesson 26 He Usually Plays Tennis
他通常打网球 …… 102
Lesson 27 Jack and His Dog
杰克和他的狗 …… 104
Lesson 28 I Always Walk
我都是走路去 …… 109
Lesson 29 Poor Dick
可怜的迪克 …… 111
Lesson 30 Money Doesn't Grow on Trees
挣钱是很辛苦的 …… 116
Lesson 31 Poor Amy
可怜的艾米 …… 118
Lesson 32 Coins for the Phone
打投币电话 …… 122
Lesson 33 She Wants to Wear Something Formal
她想穿正式的衣服 …… 125
Lesson 34 Let's Go to a Disco
咱们到迪斯科舞厅去 …… 130
Lesson 35 There's Little Food
菜很少 …… 133
Lesson 36 A Lot of Bills
许多账单 …… 138
♫ 怀念老歌园地 ♫
All I Have to Do Is Dream
我只能梦想 …… 140

Lesson 37 A Wonderful Time
美好时光 …… 147
Lesson 38 Nobody Answered the Phone
没人接电话 …… 152
Lesson 39 Homesickness
乡愁 …… 155
Lesson 40 Everybody Spoke English
大家都说英语 …… 160
Lesson 41 Going Camping
露营 …… 163
Lesson 42 Are You Having Fun?
你玩得愉快吗? …… 169
Lesson 43 Killing Two Birds with One Stone
两全其美 …… 171
Lesson 44 She Had a Bad Cold
她患了重感冒 …… 177
Lesson 45 What a Nightmare!
真是一场噩梦啊! …… 179
Lesson 46 A Terrible Headache
头痛得很厉害 …… 184
Lesson 47 Be Polite
要有礼貌 …… 186
Lesson 48 Don't Mention It
别客气 …… 191
Lesson 49 Never Talk to Strangers
千万别跟陌生人说话 …… 194
Lesson 50 You're Sally, Aren't You?

你是萨莉，对不对？ ······ 198

Lesson 51 My Girlfriend
我的女友 ······ 200

Lesson 52 Sam's OK
山姆不错 ······ 206

Lesson 53 Country Life
乡间生活 ······ 209

Lesson 54 I Like Brighter Colors
我喜欢较明亮的颜色 ······ 214

♫ 怀念老歌园地 ♫
Stoney
史东妮 ······ 216

Lesson 55 More Is Not Always Better
多未必佳 ······ 223

Lesson 56 I Want the Cheaper One
我要买那块便宜的手表 ······ 228

Lesson 57 The Elephant and the Whale
大象与鲸鱼 ······ 230

Lesson 58 The Smartest Teacher
最聪明的老师 ······ 235

Lesson 59 My Best Friend
我最好的朋友 ······ 238

Lesson 60 The Longest River in the World
世界上最长的河流 ······ 242

Lesson 61 The Hare and the Turtle
兔子与乌龟 ······ 245

Lesson 62 Practice Makes Perfect

熟能生巧 …… 251

Lesson 63 Saving a Drowning Boy

救难记 …… 254

Lesson 64 Dan's a Good Swimmer

丹很会游泳 …… 260

Lesson 65 The Fortune-teller

算命师 …… 262

Lesson 66 Will It Leave on Time?

它会准时开吗? …… 267

Lesson 67 Getting Married

结婚 …… 270

Lesson 68 Are You Going to Come?

你会来吗? …… 274

Lesson 69 Running a Bookstore

经营书店 …… 276

Lesson 70 When Will You Be Moving?

你什么时候搬家? …… 280

Lesson 71 Working Hard

努力用功 …… 283

Lesson 72 Remember to Wash

别忘了漱洗 …… 288

Lesson 73 Joe's Restaurant

乔的餐厅 …… 290

Lesson 74 You Ought to Learn to Swim

你应当学习游泳 …… 295

Lesson 75 Michael's Dream

迈克尔的梦想 …… 297

Lesson 76 I Want to Be a Doctor
我想当医生 303
Lesson 77 Rome Wasn't Built in a Day
罗马不是一天建成的 305
Lesson 78 Don't Be Discouraged
不要泄气 311
Lesson 79 Showing Off
炫耀 313
Lesson 80 I'm Good at Cooking
我擅长烹饪 317
♫ 怀念老歌园地 ♫
Tennessee Waltz
田纳西华尔兹 319

Lesson 1

Self Introduction

自我介绍

1 *Reading* 阅读

My name is Robert. My friends call me Bob. I am twenty years old. I am Chinese. I come from Beijing. There are six people in my family. I have one younger sister and two older brothers. We are not rich, but we are a happy family.

我叫罗伯特。我的朋友们都叫我鲍勃。我 20 岁，中国人，籍贯北京，家里有六口人。我有一个妹妹和两个哥哥。我们虽不富有，但家庭却很幸福。

2 Vocabulary & Idioms 单词短语注解

1. **name** [nem] *n.* 名字
   What's your name, please? 请问你叫什么名字?
2. **friend** [frɛnd] *n.* 朋友
   He has many friends. 他有许多朋友。
3. **call** [kɔl] *vt.* 称，叫(名)
   Cindy calls her doll Baby. 辛迪把她的洋娃娃叫做宝贝。
4. **Chinese** [tʃaɪˋniz] *a.* 中国人的 & *n.* 中国人
5. **come** [kʌm] *vi.* 来自
   come from... 来自于……
   I come from Japan. 我是日本人。
6. **people** [ˋpipl̩] *n.* 人们
   注意
   people 表示“人们”时，只作复数用。我们可说 two people（两个人）、three people（三个人）、many people（许多人）等，却不可说 one people。若欲表示“一个人”时，应说 one person 或 a person。
   There are many people at the station. 车站里有许多人。
   There is only <u>one people</u> in the room. (×)
   → There is only <u>one person</u> in the room. (√)
   房间里只有一个人。
7. **family** [ˋfæmәlɪ] *n.* 家庭
   He has a large family. 他家里人口很多。
8. **younger sister** 妹妹 older sister 姐姐
   younger brother 弟弟 older brother 哥哥
9. **rich** [rɪtʃ] *a.* 富有的
   The old man is rich, but he is not happy.
   这位老先生很有钱，但他却不快乐。

10. **happy** [ˈhæpɪ] *a.* 快乐的

I feel happy when I am with you. 跟你在一起时，我就感到快乐。

3 Grammar Points 语法重点

本课介绍动词 call 作不完全及物动词的用法，以及表示年龄及籍贯的说法。

1. **My friends call me Bob.** 我的朋友们都叫我鲍勃。

call [kɔl] *vt.* 称……为……

此处的 call 在语法中称为不完全及物动词；换言之，call 仍是及物动词，之后应接宾语，但意思仍不完全，故须置名词于该宾语之后，以补足句意的完整。该名词称为宾语补足语。

例 They call the little girl.... (×，句意不完整)

他们称这小女孩为……

→ They call the little girl Mary. (√)

他们称这小女孩为玛丽。

2. **I am twenty years old.** 我 20 岁。

a. 此类句子结构为：

人 + be 动词 + 数字 + year (s) + old　某人几岁了

例 My baby boy is one year old. 我的小宝贝一周岁了。

He is twenty-five years old. 他 25 岁。

b. 上列例句中的 old 亦可用 of age 取代。

He is twenty-five years old.

= He is twenty-five years of age.

* age [edʒ] *n.* 年纪

c. 谈到 age 还有一个很好的用法：

look young for one's age 看起来比实际年轻

= look younger than one really is

例 You look young for your age.

= You look younger than you really are.

你看起来比实际要年轻。

3. **I am Chinese.** 我是中国人。

= I am a Chinese.

第一例中的 Chinese 是形容词，之前不置不定冠词“a”；第二例中的 Chinese 则作名词，之前须置“a”。

4. **There are six people in my family.** 我家里有六口人。

a. there 置于句首，之后接 be 动词（is, are）时，作“有”解。句型如下：

there is + 单数名词 + 表示场所的介词短语

there are + 复数名词 + 表示场所的介词短语

例 There is a book on the desk. 桌上有一本书。

There are thirty students in my class. 我班上有 30 个学生。

b. there [ðɛr] 一词则是副词，本意为“那里”。

例 Put the book there. 把书放在那里。

4 *Substitution* 替换

1. A: What's your name?	A: 你叫什么名字？
B: My name is Peter Wang.	B: 我叫王彼得。
= I'm Peter Wang.	

---

2. A: How old are you?	A: 你几岁了？
B: I'm eighteen years old.	B: 我 18 岁。
= I'm eighteen years of age.	

---

3. A: Where are you from?	A: 你是什么地方人？
B: I am from Shanxi.	B: 我是山西人。
= I come from Shanxi.	

---

4. A: How many people are there in your family?	A: 你家里有几口人？
B: There are five people in my family.	B: 五口。
= Five.	

Lesson 2

Nice to Meet You

幸会

1 *Dialogue* 实用会话

Mike: Hi! My name is Mike.

Nancy: Hi! I'm Nancy. Nice to meet you.

Mike: Nice to meet you, too.

Nancy: Where are you from?

Mike: I'm from Shanghai. And you?

Nancy: I'm from Chicago.

迈克：嗨！我叫迈克。

南希：嗨！我叫南希。幸会。

迈克：幸会。

南希：你是什么地方人？

迈克：我是上海人。你呢？

南希：我是芝加哥人。

2 *Key Points* 重点提示

1. **(It's) Nice to meet you.** 幸会。

   = (I'm) Pleased to meet you.

   = (I'm) Glad to meet you.

2. **nice** [naɪs] *a.* 好的

3. **meet** [mit] *vt.* 遇见
4. **too** [tu] *adv.* 也
5. **Where are you from?** 你是什么地方人？
= Where do you come from?

3 请依个人情况回答下列问题

1. What do your friends call you?
My ________________________.
2. How old are you?
I ______________.
3. Are you Chinese?
Yes, ___________.
4. How many people are there in your family?
There are ____________________________.
5. How many brothers and sisters do you have?
I ____.
6. Where are you from?
I __________________.

范例
1. My friends call me Johnny.
2. I am twenty-eight years old.
3. Yes, I am Chinese.
4. There are six people in my family.
5. I have two brothers and one sister.
6. I am from Beijing.

Lesson 3

My Family

我的家人

1 *Reading* 阅读

My father is a teacher. He works during the day. My mother is a nurse. She works at night. They only see each other on the weekends.

My brothers, my sister and I don't work. We are students. Because my parents have to work, we do the housework. But we never complain.

我爸爸是老师。他白天上班。妈妈则是护士。她晚上上班。他们只有在周末才会碰面。

哥哥、妹妹和我没有上班。我们都是学生。因为爸妈要上班，家务都由我们来做。但我们从不埋怨。

2 Vocabulary & Idioms 单词短语注解

1. **father** [ˋfɑðɚ] *n.* 父亲
2. **teacher** [ˋtitʃɚ] *n.* 老师
3. **work** [wɝk] *vi.* 工作
   My mother works in a hospital. 我妈妈在医院里工作。
4. **during** [ˋdjʊrɪŋ] *prep.* 在……的时候
   Cats sleep during the day. 猫儿白天的时候睡觉。
5. **day** [de] *n.* 白天
6. **mother** [ˋmʌðɚ] *n.* 母亲
7. **nurse** [nɝs] *n.* 护士
8. **see** [si] *vt.* 看见，和……见面
   I see my friends on the weekends. 我都是在周末和朋友们见面。
9. **weekend** [ˋwikˏɛnd] *n.* 周末（星期六和星期日不需上班的时间）
   The pool is closed this weekend. 本周末这个游泳池关闭。
10. **student** [ˋstjudənt] *n.* 学生
11. **because** [bɪˋkɔz] *conj.* 因为
    Tom is not here because he is sick. 汤姆不在这里，因为他生病了。
12. **parents** [ˋpærənts] *n.* 父母
13. **do** [du] *vt.* 做
14. **housework** [ˋhausˏwɝk] *n.* 家务
    Housework is really boring. 家务实在令人乏味。
15. **never** [ˋnɛvɚ] *adv.* 从不
    Father never eats breakfast. 爸爸从来不吃早餐。
16. **complain** [kəmˋplen] *vi.* 抱怨
    Father is always busy, but he never complains.
    我爸爸总是很忙，可是他从来不抱怨。

3 Grammar Points 语法重点

本课主要介绍人称代词的种类及其用法，并介绍介词 during、代词 each other 及助动词 have to 的用法。

1. **My father is a teacher. He works during the day.**

   我爸爸是老师。他白天上班。

   上例中 He 为阳性的代词，代替 My father。

   在本课中，我们特别介绍了人称代词的用法。下面的表格可帮助读者熟悉各种人称代词的用法：

<table>
<tr><td rowspan="2">数 / 格 / 人称</td><td colspan="2">单数</td><td colspan="2">复数</td></tr>
<tr><td>主格</td><td>宾格</td><td>主格</td><td>宾格</td></tr>
<tr><td>第一人称</td><td>I 我</td><td>me 我</td><td>we 我们</td><td>us 我们</td></tr>
<tr><td>第二人称</td><td>you 你</td><td>you 你</td><td>you 你们</td><td>you 你们</td></tr>
<tr><td>第三人称</td><td>he 他</td><td>him 他</td><td rowspan="3">they
他们；她们；它们</td><td rowspan="3">them
他们；她们；它们</td></tr>
<tr><td></td><td>she 她</td><td>her 她</td></tr>
<tr><td></td><td>it 它</td><td>it 它</td></tr>
</table>

注意

a. 以上表格中主格项目内的人称代词在句中要作主语，宾格项目内的人称代词则作宾语。

   例 Peter likes music. He is a musician.

   彼得喜欢音乐。他是音乐家。

   Peter and I are teachers. We teach at the same school.

   彼得和我都是老师。我们在同一所学校任教。

   I have a younger sister. I love she very much. (×)

   → I have a younger sister. I love her very much. (√)

   我有一个妹妹。我很爱她。

   You and Peter are from Japan. You are Japanese.

   你和彼得来自日本。你们是日本人。

b. it 是代词，可用来代替任何单数的动植物或其他无生命的东西（如书、电扇等）。

   例 I see a tree there. It is very tall. 我看到那边有棵树。它很高。

   This book is interesting. I enjoy reading it.

这本书很有趣，我很喜欢看。

2. **during the day** 在白天

at night 在晚上

以上两个短语作对称用法时，亦可以用 by day 和 by night 取代。

例 John sleeps during the day and works at night.

= John sleeps by day and works by night. 约翰白天睡觉晚上工作。

3. **They only see each other on the weekends.**

他们只有在周末才会碰面。

a. 上句中的 each other 是代词，表示两者的"彼此"的意思，在句中只作宾语。句中的主语必须限定为两者。

例 John and Mary are a couple. They love each other.

约翰和玛丽是一对夫妇。他们彼此相爱。

b. one another 也是代词，但表示三者或三者以上的"彼此"，在句中也只作宾语。句中的主语必须为三个或三个以上的人物。

例 Mary and her three older sisters live together.

They love one another.

玛丽和她三个姐姐住在一起。她们彼此相亲相爱。

4. **Because my parents have to work, we do the housework.**

因为爸妈要上班，家务都由我们来做。

此处 have to 为助动词，表示"必须、不得不"的意思。must 亦为助动词，表示"必须"，但与 have to 有所区别：

must 常指义务或责任上的"必须"；have to 则有"强制"或"非做不可"的意味。

例 We must love our country. 我们必须爱国。

You have to finish all the work before you may go home.

你必须做完所有的工作才能回家。

4 Substitution 替换

1. A: What does your father do? A: 你父亲是做什么的?
   B: He is | a teacher. | a farmer. | a soldier. B: 他是老师 / 农民 / 军人。

B: He is	a teacher.	B: 他是老师 / 农民 / 军人。
	a farmer.	
	a soldier.	

---

2. A: When does he work? A: 他在什么时间工作?

B: He works	during the day.	B: 他白天工作。
	during the week.	他除周末外整星期都要工作。
	on the weekends.	他周末工作。

Lesson 4

What Do You Do?

你是做什么的？

1 *Dialogue* 实用会话

Tony: What do you do, Jenny?

Jenny: I'm a secretary. And you?

Tony: I'm a construction worker.

Jenny: Do you like your work?

Tony: Yes, I do. How about you?

Jenny: Well, I want to be an actress.

托尼：珍妮，你是做什么的？

珍妮：我是秘书。你呢？

托尼：我是建筑工人。

珍妮：你喜欢你的工作吗？

托尼：是的，喜欢。你呢？

珍妮：嗯，我想当演员。

2 *Key Points* 重点提示

1. **What do you do?** 你是做什么的？

= What's your occupation?

* occupation [ˌɑkjəˋpeʃən] *n.* 职业

2. **secretary** [ˋsɛkrəˏtɛrɪ] *n.* 秘书

3. **construction worker** [kənˋstrʌkʃən ˏwɝkɚ] *n.* 建筑工人

4. **How about you?** 你呢?

= And you?

例 A: I like music. | And you? / How about you? | 我喜欢音乐。你呢?

B: Me, too. 我也喜欢。

5. **want to +** 动词原形　想要……

例 I want to see him now. 我想要现在就见他。

He wants to be an English teacher. 他想要当英文老师。

6. **actress** [ˋæktrɪs] *n.* 女演员

actor [ˋæktɚ] *n.* 男演员

3 请于下列空格中填入适当的词

My father __1__ a farmer. I __2__ a construction worker. We __3__ very busy. We work __4__ the week. I __5__ a sister. She __6__ a student. __7__ sister __8__ to be a secretary.

解答 1. is　2. am　3. are　4. during
5. have　6. is　7. My　8. wants

Lesson 5

Tony and His Family

托尼和他的家人

1 *Reading* 阅读

I have a good friend. His name is Tony. He has an older sister. Her name is Tina. Their parents are Mr. and Mrs. Wang. Tony also has a dog. Its name is Rover.

The Wangs are my neighbors. We live on the same street. The Wangs are very nice. I am lucky because the Wangs are such good neighbors.

我有个好朋友。他叫托尼。他有个姐姐。她的名字是蒂娜。他们的父母是王氏夫妇。托尼还有条狗。它叫来福。

王家是我的邻居。我们住在同一条街。王家人很好。我很幸运,因为我有王家这么好的邻居。

2 Vocabulary & Idioms 单词短语注解

1. **have** [hæv] *vt.* 有(用于 I、you 或复数的主语之后)
   has [hæz] *vt.* 有(用于 he、she、it 等第三人称单数主语之后)
   I have a wonderful family. 我有个美满的家庭。

2. **good** [gʊd] *a.* 好的;善良的
   Judy is a good singer. 朱迪是一位好歌手。

3. **her** [hɝ] *pron.* 她的

4. **their** [ðɛr] *pron.* 他们的

5. **also** [ˋɔlso] *adv.* 也
   Bob is my teacher and he is also my friend.
   鲍勃是我的老师,也是我的朋友。

6. **dog** [dɔg] *n.* 狗

7. **the Wangs** [ðə ˋwaŋz] *n.* 王氏一家人
   = the Wang family

8. **neighbor** [ˋnebɚ] *n.* 邻居

9. **live** [lɪv] *vi.* 住
   I live in the country. 我住在乡下。

10. **same** [sem] *a.* 相同的
    注意
    使用本单词时,之前一定要置定冠词 the。
    Jane and I go to the same school. 简和我上同一所学校。

11. **street** [strit] *n.* 街

12. **very** [ˋvɛrɪ] *adv.* 很,非常地
    My neighbors are very noisy. 我的邻居非常吵。

13. **nice** [naɪs] *a.* 好的;善良的

14. **lucky** [ˋlʌkɪ] *a.* 幸运的
    The lucky boy has a new bicycle.

那个幸运的男孩有一辆新的自行车。

15. **such** [sʌtʃ] *a.* 如此的，那样的
Today is such a beautiful day. 今天天气真好。

3 Grammar Points 语法重点

本课介绍表示“有”的 have 及 there is 的用法，介绍所有格代词，介绍表示“也”的副词 too 及 also 的使用区别。

1. **I have a good friend.** 我有个好朋友。

注意

a. have 是及物动词，表示“有”的意思。使用 have 时，主语一定是表示“人或动物”的名词或代词。

例 John has two dogs. 约翰有两条狗。
They have many friends. 他们有很多朋友。

b. 在 Lesson 1 中我们曾提到“There is...”“There are...”也表示“有”的意思，但用法与 have 不同。初学英语的读者很容易犯下列错误：

中文：房间里有个男孩。
英文：In the room has a boy. (×)
理由：In the room 是表示场所的短语，不能作主语，使用时应在句首置 There is 或 There are，然后置名词，再将表示场所的短语置于句尾。

此时就须改为下面的句子结构：
There is a boy in the room. (√) 房间里有个男孩。
On the desk have three books. (×)
→ There are three books on the desk. (√) 桌上有三本书。

2. **Her name is Tina.** 她叫蒂娜。

上句中的 Her 是所有格代词，作“她的”解。使用时可将 her 视为形容词，之后接名词。

例 Mary is my classmate. Her English is very good.
玛丽是我同班同学。她的英文很棒。

我们可以从下列表格及例句了解这些所有格代词的种类及用法：

数	单数		复数	
所有格代词	my	我的	our	我们的
	your	你的	your	你们的
	his	他的	their	他们的
	her	她的	their	她们的
	its	它的	their	它们的

例 That is my book. 那是我的书。
Their teacher is strict. 他们的老师很严。
John and his younger sister love their father.
约翰和他妹妹很爱他们的爸爸。
My dog wags its tail when it sees me.
我的小狗见到我时都会摇尾巴。

3. **Tony also has a dog.** 托尼也有条狗。
= Tony has a dog, too.
also 与 too 均为副词，表示“也”的意思。但使用时，too 置于句尾，其前要有逗号。而 also 则置于一般动词前；若与 be 动词或助动词连用时，also 应置于该 be 动词或助动词之后。

例 一般动词：He likes music. I also like it. 他喜欢音乐。我也喜欢。
= He likes music. I like it, too.
be 动词：He is a student. I am also a student. 他是学生。我也是。
= He is a student. I am, too.
助动词：He can sing. I can also sing. 他会唱歌。我也会。
= He can sing. I can, too.

4 *Substitution* 替换

1. I have a good friend. 我有个好朋友。
You have a good teacher. 你有位好老师。
She has a strong brother. 她有个很壮的兄弟。
It has a beautiful tail. 它有一条漂亮的尾巴。
They have a beautiful sister. 他们有一个漂亮的姐姐。

---

2. Their parents are Mr. and Mrs. Wang. 他们的父母是王氏夫妇。
   Our teacher is Mr. Chen. 我们的老师是陈先生。
   His father is Mr. Lee. 他爸爸是李先生。
   Her mother is Mrs. Lin. 她妈妈是林太太。
   Its tail is long. 它的尾巴很长。

---

3. We live on the same street. 我们住在同一条街。
   We live in the same house. 我们住在同一幢房子。
   We live in the same building. 我们住在同一幢楼。
   We live in the same city. 我们住在同一座城市。

Lesson 6

Is This Your Dog?

这是你的狗吗？

1 Dialogue 实用会话

Mrs. Lee: Is this your dog?

Tony: Yes, it is. Why?

Mrs. Lee: Well, your dog chases my cat.

Tony: Oh, I'm sorry.

Mrs. Lee: Please keep your dog on a leash.

Tony: Yes, ma'am.

李太太：这是你的狗吗?

托　尼：是的。怎么了?

李太太：是这样的，你的狗追我的猫。

托　尼：噢，很抱歉。

李太太：请把你的狗用狗链拴好。

托　尼：是的，夫人。

2 Key Points 重点提示

1. **why** [hwaɪ/waɪ] *adv.* 为什么
2. **chase** [tʃes] *vt.* 追捕
3. **sorry** [ˋsɔrɪ] *a.* 抱歉的，遗憾的

4. **please** [pliz] *adv.* 请

please 作“请”解时，是个礼貌用语，用法有二：

a. 置于句首，之后接动词原形。

例 Please open the door. 请打开门。

千万不要造下列这种中式英文的句子：

Please you open the door. (×)

b. 置于句尾，之前加逗号。

例 Open the door, please. 请打开门。

5. **keep** [kip] *vt.* & *vi.* 保持（一种状态）

6. **leash** [liʃ] *n.* （拴狗的）链条，皮带

3 请于下列空格中填入适当的词

I __1__ a sister. __2__ name is Patty. I also __3__ a brother. __4__ name is John. We __5__ two neighbors. __6__ names are Tim and Ted. Tim has a dog. __7__ tail is beautiful. Ted has a cat. __8__ eyes are big. We all like Tim and Ted. They are __9__ good neighbors.

解答 1. have 2. Her 3. have 4. His 5. have
6. Their 7. Its 8. Its 9. our

Lesson 7

Tony and Tina

托尼和蒂娜

1 *Reading* 阅读

Tony and Tina are very different. Tony likes music. Tina doesn't. Tony is an athlete. Tina isn't.

On the other hand, Tina likes movies, but Tony doesn't. She is a good student, but he isn't.

Tony and Tina are brother and sister, but are they alike? No, they aren't. They're very different.

托尼和蒂娜非常不同。托尼喜欢音乐,蒂娜却不喜欢。托尼是个运动员,蒂娜则不是。

另一方面,蒂娜喜欢电影,但托尼不喜欢。她是好学生,但他却不是。

托尼和蒂娜是兄妹,但他们相似吗?不,他们不相似。他们大不相同。

2 Vocabulary & Idioms 单词短语注解

1. **different** [ˋdɪfərənt] *a.* 不同的
   A horse and a mule are very different. 马和骡子大不相同。
2. **like** [laɪk] *vt.* 喜欢
   The little boy likes ice cream very much. 那小男孩很喜欢冰淇淋。
3. **music** [ˋmjuzɪk] *n.* 音乐(不可数)
4. **athlete** [ˋæθlit] *n.* 运动员
5. **movie** [ˋmuvɪ] *n.* 电影
6. **but** [bʌt] *conj.* 但是
   Fred is poor, but he is happy. 弗雷德很穷,但他很快乐。
7. **alike** [əˋlaɪk] *a.* 相同的,相似的
   使用本单词时,不可置于名词前。
   John and Peter are alike brothers. (×)
   → John and Peter are alike in many ways. (√)
   约翰和彼得在许多方面很相似。

3 Grammar Points 语法重点

本课介绍省略句的形成,不定冠词 a 及 an 的用法,介词短语 on the other hand 的用法,及表示相对关系的名词之前省略冠词的用法。

1. **Tony likes music. Tina doesn't.** 托尼喜欢音乐,蒂娜却不喜欢。
   Tony is an athlete. Tina isn't. 托尼是个运动员,蒂娜则不是。
   以上两句中的"Tina doesn't."及"Tina isn't."均为省略句。省略句的功能就是省略两句重复的部分,使句子结构简单又不失清楚的含义。省略句形成的先决条件是:
   a. 两句的结构必须相同(亦即两句有相同的时态及动词),第二句方可形成省略句。
   b. 第一句若为肯定句,第二句则为否定句;第一句若为否定句,第二句则为肯定句。

形态有三：

a. be 动词

例 He is a good student. She is not a good student.
他是好学生，但她却不是。

→ He is a good student. She isn't.

= He is a good student, but she isn't.

b. 助动词（如 can、will 等）

例 He cannot do it. She can do it. 他不能做这事，但她却能。

→ He cannot do it. She can.

= He cannot do it, but she can.

c. 动词

此时省略句要按主语的人称分置助动词 do 或 does，用来代替第一句中的动词。

例 He likes music. I do not like music.
他喜欢音乐，但我却不喜欢。

→ He likes music. I don't.

= He likes music, but I don't.

I do not like music. He likes music.
我不喜欢音乐，但他却喜欢。

→ I do not like music. He does.

= I don't like music, but he does.

2. **Tony is an athlete.** 托尼是个运动员。

注意上句名词 athlete 之前的冠词是 an 而非 a。

a. 一般而言，可数名词若为单数形式时，之前要有不定冠词（a, an）表示单数的概念。

例 This is book. (×)

→ This is a book. (√) 这是一本书。

There is ox there. (×)

→ There is an ox there. (√) 那里有头公牛。

b. a 置于辅音起首的单词前，而 an 则置于元音起首的单词前。

book [bʊk], ox [ɑks], athlete [ˋæθlit]

由上列音标得知 **book** 起首为辅音，**ox** 与 **athlete** 为元音，故应说 a book、an ox、an athlete。

3. **On the other hand, Tina likes movies, but Tony doesn't.**

另一方面，蒂娜喜欢电影，但托尼则不喜欢。

on the other hand 是介词短语，表示“另一方面来说”或“话又说回来”，有副词的功能，通常置于句首，修饰整个句子。

例 He is poor at English. On the other hand, he speaks French very well.

他英文很差。但话又说回来，他法语讲得很好。

4. **Tina doesn't.** 蒂娜则不。

= Tina does not.

Tina isn't. 蒂娜不是。

= Tina is not.

No, they aren't. 不，他们不是。

= No, they are not.

They're very different. 他们大不相同。

= They are very different.

以上各句旨在强调 be 动词及助动词 do（与 I、they、you、we 或其他复数主语连用）、does（与 he、she、it 或其他单数主语连用）与 not 的缩写形式。这种缩写在英文的写作或口语中极为普遍。

a. be 动词与 not 连用时：

is not → isn't [ˋɪzn̩t]

are not → aren't [ɑrnt]

am not 无缩写形。

例 He is not a teacher. 他不是老师。

= He isn't a teacher.

They are not happy. 他们不快乐。

= They aren't happy.

b. do、does 与 not 连用时：

do not → don't [dont]

does not → doesn't [ˋdʌzn̩t]

例 They do not like music. 他们不喜欢音乐。
= They don't like music.
I do not like coffee. 我不喜欢咖啡。
= I don't like coffee.
She does not like tea. 她不喜欢茶。
= She doesn't like tea.

5. **They are brother and sister.** 他们是兄妹 / 姐弟。
上句中 brother 与 sister 是可数名词，照理本句应为：
They are a brother and a sister.
但两个名词所表示的是相对的关系，如父子、兄妹、母子等，这些名词之前的不定冠词就应省略。故我们应说：

They are	brother and sister. mother and son. father and daughter. teacher and student.	他们是兄妹 / 母子 / 父女 / 师生。

4 *Substitution* 替换

1. He likes music. 他喜欢音乐。
I like tea. 我喜欢茶。
They like coffee. 他们喜欢咖啡。

2. Tina isn't an athlete. 蒂娜不是运动员。
They aren't musicians. 他们不是音乐家。
I am not a movie star. 我不是电影明星。

3. He doesn't like movies. 他不喜欢电影。
They don't like music. 他们不喜欢音乐。
I don't speak Chinese. 我不会说中文。

Lesson 8

Do You Speak Spanish?

你会说西班牙语吗？

1 *Dialogue* 实用会话

Joe: Do you speak Spanish?

Jeannie: No, I don't.

Joe: Does he speak Spanish?

Jeannie: Yes, he does.

Joe: Is he from Spain?

Jeannie: No, he isn't. He's from Mexico.

乔: 你会说西班牙语吗?

吉妮：不，我不会。

乔: 他会说西班牙语吗?

吉妮：是的，他会。

乔: 他是西班牙人吗?

吉妮：不，他不是。他是墨西哥人。

2 *Key Points* 重点提示

1. **speak** [spik] *vt.* 说（某种语言）
2. **Spanish** [ˋspænɪʃ] *n.* 西班牙语
3. **Spain** [spen] *n.* 西班牙

4. **Mexico** [ˋmɛksɪˏko] *n.* 墨西哥

3 请于下列空格中填入适当的词

Bob and Carl are brothers, but they __1__ different. Bob __2__ quiet. Carl __3__ . Carl watches TV. Bob __4__ . Bob reads books. Carl __5__ . Bob and __6__ teacher are friends. Carl and __7__ teacher __8__ .

解答 1. are 2. is 3. isn't 4. doesn't
5. doesn't 6. his 7. his 8. aren't

Lesson 9

A Busy Family

忙碌的家庭

1 *Reading* 阅读

It's a busy day at the Wangs' house. Mr. Wang is fixing his bike. Mrs. Wang is writing a letter. Tina is reading a book. Tony is exercising.

Even the dog is busy. It's chasing a cat. The cat is running for its life.

The Wangs are busy, but they're having fun.

王家今天很忙。王先生在修他的自行车。王太太在写信。蒂娜在看书。托尼在运动。

甚至狗狗也很忙碌。它在追一只猫。猫在逃命。

王氏一家人很忙,但他们都很愉快。

2 Vocabulary & Idioms 单词短语注解

1. **busy** [ˋbɪzɪ] *a.* 忙碌的
   I am busy with my work. 我忙着工作。
2. **day** [de] *n.* 日子
3. **house** [haʊs] *n.* 房子
4. **fix** [fɪks] *vt.* 修理
   My uncle is fixing my broken watch. 我叔叔正在修理我坏掉的手表。
5. **bike** [baɪk] *n.* 自行车（=bicycle [ˋbaɪsɪkḷ] ）
6. **write** [raɪt] *vt.* 写
   I am writing a letter to my friend. 我正在写信给我的朋友。
7. **letter** [ˋlɛtɚ] *n.* 信
8. **read** [rid] *vt.* 阅读，看（文章、书等）
   My father is reading the newspaper. 我的父亲正在看报纸。
9. **book** [bʊk] *n.* 书
10. **exercise** [ˋɛksɚˏsaɪz] *vi.* 运动
    I exercise in the park every morning. 我每天早上都到公园运动。
11. **even** [ˋivən] *adv.* 甚至
    Even Father likes ice cream. 甚至连我父亲都喜欢冰淇淋。
12. **chase** [tʃes] *vt.* 追逐
    The policeman is chasing the thief. 警察在追小偷。
13. **cat** [kæt] *n.* 猫
14. **run** [rʌn] *vi.* 跑
15. **life** [laɪf] *n.* 生命
16. **fun** [fʌn] *n.* 乐趣（不可数）

3 *Grammar Points* 语法重点

本课主要介绍现在进行时的形成及用法，并介绍其他相关的重点。

1. **It's a busy day at the Wangs' house.** 王家今天很忙。

   a. It's a busy day. 今天是一个忙碌的日子。

   = It is a busy day.

   此处的 It 是代词，用来代替"今天"、"此刻"。常用于"It is + 时间名词"的句子结构中。

   例 It's Monday. 今天是星期一。

   What time is it? 现在几点了？

   It's ten o'clock. 现在是 10 点钟。

   b. at the Wangs' house 在王家的住所

   在上列短语中，at [æt] 是介词，表示"在……之处"的意思。之后所接的宾语，多为表示家(house)、车站(station)、邮局(post office)、杂货店(grocery store)等建筑物的名词。

   例 There are many people at the train station. 火车站有好多人。

   c. the Wangs' house　王家的住所

   the Wangs' 是所有格，译成"王氏一家人的"，相当于所有格代词 their（他们的）。专有名词(如 John、Peter)或表示"人"的普通名词(如 my father、the boy)形成所有格时，要在这些专有名词或普通名词之后加"'s"，之后再接名词，即：

   John's book 约翰的书

   my father's work 我父亲的工作

   the boy's dog 这个男孩的狗

   但专有名词或普通名词之后有"s"形成复数时，则表示所有格的符号"'"应置于"s"之后，即：

   the Lins' house 林家

   the boys' father 这些男孩子的父亲

   故我们应说"the Wangs' house"，而非"the Wang's house"。

2. **Mr. Wang is fixing his bike.** 王先生在修他的自行车。

   Mrs. Wang is writing a letter. 王太太在写信。

以上两句均属动词时态中现在进行时的句型。这种时态相当于中文“现在正在……”的意思，形成的方式如下：

主语 + | am / are / is | + 现在分词

a. 在造例句之前，我们得先谈谈现在分词的构成方式：动词原形加 -ing → 现在分词

   1) 绝大部分的动词原形可直接加 -ing 即成现在分词，如：
      do（做）→ doing
      teach（教书）→ teaching
   2) 但若动词原形以不发音的 e 结尾时，要先删除 e，再加 -ing，如：
      write [raɪt]（写）→ writing
      chase [tʃes]（追逐）→ chasing
      make [mek]（制造）→ making
   3) 若动词原形为单音短音节，且以一个辅音字母结尾时，应将该字母双写，再加 -ing，如：
      run [rʌn]（跑）→ running
      sit [sɪt]（坐）→ sitting

b. 有了以上了解后，我们现在就可造出下列现在进行时的例子：

   例 Mary is writing a letter. 玛丽正在写信。
   They are doing their homework. 他们正在做功课。
   I am running in the yard. 我正在院子里跑步。

3. **...but they're having fun.** ……但他们很愉快。

have fun 是固定的用语，表示“玩得愉快”、“过得愉快”之意，可不要逐字翻译成“有乐趣”。“...they're having fun.” 是现在进行时，照理应译成“他们现在正玩得愉快”，但此处为求译文顺畅，只译成“他们很愉快”即可。

例 I have fun every day. 我每天都过得很愉快。

4 Substitution 替换

1.	Mr. Wang is fixing his	bike. television. car.	王先生在修他的自行车 / 电视机 / 车子。
2.	Tina is reading	a book. a magazine. a newspaper.	蒂娜正在看书 / 杂志 / 报纸。
3.	Tony is	exercising. jogging. playing basketball.	托尼正在运动 / 慢跑 / 打篮球。

Lesson 10

What Are You Doing?

你在做什么？

1 *Dialogue* 实用会话

Betty and Bob are talking on the telephone.

Betty: Hi, Bob. What are you doing?

Bob: I'm watching TV. How about you?

Betty: I'm doing my homework.

Bob: You are a good student, Betty.

贝蒂和鲍勃在讲电话。

贝蒂：嗨，鲍勃。你在做什么？

鲍勃：我在看电视。你呢？

贝蒂：我在做功课。

鲍勃：贝蒂，你是个好学生。

2 *Key Points* 重点提示

1. **watch** [watʃ] *vt.* 看，观赏（电视、比赛等）
2. **TV** [ˈtiˈvi] *n.* 电视
   （television [ˈtɛləˌvɪʒən] 的缩写形式）
3. **homework** [ˈhomˌwɜk] *n.* 家庭作业（不可数）

3 请于下列空格中填入适当的词

The Wangs __1__ in the park. Mr. Wang is __2__ a magazine. Mrs. Wang is __3__ a song. Tony and __4__ friends are __5__ baseball. Tina is __6__ a letter. Rover is __7__ a cat. Everyone is __8__ fun in the park，except the cat.

解答 1. are 2. reading 3. singing 4. his
5. playing 6. writing (或 reading) 7. chasing 8. having

Lesson 11

My Foreign Classmates

我的外籍同学

1 *Reading* 阅读

There are several foreign students in my class. John is American. He's from the United States. Laura is Spanish. She's from Spain.

Chen and Huang are Chinese, but they are not from China. They're from Malaysia. They're overseas Chinese.

We're from different countries, but we all get along well.

我班上有几名外籍学生。约翰是美国人。他来自美国。劳拉是西班牙人。她来自西班牙。

小陈和小黄是中国人,但他们却并非来自中国。他们来自马来西亚。他们是华侨。

我们来自不同的国家,不过我们都相处得很好。

2 Vocabulary & Idioms 单词短语注解

1. **foreign** [ˋfɔrɪn] *a.* 外国的，外籍的
   I like to see foreign movies. 我喜欢看外国电影。
2. **classmate** [ˋklæsˏmet] *n.* 同班同学
3. **several** [ˋsɛvərəl] *a.* 几个的
   There are several Americans in my class. 我的班上有好几个美国人。
4. **class** [klæs] *n.* 班级
5. **American** [əˋmɛrɪkən] *a.* 美国籍的
6. **the United States (of America)**
   美利坚合众国，美国
   united [juˋnaɪtɪd] *a.* 联合的
   state [stet] *n.* 美国的一州
   美国全称为 the United States of America。一般均以 the United States、the States 或 the U.S. 称呼。
7. **Spanish** [ˋspænɪʃ] *a.* 西班牙籍的
8. **Spain** [spen] *n.* 西班牙
9. **Chinese** [tʃaɪˋniz] *a.* 中国籍的
10. **China** [ˋtʃaɪnə] *n.* 中国
11. **Malaysia** [məˋleʒə] *n.* 马来西亚
12. **overseas** [ˏovəˋsiz] *a.* 在海外的
    Amy is an overseas student. 艾米是一个留学生。
13. **country** [ˋkʌntrɪ] *n.* 国家
    I love my country. 我爱我的国家。

3 Grammar Points 语法重点

本课主要介绍表示国籍的说法。

1. **John is American.** 约翰是美国人。
Laura is Spanish. 劳拉是西班牙人。
Chen and Huang are Chinese. 小陈和小黄是中国人。
上列三句中，American、Spanish 与 Chinese 均作形容词，分别表示"美国籍的"、"西班牙籍的"、"中国籍的"；但 American 与 Chinese 均可作可数名词，此时之前应分别置不定冠词"an"和"a"，即 an American（美国人）、a Chinese（中国人），但 American 的复数形式为 Americans，而 Chinese 的复数形式仍为 Chinese。

例 John is American.　（American 为形容词）约翰是美国人。
= John is an American.　（American 为名词）
They are American.　（American 为形容词）他们是美国人。
= They are Americans.　（Americans 为名词）
Peter is Chinese.　（Chinese 为形容词）彼得是中国人。
= Peter is a Chinese.　（Chinese 为名词）
They are Chinese.　（Chinese 为形容词，亦可视作复数名词）
他们是中国人。
I see five Chinese there.　（Chinese 为复数名词）
我看到那边有五个中国人。

但 Spanish 只作形容词用，故：
He is a Spanish.（×）
→ He is Spanish.（√）他是西班牙人。
I see five Spanish there.（×）
→ I see five Spanish people there.（√）　我看到那里五个西班牙人。

因此为了避免犯类似上面的错误，英美人士多用国籍的形容词来表示某人是哪一国人。

例 He is British.
They are British. 他们是英国人。
We are Danish. 我们是丹麦人。

2. **She's from Spain.** 她来自西班牙。
= She is from Spain.
They're from Malaysia. 他们来自马来西亚。

= They are from Malaysia.

以上两句中的 She's 及 They're 分别等于 She is 及 They are。人称代词作主语与 be 动词连用时，可采用下列缩写形式，这些缩写形式在口语中最为常用：

I am → I'm [aɪm] 我是
you are → you're [jʊr] 你是 / 你们是
he is → he's [hiz] 他是
she is → she's [ʃiz] 她是
it is → it's [ɪts] 它是
we are → we're [wɪr] 我们是
they are → they're [ðer] 他们是

例 I am not a student. 我不是学生。
= I'm not a student.
He is a good teacher. 他是好老师。
= He's a good teacher.
It is a beautiful dog. 它是只很漂亮的狗。
= It's a beautiful dog.

3. **...but we all get along well.** ……不过我们都相处得很好。

以上这两个短语却有两个语法重点，兹分述如下：

a. we all 我们大家

此处的 all [ɔl] 是形容词，译成“全部的”或“所有的”，修饰三个或三个以上的人或东西。与代词连用时，置于该代词之后；与普通名词连用时，通常置于该普通名词前；与专有名词连用时，通常置于该专有名词之后。

1) 代词：

例 They all like music. 他们都喜欢音乐。
I like them all. 他们我全都喜欢。

2) 普通名词：

例 All the boys like music. 这些男孩都喜欢音乐。

3) 专有名词：

例 Peter, Paul and Mary all like music.
彼得、保罗和玛丽全都喜欢音乐。

both [boθ] 也是形容词，用来修饰两个人或东西，可译成“二者都”。

例 John and Peter are good friends. They both like music.
约翰和彼得是好朋友。他们两个都喜欢音乐。
All my parents can sing. (×，本句话暗示可能有两爸一妈或三爸五妈的)
→ Both my parents can sing. (√) 我父母都会唱歌。

b. get along 相处(along [əˈlɔŋ])
这个短语之后亦可接介词 with，再接人作宾语，即：
get along with + 人　与某人相处

例 He has a bad temper. I can't get along with him.
他脾气坏。我没法与他相处。
Do you and your sister get along well? 你和你妹妹相处得好吗？

4 Substitution 替换

1.	Laura is Spanish. I'm British. He's Swedish.	劳拉是西班牙人。 我是英国人。 他是瑞典人。
2.	She's from Spain. I'm from England. He's from Sweden.	她来自西班牙。 我来自英国。 他来自瑞典。
3.	Where's Chen from? Where does Chen come from?	小陈是哪里人？/ 小陈是哪一国人？ 小陈是哪里人？/ 小陈是哪一国人？

Lesson 12

Where's Chen from?

小陈是哪一国人？

1 *Dialogue* 实用会话

A: Where's Chen from?

B: He's from Malaysia.

A: Really? He looks Chinese.

B: As a matter of fact, he is Chinese, but he really is from Malaysia.

A: That's very interesting.

A: 小陈是哪一国人？

B: 他是马来西亚人。

A: 真的吗？他看起来像中国人。

B: 事实上，他是中国人，不过他来自马来西亚。

A: 真有趣。

2 *Key Points* 重点提示

1. **really** [ˋriəlɪ] *adv.* 真正地
2. **look** [lʊk] *vi.* 看起来（之后接形容词）

   例 He looks happy today. 他今天看起来很快乐。
3. **as a matter of fact** 事实上

   本短语有副词的功能，使用时常置于句首，再置逗号，修饰之后的整个句子。

例 He knows many English words. As a matter of fact, he is a walking dictionary.

他英文单词懂得很多。事实上,他是本活字典。

3 请于下列空格中填入适当的词

I __1__ many foreign friends. Bill __2__ from England. He's __3__. Sue is from __4__. She's Mexican. Todd and Larry __5__ from Brazil. __6__ Brazilian. We're from different __7__, but __8__ all good friends.

解答 1. have　　2. is (或 comes)　　3. British
4. Mexico　　5. are (或 come)　　6. They're
7. countries　　8. we're

Lesson 13

Nobody Is at Home

没人在家

1 *Reading* 阅读

Nobody is at home at the Wangs' house. Mr. Wang is working in his office. Mrs. Wang is shopping at the supermarket. Tony is sitting on the bus. He's on his way to the gym. Tina is studying at the library.

Rover is not at home, either. It's running around the neighborhood. It's not chasing Mrs. Lee's cat. It's chasing Mrs. Lee!

王家没有一个人在家。王先生正在办公室工作。王太太正在超级市场买东西。托尼正坐在公共汽车上。他在去健身房的路上。蒂娜正在图书馆看书。

狗儿来福也不在家。它正在住处附近到处跑。它并不是在追李太太的猫。它是在追李太太！

2 Vocabulary & Idioms 单词短语注解

1. **nobody** [ˈnoˌbadɪ] *pron.* 没有人
   Nobody likes a liar. 谁都不喜欢撒谎的人。

2. **home** [hom] *n.* 家
   Nobody is at home today. 今天没有人在家。

3. **office** [ˈɔfɪs] *n.* 办公室

4. **shop** [ʃap] *vi.* 购物，买东西
   注意
   shop 是不及物动词，之后不得接宾语。shop 需接介词 for，方可再接宾语。
   She is shopping a new dress. (×)
   → She is shopping for a new dress. (√) 她正在选购一件新服装。

5. **supermarket** [ˈsupɚˌmarkɪt] *n.* 超级市场

6. **sit** [sɪt] *vi.* 坐
   Father is sitting on the sofa. 父亲正坐在沙发上。

7. **bus** [bʌs] *n.* 公共汽车，巴士
   He takes the bus to work every day. 他每天乘公共汽车上班。

8. **way** [we] *n.* 方向，路线

9. **gym** [dʒɪm] *n.* 健身房，体育馆
   注意
   gym 是 gymnasium 的缩写形式。
   gymnasium [dʒɪmˈnezɪəm]

10. **study** [ˈstʌdɪ] *vi.* 学习
    I seldom study at home. 我很少在家里学习。

11. **library** [ˈlaɪˌbrɛrɪ] *n.* 图书馆
    I am going to the library to study. 我正要去图书馆学习。

12. **either** [ˈiðɚ] *adv.* 也

注意

either 与 too 均为副词，二者皆表“也”，但用法有别：

a. too 用于肯定句中，置于句尾，too 之前置逗号。

Mary is beautiful. Jane is, too. 玛丽很漂亮，简也很漂亮。

b. either 用于含有 not 的否定句中，置于句尾，either 之前置逗号。

He isn't happy. She isn't, either. 他不快乐，她也不快乐。

13. **neighborhood** [ˋnebɚ,hʊd] *n.* 住处附近

There is a high school in my neighborhood. 我家附近有一所高中。

3 *Grammar Points* 语法重点

本课为读者介绍现在进行时的用法，并介绍及物动词与不及物动词的区别方法。

1. 为使读者进一步熟悉现在进行时的用法，此处再强调一次，现在进行时的句型为：

   主语 + am / are / is + 现在分词

   现在进行时就相当于中文“此刻正在……”的意思。

   例 They're chatting in the living room. 他们正在客厅内聊天。

2. 本课中的现在分词 working、shopping、sitting、studying、running、chasing 分别由动词 work（工作）、shop（购物）、sit（坐）、study（学习）、run（跑）、chase（追）变化而成。这些动词除 chase 是及物动词外，其他均为不及物动词。及物动词须接宾语，意思才算完整。但不及物动词本身意思即已完整，之后无须加宾语。

   例 I work every day. 我每天工作。

   S vi. adv.

   They like music. 他们喜欢音乐。

   S vt. O

   * “S” 指主语（Subject）。

   “vi.” 指不及物动词（intransitive verb）。

   “adv.” 指副词（adverb）。

   “vt.” 指及物动词（transitive verb）。

"O"指宾语(Object)。

初学英语的读者单凭上面的定义及例句可能仍无法了解及物动词与不及物动词的区别。别急,我们可用下面的步骤帮助读者清晰了解这两种动词的不同:

第一步:先在心中想出下列的句型:

A_________B。

B被A_________。

A及B可代表任何指人或物的名词或代词。即A或B可代表"我"、"约翰"、"狗"、"书"、"钱"等。

第二步:在上列空格中填入任何一个动词,然后将两句译成中文,如果意思通顺,该动词就是及物动词,否则就是不及物动词。

我们现在用like(喜欢)作示范。此时我们将A代表"我",B代表"音乐",即成:

我like(喜欢)音乐。

音乐被我like(喜欢)。

以上译文通顺,得知like是及物动词。

同理

狗chase(追)我。

我被狗chase(追)。

以上译文通顺,得知chase是及物动词。

又例 我work(工作)他。

他被我work(工作)。

译文:我工作他。

他被我工作。

以上译文不通顺,得知work是不及物动词。

以上的两个步骤是帮助我们区别及物动词与不及物动词的简略方法,但并非完全精确。请看下例:

我sit(坐)椅子。

椅子被我sit(坐)。

以上译文虽尚称通顺,但sit并非及物动词,而是不及物动词,因为sit之后要接介词on(表示坐在无扶手的椅子上面)或in(表示坐在有扶手的椅子里面)，再接宾语。

例 He is sitting on the chair. 他正坐在椅子上。

He is sitting in the armchair. 他正坐在扶手椅里。

因此，要精确了解及物动词与不及物动词的区别，最好的方法是勤看文章，勤查字典。

3. 已知及物动词和不及物动词的区别后，就应该知道这两个动词的用法：

主语 + 及物动词(*vt.*) + 宾语(O)

主语 + 不及物动词(*vi.*)

例 They often watch TV. 他们经常看电视。
adv. vt. O

She dances well. 她舞跳得很好。
vi. adv.

以上两例中的 often (经常)、well (很好) 均是副词，在句中用来修饰动词。

4. **Nobody is at home at the Wangs' house.**

王家没有一个人在家。

be at home 是个固定用法，表示“在家里”的意思。

例 He is at home now. 他现在在家里。

5. **Mr. Wang is working in his office.** 先生正在办公室工作。

Mrs. Wang is shopping at the supermarket.

王太太正在超级市场买东西。

以上两句中的 in 及 at 均为介词，之后皆可用以表示建筑物的名词作宾语；但 in 强调“在……里面”，at 则笼统指“在……地方”。

例 I will meet you at the library. 我会在图书馆和你见面。

* 或在图书馆内，或在图书馆门口。

I will meet you in the library. 我会在图书馆内和你见面。

6. **It's running around the neighborhood.**

它正在住处附近到处跑。

around [əˋraʊnd] *prep.* 围绕

例 The children are sitting around the old man.

孩子们正围着老人而坐。

4 Substitution 替换

1. Mrs. Wang is shopping at the | supermarket. | toy store. | department store. |

   王太太正在超市 / 玩具店 / 百货商店买东西。

2. Tony is | sitting | standing | talking | on the bus.

   托尼正坐在公共汽车上。
   托尼正站在公共汽车上。
   托尼正在公共汽车上谈话。

3. Tina is studying at the library.
   We are doing our homework at the library.
   I am writing a letter at the library.
   蒂娜正在图书馆看书。
   我们正在图书馆做功课。
   我正在图书馆写信。

Lesson 14

Why Are You Smiling?

你为什么在微笑？

1 *Dialogue* 实用会话

Mary: Why are you smiling?

Tony: I'm thinking about school.

Mary: Why does that make you smile?

Tony: Because there is no school tomorrow.

Mary: Oh, I see.

Tony: Now you're smiling, too!

玛丽：你为什么在微笑?

托尼：我正想到上学的事。

玛丽：为什么那会让你笑了起来呢?

托尼：因为明天不上学。

玛丽：哦，我明白了。

托尼：现在你也在笑了!

2 *Key Points* 重点提示

1. **smile** [smaɪl] *vi.* 微笑（常与 at 连用）

   例 Look! The girl is smiling at you. 瞧！那位女孩在对着你笑呢。

2. **think about...** 想到……

   例 Sue gets sad when she thinks about home.

苏一想到家就觉得很难过。

3. **make** [mek] *vt.* 使，叫

make + 人 + 动词原形　叫某人……

例 Father makes me clean his bike every Sunday.

父亲叫我每个星期天擦拭他的自行车。

4. **I see.** 我明白了。

3 请选择下列各句中正确的一项

1. Tina is doing homework ____ the library.
   (A) on　(B) at　(C) under　(D) around
2. Mrs. Wang is shopping ____.
   (A) at the library　(B) at the Wangs' house
   (C) at the gym　(D) at the department store
3. I am ____ at the library.
   (A) reading　(B) read　(C) readed　(D) reads
4. They____ around the school yard.
   (A) are run　(B) is running
   (C) are running　(D) am running
5. Mr. Wang ____ in his office.
   (A) are reading　(B) are working
   (C) am reading　(D) is working
6. Larry smiles when he thinks ____ his girlfriend.
   (A) to　(B) for　(C) about　(D) over

解答　1. (B)　2. (D)　3. (A)　4. (C)　5. (D)　6. (C)

Lesson 15

Mrs. Lee's Kitchen

李太太的厨房

1 *Reading* 阅读

There are mice in Mrs. Lee's kitchen! There's a mouse on the kitchen table. There's a mouse behind the stove. There are mice next to the refrigerator, under the sink and inside the cupboard!

Why isn't Mrs. Lee's cat catching the mice? Because it's in a tree. It's staring at Rover with fear and shaking like a leaf.

李太太的厨房里有老鼠！厨房桌上有一只。炉子后面有一只。冰箱边、洗碗槽下，还有橱柜里面都有老鼠！

李太太的猫为何不在抓这些老鼠呢？因为它在树上。它正惊恐地盯着狗儿来福，并且抖得很厉害。

2 Vocabulary & Idioms 单词短语注解

1. **kitchen** [ˈkɪtʃɪn] *n.* 厨房

2. **mouse** [maʊs] *n.* 老鼠(单数)
   mice [maɪs] *n.* 老鼠(复数)
   a mouse 一只老鼠

two	mice	两只老鼠
three		三只老鼠
many		许多老鼠

3. **table** [ˈtebl̩] *n.* 桌子

4. **behind** [bɪˈhaɪnd] *prep.* 在……后面
   The little boy is standing behind a tall man.
   那个小男孩站在一个高大男子后面。

5. **stove** [stov] *n.* 炉子

6. **next to...** 紧靠于……，在……旁边
   There is a post office next to the bank. 那家银行旁边有一个邮局。

7. **refrigerator** [rɪˈfrɪdʒəˌretɚ] *n.* 电冰箱

8. **under** [ˈʌndɚ] *prep.* 在……下方
   My shoes are under the bed. 我的鞋就在床下。

9. **sink** [sɪŋk] *n.* 洗碗槽

10. **inside** [ɪnˈsaɪd] *prep.* 在……之内
    The lion is inside a cage. 那只狮子在笼子里。

11. **cupboard** [ˈkʌbɚd] *n.* 橱柜

12. **why** [hwaɪ / waɪ] *adv.* 为什么
    Why are you so sad? 你为什么那么难过?

13. **catch** [kætʃ] *vt.* 抓，捕捉
    The baseball player is catching the ball. 那个棒球员正在接球。

14. **because** [bɪˈkɔz] *conj.* 因为

Tom is at home because he is sick. 汤姆待在家里，因为他生病了。

15. **tree** [tri] *n.* 树

16. **stare** [stɛr] *vi.* 盯，注视（常与 at 连用）
stare at... 盯着……
It's rude to stare at people. 盯着别人看是不礼貌的。

17. **with** [wɪð] *prep.* 有，带着

18. **fear** [fɪr] *n.* 害怕，恐惧

19. **shake** [ʃek] *vi.* 抖动

20. **leaf** [lif] *n.* 叶子

21. **shake like a leaf**（因害怕、恐惧而）抖得很厉害
When I watch scary movies, I shake like a leaf.
每次看恐怖电影时，我都吓得浑身发抖。

3 *Grammar Points* 语法重点

本课介绍介词与物体的关系，并介绍特殊疑问句的造句法。

1. 注意下列介词与物体的关系：

inside + 物体　　在该物体之内
= in + 物体
behind + 物体　　在该物体的后面
under + 物体　　在该物体的下方
next to + 物体　　紧邻于该物体

例 There is a pen inside / in the box. 盒子里有支笔。
There is a dog behind the door. 门后有只狗。
He is standing under an umbrella. 他正站在雨伞下。
Mary is sitting next to the window. 玛丽正坐在窗边。

2. **There are mice in Mrs. Lee's kitchen!** 李太太的厨房里有老鼠！
我们再复习一下 There is / There are（有）与 have / has（有）的用法。我们可用中文的句子清楚了解这些用法。凡以人或动物作主语时，

就要用 have 或 has 作动词；凡以场所起首的句子，英文句首就应置 There is / There are。

例 中文：我 有只手表。
人
英文：I have a watch.
中文：这只猫 有一条长尾巴。
动物
英文：The cat has a long tail.
中文：客厅里 有一个电冰箱。
场所
英文：There is a refrigerator in the living room.
中文：书桌上 有一本书和两支铅笔。
场所
英文：There are a book and two pencils on the desk.

3. **Why isn't Mrs. Lee's cat catching the mice?**

李太太的猫为何不在抓这些老鼠呢？

本句是特殊疑问句。特殊疑问句就是用疑问副词 why（为什么）、when 何时）、how（如何）、where（何处）或疑问代词 who（谁，作主语）、whom（谁，作宾语）、what（什么）、which（哪个）等起首的问句。由于特殊疑问句需要较大的篇幅方能详细说明，我们将在往后的课文中逐步介绍。这里就疑问副词（why、when、how、where）形成的问句简单介绍如下，以使读者对特殊疑问句的造句有初步的了解：

a. 疑问词一定置于问句句首。

b. 问句要采用倒装句型。

1) 原句有 be 动词时，该 be 动词要与主语倒装。

例 中文：他为什么生气呢？
英文：He why is angry? (×)
→ Why is he angry? (√)
中文：你为什么在哭呢？
英文：You why are crying? (×)

→ Why are you crying? (√)

中文：他为什么不在做功课呢？

英文：He why isn't doing his homework? (×)

Why is not he doing his homework? (×)

→ Why isn't he doing his homework? (√)

= Why is he not doing his homework? (√)

2) 原句有助动词如 can（能够）、will（将要）、may（可以）等时，该助动词要与主语倒装。

例 中文：你何时会来呢？

英文：You when will come? (×)

→ When will you come? (√)

中文：你如何做这件事呢？

英文：You how can do it? (×)

→ How can you do it? (√)

3) 原句有一般动词时，一般动词与主语无法倒装，须按主语的人称在疑问词之后置 do 或 does，再将动词改为动词原形。

例 中文：他住在什么地方？

英文：He lives where? (×)

Where he lives? (×)

→ Where does he live? (√)

中文：他们为什么喜欢音乐？

英文：They why like music? (×)

→ Why do they like music? (√)

4. **It's staring at Rover with fear.** 它正惊恐地盯着来福。

= It's staring at Rover fearfully.

上列第一句中 with fear 这个介词短语作副词用，等于第二句中副词 fearfully [ˈfɪrfəlɪ]，用以修饰已成现在进行时短语动词的 is staring at。

4 *Substitution* 替换

1. There is a mouse on the kitchen table.
   There is a cat between the refrigerator and the stove.
   There are two cats to the right of the trash can.
   厨房桌上有一只老鼠。
   电冰箱和炉子之间有一只猫。
   垃圾箱右方有两只猫。

---

2. Why isn't Mrs. Lee's cat catching the mice?
   Why isn't she studying?
   Why aren't you cleaning your room?
   李太太的猫为何不在抓这些老鼠呢?
   她为什么没在看书呢?
   你为什么不在打扫你的房间呢?

Lesson 16

Where Are My Keys?

我的钥匙在哪里？

1 *Dialogue* 实用会话

Nick: Where are my keys?

Sandy: I don't know. Are they on the dresser?

Nick: No, they aren't.

Sandy: Are they under the bed?

Nick: No. Oh, here they are.

Sandy: Where?

Nick: In my pocket.

尼克：我的钥匙在哪里？

珊迪：我不知道。它们是不是在化妆台上？

尼克：没有，不在那里。

珊迪：是不是在床下？

尼克：没有。哦，它们在这里。

珊迪：哪里？

尼克：在我的口袋里。

2 *Key Points* 重点提示

1. **key** [ki] *n.* 钥匙
2. **dresser** [ˋdrɛsɚ] *n.* 化妆台

3. **Here they are.** 它们在这里。

   here [hɪr] *adv.* 这里

4. **pocket** [ˋpɑkɪt] *n.* 口袋

3 请选择下列各句中正确的一项

1. Bill is sitting to the______ of Mary.
   (A) in (B) on (C) right (D) next to
2. Why ______ she washing the dishes?
   (A) isn't (B) is not (C) aren't (D) are not
3. Larry is standing ______ Mary and Jane.
   (A) in (B) between (C) left (D) inside
4. Why aren't you ______ his bicycle?
   (A) clean (B) ride (C) playing (D) fixing
5. There is a trash can ______ to the refrigerator.
   (A) between (B) next (C) at (D) behind
6. What is that ______?
   (A) between the bed (B) in your pocket
   (C) to the left dresser (D) in your keys

解答 1. (C) 2. (A) 3. (B) 4. (D) 5. (B) 6. (B)

Lesson 17

My Hometown

我的家乡

1 *Reading* 阅读

My hometown is not very modern, but it's beautiful. There is a big park in the center of my hometown. There is also a swimming pool there. It is next to the park. My school is across from the swimming pool. They are all near my home. In fact, there is no place like my hometown.

我的家乡不很现代化,但它却很美。家乡的中心位置有一座大公园。那儿也有一座游泳池。它紧邻公园。我的学校就在游泳池的对面。它们离我家都很近。事实上,没有一个地方像我的家乡一样。

2 Vocabulary & Idioms 单词短语注解

1. **hometown** [ˌhomˈtaʊn] *n.* 家乡，故乡
   My hometown is far from here. 我的家乡离这里很远。

2. **modern** [ˈmɑdɚn] *a.* 现代化的
   It is very convenient to live in a modern city.
   住在现代化的城市里非常方便。

3. **beautiful** [ˈbjutəfəl] *a.* 美丽的
   The sun is shining. It's a beautiful day. 阳光灿烂，真是美好的一天。

4. **big** [bɪg] *a.* 大的
   There's a big elephant in the zoo. 动物园里有一只大象。

5. **park** [pɑrk] *n.* 公园

6. **center** [ˈsɛntɚ] *n.* 中央，中心点
   in the center of... 在……的中央位置
   Where is the town center? 市中心在哪里？
   The train station is in the center of the city. 火车站位于市中心。

7. **swimming pool** [ˈswɪmɪŋ ˌpul] *n.* 游泳池

8. **across** [əˈkrɔs] *adv.* 横越
   (be) across from... 在……的对面
   Sarah is sitting across from me. 萨拉正坐在我的对面。

9. **near** [nɪr] *prep.* 接近
   Billy lives near our school. 比利住在我们学校附近。

10. **fact** [fækt] *n.* 事实
    in fact 事实上
    I don't like hamburgers. In fact, I hate American food.
    我不喜欢汉堡包。事实上，我讨厌美式食物。

11. **place** [ples] *n.* 地方
    The library is a very quiet place. 图书馆是非常安静的地方。

12. **like** [laɪk] *prep.* 像

I want to be famous like Michael Jackson.

我希望像迈克尔·杰克逊一样有名。

3 *Grammar Points* 语法重点

本课主要介绍表示场所位置的介词用法，并介绍 in fact 之用法及 like 作介词表示“像”的用法。

1. 注意下列介词及短语介词的意思及用法：

a. near... 在……的附近

b. next to... 紧邻……，在……的旁边

例 Don't move! There is a snake next to you.

别动！你的旁边有一条蛇。

c. across from... 在……的对面

d. in the center of... 在……的中央点

注意

1) 这些介词或短语介词加了宾语之后，形成表示场所位置的介词短语，与 there is / are（有……）连用时，可置于句尾或句首。

例 There is a swimming pool near my school.

= Near my school there is a swimming pool.

我学校附近有一座游泳池。

There are several tall buildings in the center of the city.

= In the center of the city there are several tall buildings.

市中心有几幢高大的建筑物。

2) 若介词短语置于句首时，there 可省略。

例 Near my school there is a swimming pool.

= Near my school is a swimming pool.

我学校附近有一座游泳池。

In the center of the city there are several tall buildings.

= In the center of the city are several tall buildings.

市中心有几幢高大的建筑物。

2. **In fact, there is no place like my hometown.**

事实上,没有一个地方像我的家乡一样。

此处 in fact 是作副词用的介词短语,使用时置于句首,修饰 there is... 整个主句。

in fact 事实上,实际上

= as a matter of fact

例 I am tired. In fact, I am exhausted. 我很累。实际上,我累坏了。

Jim is late today. As a matter of fact, he's late every day.

吉姆今天迟到了。实际上,他每天都迟到。

3. **...there is no place like my hometown.**

……没有一个地方像我的家乡一样。

此处的 like 是介词,表示“像”的意思。

一般而言,like 有两种用法:一作及物动词,表示“喜欢”;一作介词,表示“像”。

a. 作及物动词时,句子结构如下:

主语 + like + 宾语(名词或代词)

例 The boy likes the dog. 这男孩喜欢这条狗。

Ben is selfish. We don't like him. 本很自私,我们不喜欢他。

b. 作介词时,之后亦须接宾语,形成介词短语。这个短语使用时,要置于:

1) be 动词之后

例 My teacher is like my father. 我的老师就像我的父亲。
(is: be 动词)

2) 名词之后

例 There is no place like my hometown.
(place: 名词)

没有一个地方像我的家乡一样。

3) 主语之前

例 Like John, I enjoy music. 就像约翰一样,我也喜欢音乐。
(I: 主语)

4 Substitution 替换

1. A: What is your hometown like?
   B: My hometown is not very modern, but it's beautiful.
   My hometown is small, but it's pretty.
   A: 你的家乡是什么样子？
   B: 我的家乡不是很现代化 / 很小， 但它却很美。

---

2. A: Where is your school?
   B: My school is across from the swimming pool.
   behind the post office.
   next to the bank.
   A: 你的学校在哪儿？
   B: 我的学校就在游泳池对面 / 邮局后面 / 银行隔壁。

Lesson 18

Is It near the Post Office?

就在邮局附近吗？

1 *Dialogue* 实用会话

Mary: Excuse me. Can you tell me the way to the train station, please?

Jack: Sure. It's only three blocks down the street.

Mary: Is it near the post office?

Jack: No. It's next to the fire station.

Mary: Oh, I see. Thanks.

Jack: You're welcome.

玛丽：对不起。请您告诉我车站怎么个走法，好吗？

杰克：没问题。朝这条街走下去只要走三条街就到了。

玛丽：车站就在邮局附近吗？

杰克：不是。它在消防队的隔壁。

玛丽：哦，我明白了。谢谢。

杰克：不客气。

2 *Key Points* 重点提示

1. **excuse** [ɪkˋskjuz] *vt.* 原谅

   Excuse me. 对不起 / 打扰一下。

例 Excuse me. Do you have the time?
Can you tell me what time it is?

对不起。请问现在是几点钟?

2. **tell** [tɛl] *vt.* 告诉，吩附

例 Mother is telling Bobby to clean his room.

母亲吩咐博比去打扫他的房间。

3. **sure** [ʃʊr] *adv.* 当然

4. **block** [blɑk] *n.* 街区

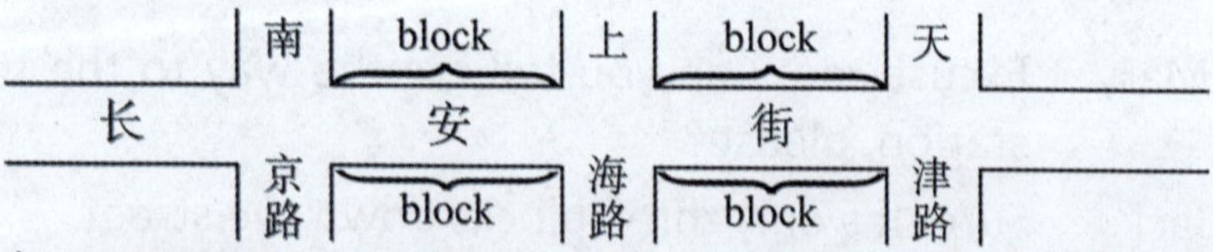

在上列路线图中，我们若想从南京路沿长安街到天津路时，就要走两个 blocks。

5. **down** [daʊn] *prep.* 朝……而下，沿着（街道）

6. **fire station** [ˈfaɪr ˌsteʃən] *n.* 消防队

7. **welcome** [ˈwɛlkəm] *a.* 受欢迎的

You are welcome. 别客气。

= Not at all.

3 请于下列空格中填入适当的词

Billy lives __1__ the center of town. There __2__ a restaurant __3__ from his house. __4__ is a police station __5__ his house. His town is not beautiful, __6__ it is safe.

解答

1. in	2. is	3. across
4. There	5. near	6. but

♫怀念老歌园地♫

Dreamin'

梦想

D4/4

By Johnny Brunette

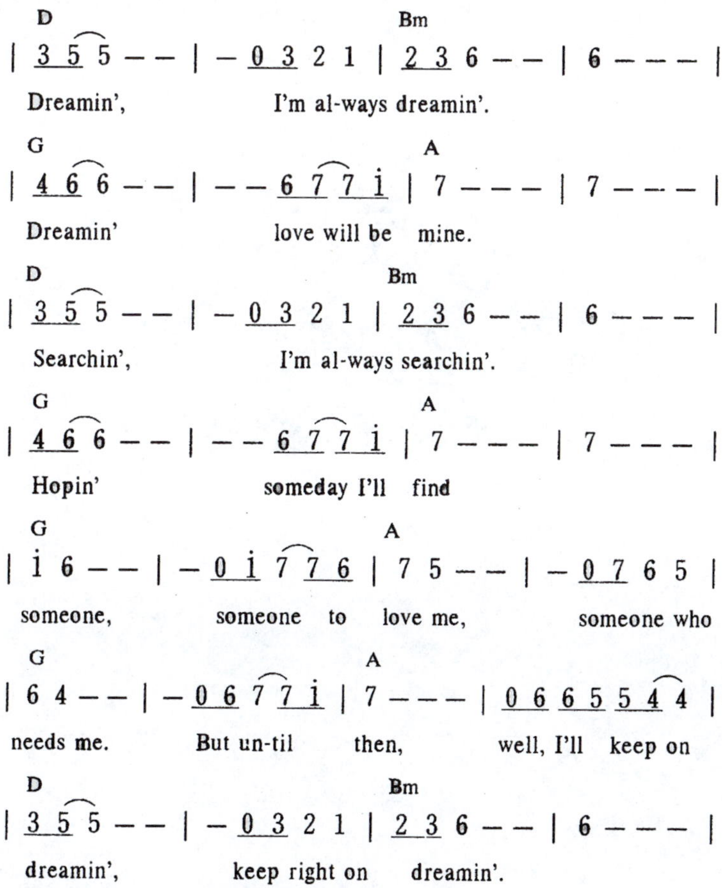

G A D

| 4 6 4 — — | — 7 6 7 1̇ 2̇ | 1̇ — 0 7 1̇ 7 |

Dreamin', till my dreamin' comes true. Oh......

Bm G A

| 6 — 0 5 6 5 | 4 — 0 6 6 1̇ | 7 — — — ‖

oh..............................oh..............................oh...

♫怀念老歌园地♫

Dreamin'

梦想

1 Lyrics 歌词

Dreamin', I'm always dreamin'. Dreamin' love will be mine. Searchin', I'm always searchin'. Hopin' someday I'll find someone, someone to love me, someone who needs me. But until then, well, I'll keep on dreamin', keep right on dreamin'. Dreamin', till my dreamin' comes true. Oh...

梦想，我总是在梦想。梦想我会找到心爱的人。寻找，我总是在寻找，希望有一天我能找到一个爱我、需要我的人。但是，在那一天来临前，我会一直梦想下去，直到美梦成真。哦……

2 Vocabulary & Idioms 单词短语注解

1. **dreamin'** [ˋdrimɪn] *vi.* 梦想（dream 的现在分词）
   = dreaming [ˋdrimɪŋ]
   * 本歌曲中之 dreamin' 实应写成 dreaming，但在口语或歌词中，常将 -ing 形成的现在分词说成或写成 -in'，以求发音的方便，如下：

singing → singin'
doing → doin'
dreaming → dreamin'
dream [drim] *vi.* 梦想，梦到 & *vt.* 做（梦）& *n.* 梦，梦想
a. dream 作不及物动词时，通常有两种用法：
1) dream of / about + 动名词　梦想要……
例 Stan dreams of being a millionaire. 斯坦梦想成为百万富翁。
2) dream of / about + 名词（或代词）　梦到……
例 I dreamed of you last night. 昨晚我梦到你。
b. dream 作及物动词时，常用同系名词 dream 作宾语，此时动词 dream 可用 have 取代。此外也可用 that 引导的名词性从句作宾语。
例 She dreamed a bad dream last night. 昨晚她做了一个噩梦。
= She had a bad dream last night.
I dreamed that we were swimming together.
我梦见我们在一起游泳。
c. dream 作名词当主语时，可使用动词短语 come true，表示"梦想实现"的意思。
例 His dream came true when he became a doctor.
他成为医生时便实现了他的梦想。

2. **Dreamin' love will be mine.**
= I am dreaming that love will be mine.
= I am dreaming that I will find my love someday.
我梦想着有一天我会找到心爱的人。

3. **Searchin', I'm always searchin'.**
= I am always searching for the girl that I love.
我总是一直在寻找我所爱的女孩。
search [sɜtʃ] *vi.* 寻找，搜索 & *n.* 寻觅
a. search 作不及物动词时，常与介词 for 连用。
例 The police are searching for the criminal.
警方正在搜索那名罪犯。

b. search 作名词时，有一固定用法 be in search of，即等于 search for。

例 Pat is still in search of a better job.
帕特仍然在找一份较好的工作。

4. **Hopin' someday I'll find someone, someone to love me, someone who needs me.**

= I am hoping that someday I will find someone who loves and needs me.
希望有一天我能找到一个爱我并需要我的人。

hope [hop] *vt.* & *vi.* 希望

a. hope 作及物动词时，通常有下列用法：

1) 以 that 引导的名词性从句作宾语

例 Betty hopes that her son will return home this year.
贝蒂希望她儿子今年会回家。

2) 以不定式短语（to + 动词原形）作宾语

例 I hope to meet you again when I visit Tokyo next week.
我希望在下个礼拜去东京时能再见到你。

b. hope 作不及物动词时，通常和介词 for 连用。

hope for + 名词　希望得到……

例 I always hope for the best and prepare for the worst.
我总是抱着乐观的态度，并为最坏的情形做准备。

5. **But until then, well, I'll keep on dreamin', keep right on dreamin'.**

= But before that day comes, I will keep on dreaming.

= But I will keep on dreaming until the day comes.
但是我将继续不断地梦想下去，直到那一天的到来。

a. until [ən`tɪl] *prep.* 直到 & *conj.* 直到……时，在……之前

1) until 在上句中为介词，以时间副词 then 作宾语，表“直到那时”。

例 The boss said that I could not leave until I finish my work.
老板说我要完成工作才能离开。

2) 但 until 亦常作副词连词，引导状语从句。

例 I will not go away until he comes.
在他来之前，我是不会走开的。

3) not until 置于句首引导状语从句时，其后之主句要倒装。

例 Not until he comes will I go away. 直到他来时，我才会走开。

b. keep on + 现在分词　继续做某事
= keep + 现在分词

例 Derek kept on running even though the race was already over.
即使赛跑已经结束了，德里克还一直跑下去。

c. right [raɪt] 在本文中作副词，修饰 keep on，为强调用法，表“一直”。

例 Go right on to the end of the street and you will see the post office.
一直走到街尾，你就会看到邮局了。

6. **Dreamin', till my dreamin' comes true.**

= I will keep on dreaming until my dream comes true.
我会一直梦想下去，直到梦想成真。

a. till [tɪl] *conj.* & *prep.* 直到……时
= until

例 I will stay here till the winter is over.
我将待在这里直到冬天结束。

b. 本句中第一个 Dreamin' 是现在分词，等于“I'll keep on dreaming”，第二个 dreamin' 为动名词，等于名词 dream，在 till 引导的状语从句中作主语。

c. come true　实现
= be realized
realize [ˋriəˏlaɪz] *vt.* 实现；了解，领悟

例 The fortune-teller's words never came true.
那位算命师所说的话从未实现过。
Do you realize what you have just said?
你了解自己刚刚所说的话吗？

Lesson 19

I Have Two Friends

我有两个朋友

1 *Reading* 阅读

I have two friends. One is short, and the other is tall.

My short friend is fat, bald and ugly, but his girlfriend is beautiful. My tall friend is handsome, intelligent and strong, but his girlfriend is ugly.

Oh, one more thing: my short friend is rich, but my tall friend is poor.

我有两个朋友。一个是矮个子，另一个是高个子。

我那位矮个子朋友肥胖、秃头、长得又丑，但他的女友很美。我那位高个子朋友英俊、聪明、身体又壮，但他的女友很丑。

哦，另外还有一点：我那位矮个子朋友很有钱，但是我那位高个子朋友则很穷。

2 Vocabulary & Idioms 单词短语注解

1. **short** [ʃɔrt] *a.* 矮的，短的
My parents are short, but I am tall. 我的父母亲很矮，但我却很高。
Bob is writing a short letter to his grandmother.
鲍勃正在写一封简短的信给他的祖母。

2. **other** [ˋʌðɚ] *a.* 剩余的，其他的
在本文中 other 与 the 连用，形成代词 the other（另外一个）。
one...the other... 一个……另一个……
I have two sons. One is a doctor, and the other is a lawyer.
我有两个儿子。其中一个是医生，另一个是律师。

3. **tall** [tɔl] *a.* 高的
Basketball players are very tall. 篮球运动员都很高。

4. **fat** [fæt] *a.* 肥胖的
Fat people can't run fast. 胖的人都跑不快。

5. **bald** [bɔld] *a.* 秃头的

6. **ugly** [ˋʌglɪ] *a.* 丑陋的，难看的
The ugly boy doesn't have a girlfriend. 那丑男孩没有女朋友。

7. **girlfriend** [ˋgɝlˏfrɛnd] *n.* 女朋友

8. **handsome** [ˋhænsəm] *a.* 英俊的
The handsome actor is very famous. 那位英俊的演员非常有名。

9. **intelligent** [ɪnˋtɛlədʒənt] *a.* 聪明的
The intelligent boy is reading a novel. 那个聪明的男孩正在看小说。

10. **strong** [strɔŋ] *a.* 强壮的
Boxers are very strong. 拳击手都很强壮。

11. **rich** [rɪtʃ] *a.* 富有的
The rich man is a banker. 那个有钱人是个银行家。

12. **poor** [pʊr] *a.* 贫穷的
I don't have any money. I am very poor. 我没有半毛钱，我很穷。

3 Grammar Points 语法重点

本课主要介绍代词“one...the other...”的用法，并介绍并列连词 and 的用法。

1. **I have two friends. One is short, and the other is tall.**
   我有两个朋友。一个是矮个子，另一个是高个子。
   注意下列代词的用法：
   a. 两者：one...the other...
   一个……另一个……
   例 I have two brothers. One is a teacher, and the other is a soldier.
   我有两个哥哥。一个是老师，另一个是军人。
   b. 三者：one...another...the other...
   一个……一个……另一个……
   例 Her three sisters are busy now. One is cooking in the kitchen, another is fixing her bike in the yard, and the other is studying in the living room.
   她的三个姐姐现在都很忙。一个正在厨房做饭，一个正在院子里修她的自行车，另一个则正在客厅里看书。

2. **My short friend is fat, bald and ugly.**
   我那位矮个子朋友肥胖、秃头、长得又丑。
   上句中的 and 是并列连词，表示“和”、“以及”的意思，连接 fat、bald 及 ugly 三个平行对等的形容词。and 可连接平行的单词、短语、从句或句子。
   例 John and David are good friends. 约翰和大卫是好朋友。
   (John: n.; David: n.)
   She is beautiful and helpful. 她美丽又乐于助人。
   (beautiful: a.; helpful: a.)
   She sings and dances very well. 她唱歌跳舞都很好。
   (sings: v.; dances: v.)
   I like him because he is intelligent and because he is helpful.
   (because he is intelligent: 状语从句; because he is helpful: 状语从句)
   我喜欢他，因为他很聪明，也因为他乐于助人。

She sings well, and she is good at dancing.
句子 句子
她歌唱得很好，跳舞也很行。

注意

a. and 连接两个平行单词时，and 之前不得置逗号。

例 My friend is handsome, and intelligent. (×)
→ My friend is handsome and intelligent. (√)
我的朋友英俊又聪明。

b. and 连接三个平行单词时，第一个单词与第二个单词之间置逗号，and 则置于第二个单词与第三个单词之间，and 之前则可置逗号，但通常予以省略。

例 My friend is handsome, intelligent, and strong. (可)
→ My friend is handsome, intelligent and strong. (常用)
我的朋友英俊、聪明、身体强壮。

c. and 连接平行的句子时，and 之前通常置一逗号；but 亦为并列连词，表示“但是”、“不过”的意思，用来连接平行的句子时，but 之前通常也置一逗号。

例 He loves Jane, and (he) is planning to marry her this year.
他很爱简，且正计划今年要跟她结婚。
He likes music, but his girlfriend hates it.
他喜欢音乐，但他的女友讨厌音乐。

3. **Oh, one more thing: my short friend is rich, but my tall friend is poor.**

= Oh, there is one more thing: my short friend...
哦，另外还有一点：我那位矮个子朋友……。
more [mɔr] *a.* 更多的
one more.... 再一个……
two more... 再两个……
three more... 再三个……
⋮ ⋮

例 We need five more apple pies for the party.
我们的宴会还需要五个苹果派。

4 Substitution 替换

1. His girlfriend is beautiful. 他的女友很漂亮。
His girlfriend is polite. 他的女友很有礼貌。
Her boyfriend is hardworking. 她的男友工作很努力。
Her boyfriend is handsome. 她的男友很英俊。

---

2. I have two friends. One is short, and the other is tall.
I have two sisters. One is a teacher, and the other is a musician.
He has two dogs. One is black, and the other is yellow.
我有两个朋友。一个是矮个子，另一个是高个子。
我有两个姐姐。一个是老师，另一个是音乐家。
他有两条狗。一条是黑色的，另一条是黄色的。

---

3. My tall friend is handsome, intelligent and strong.
My tall friend is young, healthy and successful.
My tall friend is lazy, selfish and boring.
我那位高个子朋友既英俊、聪明、身体又壮。
我那位高个子朋友既年轻、健康、事业又成功。
我那位高个子朋友既懒惰、自私、又令人生厌。

Lesson 20

She Is Beautiful

她很漂亮

1 *Dialogue* 实用会话

John: Wow! Who is that lady next to Bob? She's pretty.

Tina: Do you really think so?

John: Sure. Look at her lovely blond hair and blue eyes.

Tina: You're right. She is beautiful.

John: Well, who is she?

Tina: She's my mother.

约翰：哇！鲍勃身旁的那位小姐是谁呀？她好漂亮。

蒂娜：你真的这么认为吗？

约翰：当然。瞧瞧她那漂亮的金发和蓝眼睛。

蒂娜：你说对了。她很美。

约翰：那么，她是谁呢？

蒂娜：她是我妈妈。

2 *Key Points* 重点提示

1. **lady** [ˋledɪ] *n.* 小姐，女士
2. **pretty** [ˋprɪtɪ] *a.* 漂亮的（= beautiful）

3. **think so** 如此想法
此处 so 是代词，代替前面的句子“She's pretty.”。

4. **look** [lʊk] *vi.* 看
look at... 注视……，注意看……
例 The boys are looking at the pretty girl.
男孩们正注视着那位漂亮的女孩。

5. **lovely** [ˈlʌvlɪ] *a.* 美丽的（= beautiful）
例 My best friend has a lovely daughter. 我最好的朋友有个漂亮的女儿。

6. **blond** [blɑnd] *a.* 金色的（头发）

7. **hair** [hɛr] *n.* 头发

8. **blue** [blu] *a.* 蓝色的

9. **eye** [aɪ] *n.* 眼睛

3 请选择下列各句中正确的一项

1. Mary has two sons. One is a college student, and ______ is a soldier.
(A) another (B) other
(C) the other (D) an other
2. __________ is the boy there?
(A) Who's (B) Who (C) Where (D) There
3. Tom's ________ is a musician.
(A) girl's friends (B) girlfriend
(C) boys' friends (D) friends
4. Can I have ________ cup of coffee?
(A) more (B) one more
(C) more one (D) two more
5. __________ the girl next to the window. She is beautiful.
(A) Look (B) Look into
(C) Look look (D) Look at

6. Roger thinks Jane has lovely eyes. This sentence means ________.
   (A) Roger loves Jane
   (B) Roger loves Jane's eyes
   (C) Roger thinks Jane's eyes are beautiful
   (D) Roger thinks Jane's hair is beautiful

解答 1. (C) 2. (B) 3. (B) 4. (B) 5. (D) 6. (C)

Lesson 21

I Don't Know Anyone

我谁都不认识

1 *Reading* 阅读

I don't know anyone at this party. There's a strange man. He has a big nose and small ears. I don't know him. There are two women. They're wearing glasses. I don't know them, either.

There is a cute young girl. She has long hair and fair skin. She's dancing with someone. I like her, but everyone else does, too.

这个宴会上的人我一个也不认识。有个陌生人。他鼻大耳小。我不认识他。有两个女人。她们都戴着眼镜。我也不认识她们。

有位可爱的年轻女孩。她留着长发皮肤白皙。她正跟某个人跳舞。我喜欢她,但其他的人也都喜欢她。

2 Vocabulary & Idioms 单词短语注解

1. **know** [no] *vt.* 认识
   Do you know the way to my house? 你知道去我家的路吗?
2. **anyone** [ˋɛnɪˏwʌn] *pron.* 任何一个人
   Does anyone want an orange? 有没有人想要橙子呢?
3. **party** [ˋpɑrtɪ] *n.* 宴会,(社交性或娱乐性的)聚会
4. **strange** [strendʒ] *a.* 陌生的;奇怪的
   Tim's girlfriend has a strange voice. 蒂姆女友的声音很奇怪。
5. **big** [bɪg] *a.* 大的
6. **nose** [noz] *n.* 鼻子
7. **small** [smɔl] *a.* 小的
8. **ear** [ɪr] *n.* 耳朵
9. **women** [ˋwɪmən] *n.* 女人(复数)
   woman [ˋwumən] *n.* 女人(单数)
   one woman 一个女人
   two women 两个女人
10. **wear** [wɛr] *vt.* 穿,戴(帽子、耳环、鞋、衣服、皮带等任何可穿戴在身上的东西)
    I like to wear jeans. 我喜欢穿牛仔裤。
11. **glasses** [ˋglæsɪz] *n.* 眼镜
    glass 可作"玻璃"或"玻璃杯"解,作"玻璃"解时,是不可数名词;作"玻璃杯"解时,则为可数名词。
    a piece of glass 一片玻璃
    two pieces of glass 两片玻璃
    a glass 一个玻璃杯
    two glasses 两个玻璃杯
    但 glasses 亦可作"眼镜"解,由于眼镜的镜片有两片,故用来指"眼镜"时,glasses 用复数。

a pair of glasses 一副眼镜

two pairs of glasses 两副眼镜

12. **cute** [kjut] *a.* 可爱的

Everybody likes cute children. 每个人都喜欢可爱的小孩。

13. **young** [jʌŋ] *a.* 年轻的

The young man is very polite. 那个年轻人很有礼貌。

14. **long** [lɔŋ] *a.* 长的

John likes girls with long hair. 约翰喜欢长头发的女孩。

15. **fair** [fɛr] *a.*（皮肤）白皙的

注意

本文的 fair 专指皮肤的白皙，此处不可用 white（白的）来取代。因为 white skin 是指白种人的白皮肤。

16. **skin** [skɪn] *n.* 皮肤（不可数）

17. **dance** [dæns] *vi.* 跳舞

Do you know how to dance? 你知道怎么跳舞吗？

18. **someone** [ˋsʌmˏwʌn] *pron.* 某个人

19. **else** [ɛls] *adv.* 另外，别的（置于 everybody、somebody、nobody 之后）

everybody else 其他每个人

= everyone else

somebody else 另外一个人

= someone else

nobody else 没有其他的人

= no one else

I like my teacher, but everyone else doesn't.

我喜欢我的老师，但是其他人都不喜欢。

Sorry, I can't help you. Please ask someone else.

抱歉，我没办法帮你。请你找别人吧！

James smokes, but no one else in the office does.

詹姆斯抽烟,但是办公室里的其他人都不抽烟。

3 Grammar Points 语法重点

本课介绍 not 形成的否定句,并介绍代词 anyone 与 someone 的区别。

1. **I don't know anyone at this party.**

   这个宴会上的人我一个也不认识。

   本句为以副词 not 形成的否定句子结构。否定句均由肯定句变化而成,有下列三种形态:

   a. 句中有 be 动词时,not 置于该 be 动词之后。

   例 He is intelligent. (肯定)
   他聪明。
   He is not intelligent. (否定)
   = He isn't intelligent.
   他不聪明。

   b. 句中有助动词如 can(能够)、will(将要)、may 可以)、must(必须)等时,not 置于该助动词之后。

   例 He will come today. (肯定)
   他今天会来。
   He will not come today. (否定)
   = He won't come today.
   他今天不会来。
   The boy can sing. (肯定)
   这男孩会唱歌。
   The boy cannot sing. (否定)
   = The boy can't sing.
   这男孩不会唱歌。

   * can 与 not 连用时,应写成 cannot 而非 can not,但 will、may、must 等助动词与 not 连用时,则仍为 will not、may not、must not。

   c. 句中只有一般动词而无 be 动词或助动词时,应先在主语之后按人称变化分置助动词 do 或 does,再加 not,原来的动词均改为动词原形。

例 She loves David. (肯定)

她爱大卫。

此时主语 She 为第三人称单数代词，故 She 之后应置 does，再加 not，然后将 loves 改为 love，即：

She does not love David. (否定)

= She doesn't love David.

她不爱大卫。

例 They like music. (肯定)

他们喜欢音乐。

此时主语 They 为第三人称复数代词，故 They 之后应置 do，再加 not，like 的原形仍为 like，即：

They do not like music. (否定)

= They don't like music.

他们不喜欢音乐。

2. **anyone / someone** 任何一个人 / 某个人

以上两个代词分别等于 anybody 及 somebody。anyone 或 anybody 用于否定句或疑问句中，someone 或 somebody 则用于肯定句中。

例 I don't know anybody in the classroom. (否定)

教室里的人我都不认识。

There isn't anyone in the room. (否定)

房间里一个人都没有。

Does anyone know the answer? (疑问)

有人知道这答案吗？

Can anybody do it? (疑问)

这件事有人会做吗？

There is someone there. (肯定)

那里有个人。

Somebody is talking to Mary. (肯定)

有人在跟玛丽说话。

不过 anybody 或 anyone 若作主语时，仍可用于肯定句中，作强调的用法。

例 Anybody can answer the question. 任何人都能回答这个问题。

If he can do it, anyone can.

他若能做这件事，那么任何人都能够做了。

4 Substitution 替换

1. He has a big nose and small ears. 他鼻大耳小。
He has a round face and a big mouth. 他脸圆嘴大。
She has a thin face and round eyes. 她脸瘦眼圆。

---

2. They're wearing glasses. 他们都戴着眼镜。
He's wearing a yellow suit. 他穿着一套黄色的西装。
She's wearing a purple hat. 她戴着一顶紫色的帽子。

Lesson 22

Do You Want to Dance?

你想跳舞吗？

1 *Dialogue* 实用会话

Bob: Hello. Do you want to dance?

Jane: No, thanks.

Bob: Do you want a drink?

Jane: No, thank you.

Bob: What do you want?

Jane: I just want you to go away.

鲍勃：你好。你想跳舞吗?

简：不想，谢谢。

鲍勃：你想喝一杯（酒）吗?

简：不想，谢谢你。

鲍勃：你想要什么?

简：我只想要你离开。

2 *Key Points* 重点提示

1. **want** [wɑnt] *vt.* 要，欲

   a. want to + 动词原形　想要……

   例 I want to see him now. 我想现在就见到他。

   b. want + 名词　要……

例 The little boy wants more toys. 这小男孩想要更多的玩具。

c. want + 人 + to + 动词原形　要某人……

例 He wants me to mail the letter for him. 他要我为他寄这封信。

2. **drink** [drɪŋk] *n.* 酒

drink 可作"饮料"或"酒"解,但在现代美语中,多作"酒"解,尤其常见使用于下列短语中:

have / want / get + a drink 喝一杯(酒)

例 I want a drink after work. 下班后我想喝杯酒。

3. **go away** 离开

例 Don't bother me! Please go away. 别烦我! 请你走开。

3 请选择下列各句中正确的一项

1. I don't know ______ here.
   (A) anyone　(B) someone
   (C) another one　(D) the other
2. He isn't polite. She isn't, ______.
   (A) also　(B) too　(C) either　(D) polite
3. They like music. I ______, too.
   (A) am　(B) can　(C) don't　(D) do
4. The question is easy. ______ can answer it.
   (A) Some body　(B) No one
   (C) Every body　(D) Anyone
5. He's wearing ______.
   (A) a piece of glass　(B) a glass
   (C) glasses　(D) glass
6. Mother wants you ______ the dishes for her.
   (A) to wash　(B) washing
   (C) wash　(D) to washes

解答　1. (A)　2. (C)　3. (D)　4. (D)　5. (C)　6. (A)

Lesson 23

The Book Is Mine

这本书是我的

1 *Reading* 阅读

This is my English book. It belongs to me. It is mine. That is your English book. It belongs to you. It is yours. Those books aren't ours. They belong to those boys over there. They are theirs. Why do we all have different books? Because we belong to different classes.

这是我的英文书。它属于我。它是我的。那是你的英文书。它属于你。它是你的。那些书不是我们的。它们属于那边那些男孩的。那些书是他们的。我们大家的书为什么不一样？因为我们属于不同的班级。

2 Vocabulary & Idioms 单词短语注解

1. **English** [ˋɪŋglɪʃ] *n.* 英文，英语
   John is Chinese, but he speaks English well.
   约翰是中国人，不过他英文说得很好。
2. **belong** [bɪˋlɔŋ] *vi.* 属于（与介词 to 连用）
   belong to... 属于……
   Put that umbrella down. It doesn't belong to you.
   把那把雨伞放下。它不属于你的。
3. **mine** [maɪn] *pron.* 我的
4. **yours** [jʊrz] *pron.* 你的，你们的
5. **those** [ðoz] *pron.* 那些
6. **ours** [aʊrz] *pron.* 我们的
7. **theirs** [ðɛrz] *pron.* 他们 / 她们 / 它们的
8. **different** [ˋdɪfərənt] *a.* 不同的
   I like many different kinds of books. 我喜欢很多不同种类的书。
9. **class** [klæs] *n.* 班级；课
   What time is your history class? 你的历史课是在什么时候呢？

3 Grammar Points 语法重点

本课介绍指示代词及名词性所有格代词的种类及用法。

1. **This is my English book.** 这是我的英文书。
   That is your English book. 那是你的英文书。
   Those books aren't ours. 那些书不是我们的。
   上列句中的 This、That 及 Those 均为指示代词。
   英语中的指示代词常用的有四个：this [ðɪs]（这个）、that [ðæt]（那个）、these [ðiz]（这些）、those [ðoz]（那些）。请读者注意下列要点：
   a. this 及 that 代替单数名词或不可数名词，these 及 those 则代替

复数名词。

例 This is my bike. 这是我的自行车。
单数名词

That is your money. 那是你的钱。
不可数名词

These are your books. 这些是你的书。
复数名词

Those are his pencils. 那些是他的铅笔。
复数名词

b. 以上指示代词亦有定冠词的功能,之后可接名词。

例 This bike belongs to me. 这辆自行车属于我的。

These girls are cute. 这些女孩子很可爱。

c. this 及 these 指较近的人或事物;that 及 those 则指较远的人或事物。

例 This book belongs to me, and that book belongs to him.
这本书属于我的,那本书则属于他的。

I don't like these flowers. I like those flowers next to the window.
我不喜欢这些花。我喜欢紧靠窗户的那些花。

d. this、that、these、those 在文章第一次出现之后,第二次使用时为避免重复,this 及 that 应用 it 代替,these 及 those 则用 they 代替。

例 This is my English book. This belongs to me.(劣)
→ This is my English book. It belongs to me. (佳)
这是我的英文书。它属于我。

These books are mine. These don't belong to you.(劣)
→ These books are mine. They don't belong to you.(佳)
这些书是我的。它们不属于你。

2. **It is mine.** 它是我的。
It is yours. 它是你的。
Those books aren't ours. 那些书不是我们的。
上列句中的 mine、yours 及 ours 均为名词性所有格代词,与我们稍早所介绍的形容词性所有格代词有所不同。列表如下：

数 / 中译 / 形态	单数		
	我的	你的	他(她、它)的
形容词性所有格代词	my	your	his / her / its
名词性所有格代词	mine	yours	his / hers / its

数 / 中译 / 形态	复数		
	我们的	你们的	他(她、它)们的
形容词性所有格代词	our	your	their
名词性所有格代词	ours	yours	theirs

注意事项：

a. 形容词性所有格代词相当于形容词，之后一定要接名词；而名词性所有格代词则相当于名词，之后不可再接名词。

例 The book is my. (×, my 是形容词性所有格代词，之后须接名词)
→ This is my book. (√) 这是我的书。
→ The book is mine. (√) 这本书是我的。

例 Our school is big, but their is small. (×, their 是形容词性所有格代词，之后须接名词)
→ Our school is big, but their school is small. (√, 但 school 一词在句中重复是一缺点)
→ Our school is big, but theirs is small. (佳)
我们的学校很大，但他们的却很小。

b. his 及 its 可同时作形容词性或名词性所有格代词；her 属形容词性所有格代词，hers 则属名词性所有格代词。

例 I don't like her car. I like his. (her 为形容词性所有格代词，his 为名词性所有格代词)
我不喜欢她的车。我喜欢他的。

I like his car. I don't like hers.（his 为形容词性所有格代词，hers 为名词性所有格代词）

我喜欢他的车。我不喜欢她的。

I have a dog. Its mouth is big, but mine is bigger than its.（Its 是形容词性所有格代词，its 则为名词性所有格代词）

我有一只狗。它的嘴很大，但我的嘴比它的大。

c. 勿将 it's 与 its 混为一谈。

its（它的）是所有格代词；it's 则为 it is（它是）的缩写形式。

例 I have a dog. It's tail is long. (×)

→ I have a dog. Its tail is long. (√)

我有一只狗。它的尾巴是长的。

I have a dog. Its very strong. (×)

→ I have a dog. It's very strong. (√)

= I have a dog. It is very strong.

我有一只狗。它很强壮。

3. **They belong to those boys over there.**

它们属于那边那些男孩子的。

there（那里）、here（这里）皆为表示场所的副词，使用时，通常置于句尾。

例 I see a boy there. 我看到那边有个男孩。

There is a dog here. 这里有只狗。

但在口语中，老美常在 there 及 here 之前另加一副词 over [ˋovɚ]，强调 there 或 here。故以上两句亦可改为：

I see a boy over there.

There is a dog over here.

4 Substitution 替换

1. This is my English book. It belongs to me.

That is her pen. It belongs to her.

These are his pencils. They belong to him.

这是我的英文书。它属于我。
那是她的笔。它属于她。
这些是他的铅笔。它们属于他。

---

2. Those books aren't ours. They belong to those boys over there.
These notebooks aren't yours. They belong to those girls over there.
That ball isn't hers. It belongs to this boy over here.
那些书不是我们的。它们属于那边那些男孩子。
这些笔记本不是你们的。它们属于那边那些女孩。
那个球不是她的。它属于这边这个男孩子。

Lesson 24

It's Mine
它是我的

1 *Dialogue* 实用会话

Teacher: Whose test paper is this?

Bob: It's mine, ma'am.

Teacher: And whose test paper is this?

Bob: It's Tony's, ma'am.

Teacher: And why are your answers exactly the same as his?

Bob: Because Tony has eyes in the back of his head.

老师：这是谁的测验卷？

鲍勃：这是我的，老师。

老师：那么，这又是谁的测验卷？

鲍勃：那是托尼的，老师。

老师：那么，为什么你的答案与他的完全一样呢？

鲍勃：因为托尼的脑袋后面长了眼睛。

2 *Key Points* 重点提示

1. **whose** [huz] *pron.* 谁的

本词乃所有格疑问代词，用于问句中，置于该问句句首。whose 可作形容词性或名词性所有格代词；作形容词性所有格代词时，之后接名词；作名词性所有格代词时，之后不接名词。

例 This is whose dog?（×，whose 因属疑问代词，故应置于句首）
→ Whose dog is this?（√，此处 whose 为形容词性所有格代词，之后接名词 dog）
这是谁的狗？

例 This dog is whose?（×，whose 因属疑问代词，故应置于句首）
→ Whose is this dog?（√，此处 whose 为名词性所有格代词，之后不接名词）
这只狗是谁的？

2. **test paper** [ˋtɛst ˏpepɚ] *n.* 测验卷，试卷

3. **ma'am** [mæm] *n.* 夫人，女士（对妇女的尊称语，此指女老师）

注意

a. ma'am 是 madam [ˋmædəm] 的缩写形式。

b. sir [sɝ] 指对男士（含男老师）的尊称。

4. **answer** [ˋænsɚ] *n.* 答案

5. **exactly** [ɪgˋzæktlɪ] *adv.* 完全地

6. **same** [sem] *a.* 相同的

注意

a. same 之前始终要置定冠词 the，常用于下列句型中：

A is the same as B　A 和 B 相同

（句中的 as [æz] 是连词，译成 "和"）

例 This book is the same as mine. 这本书和我的那本相同。

b. the same 之前可置副词 exactly、much、about，表示相同的程度的深浅之别。

exactly the same 完全相同

much the same 很相同

about the same 大致相同

例 My bike is exactly the same as John's.
我的自行车和约翰的完全相同。

7. **in the back of** 在……之后

例 I sit in the back of the class, and Mary sits in the front.
我坐在教室后面，而玛丽坐在前面。

3 请选择下列各句中正确的一项

1. ________ is her pencil over there.
   (A) Those (B) These (C) That (D) This
2. ________ is my book bag over here.
   (A) Those (B) These (C) That (D) This
3. ________ shoes over here are his.
   (A) Those (B) These (C) That (D) This
4. ________ earrings over there are Sally's.
   (A) Those (B) These (C) That (D) This
5. Whose cigarettes are these? ______ Peter's.
   (A) They're (B) This's (C) That's (D) It's
6. Bob's car is ______ color as mine.
   (A) exactly same (B) same
   (C) exactly the same (D) very same

解答 1. (C) 2. (D) 3. (B) 4. (A) 5. (A) 6. (C)

Lesson 25

My Father

我的父亲

1 *Reading* 阅读

My father does the same thing every morning. He gets up at six o'clock. He washes, brushes his teeth and combs his hair. Then, he puts on his clothes and eats breakfast. At six thirty he listens to the news on the radio. At exactly seven o'clock he leaves the house. My father has very regular habits.

我父亲每天早上都做相同的事。他 6 点起床。他洗脸、刷牙、梳头发。然后他就穿衣吃早饭。他 6 点半听收音机播报的新闻。他 7 点整出门。我父亲有很规律的习惯。

2 Vocabulary & Idioms 单词短语注解

1. **every** [ˋɛvrɪ] *a.* 每个
   He visits his teacher every Sunday. 他每个星期天都会去看他的老师。
2. **morning** [ˋmɔrnɪŋ] *n.* 早上
3. **wash** [wɑʃ] *vi.* 洗脸，洗手
   My kung fu teacher always washes in cold water.
   我的功夫课老师总是以冷水盥洗。
4. **brush** [brʌʃ] *vt.* 刷
5. **teeth** [tiθ] *n.* 牙齿（tooth [tuθ] 的复数形式）
   one tooth 一颗牙齿
   two teeth 两颗牙齿
6. **comb** [kom] *vt.* 用梳子梳（comb 也可作名词，表示“梳子”的意思）
   Comb your hair. It's a mess. 把头发梳一梳吧！乱七八糟的。
7. **hair** [hɛr] *n.* 头发（不可数）
8. **then** [ðɛn] *adv.* 然后
9. **clothes** [kloz] *n.* 衣服
   注意
   a. clothes 是复数，表示“衣服”，但却是不可数名词。不可说：
      a cloth (×)
      two clothes (×)
      three clothes (×)
      但可说：some clothes 一些衣服
      many clothes 许多衣服
   b. clothes 是衣服的总称。以下名词则为可数名词。
      上衣：shirt [ʃɝt] *n.* 衬衫
      a shirt，two shirts
      blouse [blaʊs] *n.* 女人的圆领衬衫
      a blouse，two blouses

coat [kot] *n.* 西装的上装

a coat, two coats

裤子 : trousers [ˋtraʊzɚz] *n.* 长裤(由于裤管有两个,故始终用复数)

a trouser (×)

two trousers (×)

a pair of trousers 一条裤子

two pairs of trousers 两条裤子

shorts [ʃɔrts] *n.* 短裤

a shorts (×)

two shorts (×)

a pair of shorts 一条短裤

two pairs of shorts 两条短裤

裙 : skirt [skɜt] *n.* 裙子

a skirt, two skirts

套装 : suit [sut] *n.* 男西装(上装及裤子); 女套装(上装及裙子)

a suit, two suits

dress [drɛs] *n.* 女用服装(一件式)

a dress, two dresses

10. **eat** [it] *vt.* 吃

I usually eat a sandwich for lunch. 我午餐通常吃一个三明治。

11. **breakfast** [ˋbrɛkfəst] *n.* 早餐

12. **listen** [ˋlɪsn̩] *vi.* 倾听(与介词 to 连用,方可置宾语)

He is listening music. (×)

→ He is listening to music. (√) 他正在听音乐。

13. **news** [njuz] *n.* 新闻,消息(不可数)

a piece of news 一则消息

That's a very good news. (×)

→ That's very good news. (√) 那是很好的消息。

→ That's a very good piece of news. (√) 那是一则好消息。

14. **radio** [ˋredɪ͵o] *n.* 收音机

15. **o'clock** [əˋklɑk] *n.* ……点钟
eight o'clock 8 点钟

16. **leave** [liv] *vt.* 离开
What time does the train leave the station? 火车什么时候离开车站?

17. **regular** [ˋrɛgjələ] *a.* 有规律的
My father goes to bed at regular hours. 我父亲的睡觉时间很规律。

18. **habit** [ˋhæbɪt] *n.* 习惯
Smoking is a bad habit. 抽烟是个坏习惯。

3 *Grammar Points* 语法重点

本课主要介绍一般现在时的用法。

1. 稍早我们曾介绍了现在进行时的形态及用法。我们现在将两种时态作个比较:
一般现在时:
例 He has breakfast at seven every morning. 他每天早上 7 点吃早饭。
现在进行时:
例 He is having breakfast now. 他现在正在吃早饭。
第一句中的 has (吃) 等于 eats,是一般现在时,所表示的动作并非"正在发生的动作",而是"常态的动作";而第二句 is having (正在吃) 等于 is eating,则表示"现在正在发生的动作"。

2. **My father does the same thing every morning.**
= Every morning my father does the same thing.
我父亲每天早上都做相同的事。
上句中的 every morning 是时间副词。英文中的时间副词可置于句首或句尾,但多半置于句尾。中文里的时间副词,则多置于主语之后。比较下列句子:
中文:我今天很忙。
英文:I today am busy. (×)

→ I am busy today. (√)

= Today I am busy.

3. **He gets up at six o'clock.** 他6点钟起床。

= He rises at six o'clock.

a. get up 起床(= rise [raɪz])

go to bed 睡觉

例 A farmer usually gets up early in the morning.

农民通常一大早就起床。

b. at six o'clock 在6点钟

= at six

英文里表示“在……点钟”时,要使用介词 at,之后接数字,名词 o'clock 通常可省略。

例 He gets up at five (o'clock) every morning.

他每天早上5点起床。

4. **Then, he puts on his clothes and eats breakfast.**

然后,他就穿衣吃早饭。

put on 穿戴(衣、帽、鞋、袜子、耳环等可佩戴在身上的任何东西)

take off 脱下(上列的任何东西)

例 Put on your bathing suit and let's go swimming.

穿上泳装,咱们去游泳吧。

Take off your shoes. They're dirty. 把鞋脱掉,它们太脏了。

注意

wear [wɛr] 与 put on 均表示“穿”的意思, 但 wear 强调“穿着了……”(已穿好的状态),而 put on 则强调“穿上……”(穿的动作)。

例 After I wash, I put on my school uniform.

盥洗过后,我穿上学校的制服。

Bob wears a suit and tie to work. 鲍勃上班时穿西装打领带。

5. **At exactly seven o'clock he leaves the house.**

= He leaves the house at exactly seven (o'clock).

他7点整出门。

exactly [ɪgˋzæktlɪ] *adv.* 精确地

此处 exactly 置于表几点钟的名词之前，表示"几点整"之意。

例 Please see me at exactly nine (o'clock) tonight.

请于今晚 9 点整见我。

4 Substitution 替换

1. He gets up at six o'clock every morning.
   He wakes up at six o'clock every morning.
   He rises at six o'clock every morning.
   他每天早上 6 点起床 / 醒来 / 起来。

---

2. At exactly seven o'clock he leaves the house.
   At about nine o'clock she goes to work.
   At around seven fifteen I go to school.
   他 7 点整出门。
   她大约 9 点上班。
   我大约 7 点 15 分上学。

Lesson 26

He Usually Plays Tennis

他通常打网球

1 *Dialogue* 实用会话

Jeff: What do you usually do on Sundays?

Betty: I usually go for a walk in the mountains.

Jeff: Does your husband go with you?

Betty: No. He doesn't.

Jeff: What does he do?

Betty: He usually plays tennis.

杰弗：你星期天通常做些什么事?

贝蒂：我通常到山中走一走。

杰弗：你先生跟你一块儿去吗?

贝蒂：不。他不去。

杰弗：他做什么呢?

贝蒂：他通常打网球。

2 *Key Points* 重点提示

1. **What do you usually do on Sundays?**

   你星期天通常做些什么事?

   on Sunday 这个星期天

   on Sundays 每逢星期天

例 Do you want to go to the beach on Sunday?
你这个星期天要去海滩吗？
I practice the piano on Sundays. 我每个星期天都练习弹钢琴。

2. **go for a walk** 散步
= take a walk
walk [wɔk] *n.* 散步
例 Let's go for a walk in the countryside tomorrow.
咱们明天到乡下去走走吧。

3. **mountain** [ˋmaʊntn̩] *n.* 山

4. **husband** [ˋhʌzbənd] *n.* 丈夫

5. **tennis** [ˋtɛnɪs] *n.* 网球

3 请选择下列各句中正确的一项

1. Patty ______ up at eight o'clock.
(A) wake (B) rises (C) wakes (D) waking
2. At seven o'clock I ______ my homework.
(A) does (B) do (C) writes (D) doing
3. ________ your coat. It's cold outside.
(A) Take off (B) Put on
(C) Wear (D) Put down
4. Carl ______ his dog on Sundays.
(A) wash (B) walk (C) walking (D) washes
5. I ______ a shower in the morning.
(A) do (B) take (C) wash (D) make
6. I usually watch TV ______.
(A) for Saturdays (B) in Saturdays
(C) on Saturdays (D) at Saturdays

解答 1. (C) 2. (B) 3. (B) 4. (D) 5. (B) 6. (C)

Lesson 27

Jack and His Dog

杰克和他的狗

1 *Reading* 阅读

Jack seldom gets together with his friends. He usually stays at home with his pet dog, Lucky. They sometimes go for long walks in the park. Although Jack is often alone, he is never lonely. He always tells his friends that a dog is man's best friend.

杰克很少与朋友在一起。他通常跟他的爱犬乐奇待在家里。他们有时候在公园里散步,走上好一阵子。虽然杰克经常孤单一人,他却从不感寂寞。他总是告诉他的朋友说狗是人类最好的朋友。

2 Vocabulary & Idioms 单词短语注解

1. **seldom** [ˋsɛldəm] *adv.* 很少
   I seldom go to the movies. 我很少去看电影。

2. **together** [təˋgɛðɚ] *adv.* 一起
   get together 在一起
   Carl and I are working on this project together.
   卡尔和我正一起做这项计划。

3. **usually** [ˋjuʒʊəlɪ] *adv.* 通常
   I usually jog in the morning. 我通常在早上慢跑。

4. **stay** [ste] *vi.* 待在，停留在
   Susie often stays at her grandmother's house on Saturdays.
   苏西星期六经常待在她奶奶家里。

5. **pet** [pɛt] *n.* 宠物
   a pet dog 爱犬
   a pet cat 宠猫

6. **sometimes** [ˋsʌmˏtaɪmz] *adv.* 有时候
   Patty sometimes falls asleep in class. 帕蒂有时候会在课堂上睡着。

7. **go for a walk** 去散步
   = go for a stroll
   * stroll [ˋstrol] *n.* 散步
   I usually go for a walk after dinner. 我通常在吃完晚饭后会去散步。

8. **park** [pɑrk] *n.* 公园

9. **although** [ɔlˋðo] *conj.* 虽然
   Although Jane eats a lot of ice cream, she is not fat.
   虽然简吃了很多冰淇淋，但是她并不胖。

10. **often** [ˋɔfən] *adv.* 经常
    Chris is often late for work. 克里斯上班经常迟到。

11. **alone** [əˋlon] *a.* 单独的，独自的

Are you alone, or is somebody with you?
你是一个人呢，还是有人跟你作伴？

12. **never** [ˋnɛvɚ] *adv.* 绝对不，从不
Mother is always happy. She is never sad.
我母亲总是很快乐。她从不会感到难过。

13. **lonely** [ˋlonlɪ] *a.* 寂寞的

14. **always** [ˋɔlwez] *adv.* 始终
I always play ping-pong on Saturday mornings.
我总是在星期六早上打乒乓球。

15. **tell** [tɛl] *vt.* 告诉
My teacher often tells us to study hard.
我的老师常常告诉我们要用功读书。

16. **man** [mæn] *n.* 人类(之前不置冠词)

17. **best** [bɛst] *a.* 最好的(good 的最高级)
Tim is the best basketball player on our team.
蒂姆是我们队里最好的篮球运动员。

3 Grammar Points 语法重点

本课主要介绍频率副词与一般现在时的关系，并介绍双重连接的错误句子结构及改正之道。

1. 本课出现了许多频率副词，计有 seldom(很少)、usually(通常)、often(经常)、sometimes(有时候)、never(从不)、always (始终)等。频率副词通常使用在一般现在时中。注意这些频率副词在句中的位置：
   a. 句中有 be 动词时，频率副词置于该 be 动词之后。
   例 John is always busy. 约翰总是很忙。
   Chris is helpful. He is never selfish.
   克里斯很乐于助人。他从不自私。
   Because they live far away from here, they are sometimes late

for work.
因为他们住的地方离这里很远,所以他们有时候上班会迟到。

b. 句中有一般动词时,频率副词置于该动词之前。

例 He usually goes to bed late. 他通常很晚才睡觉。

I seldom talk to him. 我很少跟他说话。

2. **Although Jack is often alone, he is never lonely.**

= Jack is often alone, but he is never lonely.
虽然杰克经常单独一个人,但是他从不感到寂寞。
请读者注意下列要点:

a. although 亦可用 though [ðo] 代替,均表"虽然",作副词连词,引导状语从句,修饰主句。我们因受中文语法"虽然……但是……"的影响,而可能在英文里亦说"although(或 though)...but...",但这是错误的用法,因为英文的语法规定两句之间的连词只能有一个。"although(或 though)...but..."之中,although(或 though)与 but 均为连词,形成错误的双重连接句子结构。故若采用 although(或 though),则 but 应予省略;若采用 but,则 although(或 though)就应省略。

例 Though he is nice, but I don't like him. (×)
→ Though he is nice, I don't like him. (√)
= He is nice, but I don't like him.
虽然他人不错,但是我不喜欢他。

b. "Because...so..."(因为……所以……)亦是错误的双重连接句子结构。故若采用 because 时,则不可再用 so; 若采用 so 时,则不可再用 because。

例 Because he is nice, so we all like him. (×)
→ Because he is nice, we all like him. (√)
= He is nice, so we all like him.
因为他人不错,所以我们都喜欢他。

4 Substitution 替换

1. He seldom gets together with his friends.

   He doesn't usually get together with his friends.

   He often gets together with his friends.

   他很少 / 不常 / 经常与朋友在一起。

---

2. They sometimes go for a walk in the park.

   They rarely go for a drive in the country.

   They often go for a stroll at the seashore.

   他们有时到公园里散步。

   他们很少在乡下开车兜风。

   他们经常在海边散步。

Lesson 28

I Always Walk

我都是走路去

1 *Dialogue* 实用会话

Chris: How do you go to school, Judy?

Judy: I usually take a bus, but sometimes I ride my bicycle. What about you?

Chris: I live near our school, so I always walk.

Judy: You're lucky.

克里斯：朱迪，你是怎么上学的？

朱　迪：我通常乘公共汽车，但有时候我骑自行车。你呢？

克里斯：我住在我们学校附近，因此我都是走路去。

朱　迪：你真幸运。

2 *Key Points* 重点提示

1. **take a bus** 乘公共汽车
   take a train 乘火车
   take a taxi 乘出租车
2. **ride** [raɪd] *vt.* 骑乘
   例 Do you know how to ride a motorcycle? 你知道怎么骑摩托车吗？
3. **near** [nɪr] *prep.* 在……附近
4. **lucky** [ˋlʌkɪ] *a.* 幸运的

例 Roger has a beautiful girlfriend. He is very lucky.
罗杰有个很漂亮的女友,他真是幸运。

3 请选择下列各句中正确的一项

1. Mark is very lazy. He is ______ late for class.
   (A) rarely (B) never (C) seldom (D) always
2. Paul is very hardworking. He ______ watches TV.
   (A) rarely (B) always (C) usually (D) often
3. Mary ______ walks to school. She always takes a bus.
   (A) never (B) often
   (C) sometimes (D) usually
4. Jack is very shy. He ______ talks to people.
   (A) always (B) usually (C) often (D) seldom
5. Bill is afraid of cold weather. He ______ swims in the winter.
   (A) always (B) usually (C) never (D) often

解答 1. (D) 2. (A) 3. (A) 4. (D) 5. (C)

Lesson 29

Poor Dick

可怜的迪克

1 *Reading* 阅读

There are holes in Dick's shoes. He needs new shoes. Dick doesn't want cheap shoes. He wants expensive shoes, but he doesn't have any money. He needs a job. He is looking for one, but he isn't having any luck. No one wants to give him a job because his shoes have holes in them. Poor Dick!

迪克的鞋有破洞。他需要新鞋。迪克不想要便宜的鞋。他想要贵的鞋,但他没钱。他需要一份工作。他正在找工作,但他的运气不好。因为他的鞋有破洞,所以没有人给他工作。可怜的迪克!

2 Vocabulary & Idioms 单词短语注解

1. **hole** [hol] *n.* 破洞；小洞
2. **shoe** [ʃu] *n.* 鞋
   a pair of shoes 一双鞋
   I want to buy a pair of black leather shoes. 我想买一双黑皮鞋。
3. **need** [nid] *vt.* 需要
   Do you need any help? 你需要任何帮助吗？
4. **want** [wɑnt] *vt.* 想要
   I want to study abroad. 我想去国外念书。
5. **cheap** [tʃip] *a.* 便宜的，廉价的
   Most vegetables are cheap in the summer.
   大部分的蔬菜在夏天都很便宜。
6. **expensive** [ɪkˋspɛnsɪv] *a.* 昂贵的
   This diamond ring is very expensive. 这枚钻戒非常昂贵。
7. **any** [ˋɛnɪ] *a.* 任何的
8. **money** [ˋmʌnɪ] *n.* 钱
9. **job** [dʒɑb] *n.* 工作
   Do you have a full-time job? 你有全职的工作吗？
10. **look** [lʊk] *vi.* 寻找（与介词 for 连用）
    look for... 寻找……
    What is she looking for? 她在寻找什么？
11. **luck** [lʌk] *n.* 幸运
12. **poor** [pʊr] *a.* 可怜的
    Poor Billy has a terrible cold. 可怜的比利感冒得很厉害。

3 Grammar Points 语法重点

本课介绍 no 与 not 的区别、代词 one 的用法，并复习连词 but 及 because 的用法。

1. **He wants expensive shoes, but he doesn't have any money.**

= He wants expensive shoes, but he has no money.

他想要贵的鞋，但他没钱。

no 与 not 对初学英文的读者来说，有时是个头痛的问题。请先看下例：

I have not money. (×)

→ I have no money. (√) 我没有钱。

其实 no 与 not 很容易分辨：

a. no 是形容词，表示"没有一个"，而 not 则是副词，表示"不"的意思。

b. no 就等于 not any（没有任何一个）。换言之，no 之后可直接置名词，而 not 则须先接形容词 any，才可接名词。

例 I have not any money.（可）我没有钱。

= I have no money.（佳，no 比 not any 更简洁）

注意

上列第一句中，not 亦可置于动词 have 之前，形成否定句。但 not 不能直接修饰动词，须于其前按主语人称分置助动词 do 或 does，再将动词改为原形。

例 He not has any money. (×)

→ He does not have any money. (√) 他没有钱。

= He doesn't have any money.

= He has no money.

2. **He wants expensive shoes, but he doesn't have any money.**

他想要贵的鞋，但他没钱。

He is looking for one, but he isn't having any luck.

他正在找工作，但他的运气不好。

以上两句中的 but 是并列连词，这种连词连接两个句子。就写作习惯而言，but 之前应置逗号。不过，现在的英美文章中，亦常见将 but 之前的逗号省略。

3. **He needs a job. He is looking for one, but he isn't having any luck.**

他需要一份工作。他正在找工作，但他的运气不好。

a. 上列第二句中的 one 是代词，代替前面的名词 a job。

原句实为：

He needs a job. He is looking for a job, but...

但 a job 重复了一次，就修辞而言应予避免，故用 one 代替。这个 one 专用来代替前面提到的单数可数名词。

例 I need a good English dictionary, but I can't afford a good English dictionary now. (劣)

→ I need a good English dictionary, but I can't afford one now. (佳)

我需要一本好的英文字典，但我现在买不起。

b. one 亦可与形容词连用。

例 I don't like this red pen. Give me a yellow pen. (劣)

= I don't like this red pen. Give me a yellow one. (佳)

我不喜欢这支红色的笔。给我一支黄色的笔。

4. **No one wants to give him a job because his shoes have holes in them.**

因为他的鞋有破洞，所以没有人给他工作。

本句中的 because 是从属连词，引导状语从句，修饰主句。Because 引导的从句可置于主句前后。就写作习惯而言，置于主句之前时，主句与从句之间应置逗号；若置于主句之后时，则主句与从句之间不置逗号。

例 Because he is knowledgeable, he has my respect.

= He has my respect because he is knowledgeable.

因为他有学问，所以我尊敬他。

其他从属连词如 although(= though，虽然)、when (当……的时候)、if (如果) 等用法皆同。

例 Although he is rich, I don't envy him. 虽然他有钱，可我不嫉妒他。

= I don't envy him although he is rich.

If I have time, I will do it. 我若有时间,就会做这件事。

= I will do it if I have time.

4 Substitution 替换

1. He wants expensive shoes, but he doesn't have any money.
   The food is good, but I have no appetite.
   The bike is great, but it's too expensive.
   他想要贵的鞋，但他没钱。
   这菜不错，但我没胃口。
   这辆自行车很棒，但它太贵了。

---

2. No one wants to give him a job because his shoes have holes in them.
   No one likes him because he is lazy.
   He has no friends because he is selfish.
   因为他的鞋有破洞，所以没有人给他工作。
   因为他懒，所以没人喜欢他。
   因为他自私，所以他没朋友。

Lesson 30

Money Doesn't Grow on Trees

挣钱是很辛苦的

1 *Dialogue* 实用会话

Sam: Mother, can you buy me a new bike?

Mother: No, Sam. I can't.

Sam: But all my friends have new bicycles.

Mother: You can ride their bikes.

Sam: Why can't I have a new bike?

Mother: Because money doesn't grow on trees.

山姆：妈，您可不可以买一辆新的自行车给我?

妈妈：不可以，山姆。我办不到。

山姆：但是我所有的朋友都有新车。

妈妈：你可以骑他们的车子呀！

山姆：我为什么不能有辆新车呢?

妈妈：因为钱不会长在树上嘛（喻挣钱是很辛苦的）。

2 *Key Points* 重点提示

1. **buy + 人 + 物**　买某物给某人

 = buy + 物 + for + 人

 例 Romeo buys his wife flowers every day.

 = Romeo buys flowers for his wife every day.

罗密欧每天都买花送他太太。

2. **ride** [raɪd] *vt.* 骑（马、自行车等），乘坐（公共汽车、火车等）

例 Can you ride a horse? 你会骑马吗？

I always ride the train to work. 我总是乘火车上班的。

3. **grow** [gro] *vi.* 生长

例 All flowers need water to grow. 花都需要水才能生长。

3 请选择下列各句中正确的一项

1. Mary doesn't like this dress. She likes ______ over there.

   (A) the red one　　(B) the red

   (C) red　　(D) a red

2. John is looking ______ a good English dictionary.

   (A) on　　(B) around　　(C) into　　(D) for

3. He can't come ______ he is busy now.

   (A) though　　(B) but　　(C) because　　(D) although

4. He is sad because he ______ money.

   (A) has no any　　(B) not has

   (C) not has any　　(D) doesn't have any

5. Tim often ______ his children.

   (A) buys toys　　(B) buys toys for

   (C) buys for his toys　　(D) buys toys to

解答　1. (A)　2. (D)　3. (C)　4. (D)　5. (B)

Lesson 31

Poor Amy

可怜的艾米

1 *Reading* 阅读

Amy can't pay this month's rent. She needs some help. Unfortunately, none of her friends can help her. They don't have any money, either. Poor Amy is really depressed. She has no money, and the landlord is knocking at the door. Amy is very nervous. She shouts, "No one is home!"

艾米这个月的房租付不出来。她需要一些帮助。不幸的是，她的朋友没有一个能帮助她。他们也没钱。可怜的艾米真的很沮丧。她没钱，而房东这时正在敲门。艾米很紧张。她叫道："没人在家！"

2 Vocabulary & Idioms 单词短语注解

1. **pay** [pe] *vt.* 付(钱)
   Can you pay the telephone bill today? 你今天可以去付电话费吗?

2. **rent** [rɛnt] *n.* 房租

3. **help** [hɛlp] *n.* & *vt.* 帮助
   Thank you very much for your help. 非常感谢你的帮忙。
   Help your mother (to) wash the dishes. 去帮你母亲洗碗。

4. **unfortunately** [ʌnˋfɔrtʃənɪtlɪ] *adv.* 不幸的是
   I should see a doctor. Unfortunately, I don't have any time.
   我应该去看医生。不幸的是,我没有时间。

5. **none** [nʌn] *pron.* 没有一个
   none of + the + 复数名词　……之中没有一个
   None of the students know the answer. 这些学生中没有一个知道答案。

6. **really** [ˋriəlɪ] *adv.* 真正地
   Sam really loves studying English. 山姆真的很爱学英文。

7. **depressed** [dɪˋprɛst] *a.* 沮丧的,难过的
   Carl is depressed because his bicycle is broken.
   卡尔很沮丧,因为他的自行车坏了。

8. **landlord** [ˋlænd,lɔrd] *n.* 房东
   tenant [ˋtɛnənt] *n.* 房客

9. **knock** [nɑk] *vi.* 敲(门)
   knock the door (×)
   knock <u>at</u> the door (√) 敲门

10. **nervous** [ˋnɝvəs] *a.* 紧张的
    Exams make me very nervous. 考试使我很紧张。

11. **shout** [ʃaʊt] *vt.* 高呼,大声说出
    My teacher often shouts, "Shut up!" when we are noisy.
    当我们吵闹时,老师常会大叫:"闭嘴!"

3 Grammar Points 语法重点

本课介绍形容词 some 及代词 none 的用法。

1. **She needs some help.** 她需要一些帮助。

   此处 some [sʌm] 为形容词，表示“一些”。此外，亦可表示“某个”的意思，用法如下：

   a. 作“一些”解时，之后可接复数可数名词（如 friends、books）或不可数名词（如 money、help）。

   例 Peter has some very good English books.
   彼得有一些很棒的英文书。
   I have some money. 我有一些钱。

   b. 作“某个”解时，之后接单数可数名词。此时的 some 相当于不定冠词 a 或 an。

   例 Some guy is looking for you. 某个家伙正在找你。
   = A guy is looking for you.

2. **...none of her friends can help her.**

   ……她的朋友没有一个能帮助她。

   本句中的 none 是代词，可用来代替人或物，指三个或三个以上的人或东西中“没有一个”，用法如下：

   none of + the (these、those、my、your、his...) + 复数名词 + 复数（或单数）动词

   例 None of my friends like (s) music.
   我的朋友中没有一个喜欢音乐。
   None of those books are / is interesting.
   那些书中没有一本是有趣的。

4 Substitution 替换

1. She needs some help.
   We need some pens.
   My tired mother needs some sleep.

她需要一些帮助。
我们需要一些笔。
我那疲惫的母亲需要一些睡眠。

---

2. Unfortunately, none of | her friends can help her. | his classmates can go. | my co-workers can come. |

不幸的是，她的朋友没有一个能帮助她。
不幸的是，他的同学没有一个能去。
不幸的是，我的同事没有一个能来。

Lesson 32

Coins for the Phone

打投币电话

1 *Dialogue* 实用会话

Roy: Hi, Connie! Do you have any change?

Connie: What for?

Roy: I want some coins for the pay phone.

Connie: I see. Here you are.

Roy: Thank you.

Connie: You're welcome.

罗伊：嗨，康妮！你有零钱吗？

康妮：干嘛？

罗伊：我想要些硬币打投币电话。

康妮：我明白了。给你！

罗伊：谢谢你。

康妮：别客气。

2 *Key Points* 重点提示

1. **change** [tʃendʒ] *n.* 零钱（不可数）

   注意

   上面括号内"不可数"三个字，并非指零钱不能数；零钱当然可数，如 1 美元（a dollar）、2 美元（two dollars）、3 毛钱（three dimes）

等；“不可数”这三个字乃指change这个英文单词不能数。我们不能说一个零钱（a change）、两个零钱（two changes）。change作“零钱”解时，无复数形式。

中文：你有多少零钱？

英文：How many changes do you have? (×)

→ How much change do you have? (√)

中文：我有20美元的零钱。

英文：I have twenty dollars in change. (√)

2. **Do you have any change?** 你有零钱吗？

I want some coins for the pay phone. 我想要些硬币打投币电话。

any与some均可作数量形容词，之后均可置可数或不可数名词，但用法有别：

a. any使用于疑问句或否定句中；

b. some使用于肯定句中。

1) 疑问句：

例 Do you need any help? 你需要帮助吗？

2) 否定句：

例 He doesn't need any help. 他不需要任何帮助。

3) 肯定句：

例 He needs some help. 他需要一些帮助。

3. **What for?** 为什么？

= Why?

4. **coin** [kɔɪn] *n.* 硬币

5. **pay phone** [ˋpe ˏfon] *n.* 投币电话，付费电话

6. **I see.** 我明白了。

= I understand.

* understand [ˏʌndɚˋstænd] *vi.* 了解

例 A: Bill is studying for his test. 比尔正在为他的考试而学习。

B: Oh, I see. 哦，我知道了。

7. **Here you are.** 给你！

例 A: Please pass me the salt. 请把盐递给我。

B: Here you are. 给你！

3 请选择下列各句中正确的一项

1. He doesn't have ______ friends.

(A) some (B) any (C) no (D) none

2. ______ can sing.

(A) None my friends (B) None of my friends

(C) None of friends (D) No of friends

3. ______ does he have?

(A) How many change (B) How many changes

(C) How much change (D) How much changes

4. I don't have ______ with me.

(A) some moneys (B) any moneys

(C) some money (D) any money

5. I have ______ questions.

(A) some (B) any (C) none (D) no any

解答 1. (B) 2. (B) 3. (C) 4. (D) 5. (A)

Lesson 33

She Wants to Wear Something Formal

她想穿正式的衣服

1 *Reading* 阅读

Judy is looking for something nice to wear for a job interview. She wants to wear something formal. Unfortunately, she doesn't have anything except casual clothes. Judy is worried. She has nothing suitable to wear, so she puts on her best casual clothes. She goes to the interview. Guess what? Judy gets the job!

朱迪正在寻找求职面试时要穿的一件好衣服。她想要穿正式的衣服。不幸的是，她除了休闲装以外，没别的衣服。朱迪很焦急。她没有适合的衣服可穿，于是她穿上了她最好的休闲装。她面试去了。你猜怎么样？朱迪得到了那份工作！

2 Vocabulary & Idioms 单词短语注解

1. **interview** [ˋɪntɚˏvju] *n.* 面试
I am nervous at interviews. 我面试时都会紧张。

2. **formal** [ˋfɔrml̩] *a.* 正式的
People wear formal clothes at weddings. 婚礼时人们都穿着正式的服装。

3. **except** [ɪkˋsɛpt] *prep.* 除……之外
My father works every day except on Sundays.
我父亲除了星期天外，每天都要工作。

4. **casual** [ˋkæʒuəl] *a.* 休闲的
casual clothes 便服，休闲装

5. **worried** [ˋwɝɪd] *a.* 忧虑的，焦急的
I am worried about my sick mother. 我很担心我生病的母亲。

6. **suitable** [ˋsutəbl̩] *a.* 适合的
Shorts are not suitable for cold weather. 短裤不适合在寒冷的天气时穿。

7. **guess** [gɛs] *vt.* 猜
Can anyone guess the answer? 有谁能猜出答案吗?

3 Grammar Points 语法重点

本课介绍“something / anything / nothing + 形容词”的后位修饰结构，以及介词 except 的用法。

1. **something** [ˋsʌmθɪŋ] *pron.* 某物，某事
anything [ˋɛnɪˏθɪŋ] *pron.* 任何事物
nothing [ˋnʌθɪŋ] *pron.* 无事，无物
以上三词均为代词，可代替物或事情；代替物时，可指衣服(如本文)、桌子、手表等任何具体的东西。使用时应注意下列事项：
a. 形容词修饰一般名词时，通常置于该名词前。但形容词修饰 something、anything、nothing 等代词时，该形容词应置于这些代词之后，这种结构称为后位修饰。

例 He is a boy good. (×)
→ He is a good boy. (√) 他是好孩子。
I have good something for you. (×)
→ I have something good for you. (√) 我有好东西给你。
I can't find good anything at the store. (×)
→ I can't find anything good at the store. (√)
在那家商店我找不到任何好货。
He is doing wrong nothing. (×)
→ He is doing nothing wrong. (√) 他没有做不对的事。

b. something、anything、nothing 无复数形式。

例 I have somethings to do. (×)
→ I have something to do. (√) 我有事要做。

c. something 使用于肯定句中; anything 使用于否定句及疑问句中; nothing 本身具否定意味,不可再与否定句连用形成双重否定。

1) something

例 I don't have something important to tell you.
(×, something 不可用于否定句中)
→ I have something important to tell you.
(√, something 用于肯定句中)
我有重要的事要告诉你。

2) anything

例 Do you have anything important to tell me?
(√, anything 用于疑问句中)
你有任何重要的事要告诉我吗?
I don't have anything important to tell you.
(√, anything 用于否定句中)
我没有重要的事要告诉你。

3) nothing

例 I don't have nothing important to tell you.
(×, nothing 已具否定意思, 故不得再与否定副词 not 连用, 否则形成错误的双重否定)
→ I have nothing important to tell you. (√)

= I don't have anything important to tell you.
我没有重要的事要告诉你。

2. **Unfortunately, she doesn't have anything except casual clothes.**

不幸的是,她除了休闲装以外,没别的衣服。

本句的 except 是介词,表示"除……之外",使用时要置于有 all(所有的)、no(没有一个)、any(任何一个)、every(每一个)等含有完全意义的形容词所修饰的名词之后。

例 All the boys like music except John.
除了约翰以外,所有男孩都喜欢音乐。
He has nothing except money. 他除了钱以外,什么都没有。
He likes everybody except me. 他除了我以外,谁都喜欢。
I don't like anyone except Mary. 我除了玛丽以外,谁都不喜欢。

了解上述有关 except 的用法后,我们就不可再造下列错误的句子:

例 Many boys are good except him. (×, many 表"许多",不含有完全的意义,故不能与 except 连用)
→ All the boys are good except him. (√)
除了他以外,所有男孩都很好。
I like some girls here except Mary. (×, some 表"一些",不含有完全的意义,故不能与 except 连用)
→ I like every girl here except Mary. (√)
= I like all the girls here except Mary.
除了玛丽以外,这里的女孩我都喜欢。

4 Substitution 替换

1. She wants to wear something formal.
She wants to wear something simple.
She doesn't want to wear anything uncomfortable.
她想要穿正式的衣服。
她想要穿简朴的衣服。

她不想穿不舒适的衣服。

---

2. She has nothing suitable to wear.
   I have no suitable clothes to wear.
   He doesn't have anything suitable to wear.
   她没有适合的衣服可穿。
   我没有适合的衣服可穿。
   他没有适合的衣服可穿。

Lesson 34

Let's Go to a Disco

咱们到迪斯科舞厅去

1 *Dialogue* 实用会话

Peter: Hi, Paula! What are you doing?

Paula: Nothing special.

Peter: Let's do something together.

Paula: Do you have anything in mind?

Peter: Let's go to a disco.

Paula: Great! Can your handsome brother come too?

彼得：嗨，波拉！你在做什么？

波拉：没什么特别的事。

彼得：咱们一块做些事好了。

波拉：你有什么想法没有？

彼得：咱们到迪斯科舞厅去。

波拉：太棒了！你那英俊的哥哥是否也可以来？

2 *Key Points* 重点提示

1. **special** [ˋspɛʃəl] *a.* 特别的

2. **together** [təˋgɛðɚ] *adv.* 一起

   例 Do you want to go to the party together?

你想要一起去参加宴会吗?

3. **mind** [maɪnd] *n.* 头脑，心里

have...in mind 心里想着……

例 Do you have anybody in mind for the job?

这工作你心里有人选没有?

4. **disco** [ˈdɪsko] *n.* 迪斯科舞厅

5. **handsome** [ˈhænsəm] *a.* （指男士）英俊的

例 You look very handsome today. 你今天看起来很英俊。

3 请选择下列各句中正确的一项

1. I don't have ______ to eat.

(A) anything (B) nothing

(C) something (D) any

2. We have ______ to do.

(A) anything (B) some

(C) nothing (D) none

3. I have ______ to say.

(A) anything (B) anythings

(C) somethings (D) something

4. Do you want ______ to eat?

(A) any (B) anything

(C) some (D) none

5. I have nothing to wear ______ dirty clothes.

(A) and (B) except

(C) some (D) no

6. Sam : Let's get something to eat.

Sally: OK. Do you ______?

(A) any place have in mind

(B) any place in mind

(C) have in mind

(D) have any place in mind

解答 1. (A) 2. (C) 3. (D) 4. (B) 5. (B) 6. (D)

Lesson 35

There's Little Food

菜很少

1 *Reading* 阅读

Fred's having a party, but he's very embarrassed. There are many people at his party, but there's very little food. There's very little meat. There isn't much rice, either. There are only a few cans of coke and a little orange juice. However, everyone is happy at the party because there's plenty of beer.

弗雷德在开宴会，但是他觉得很不好意思。赴宴的人很多，不过菜却很少，肉也很少，饭也不够多。只有几罐可乐和一些橙汁。不过，因为啤酒很多，所以宴会上每个人都很高兴。

2 Vocabulary & Idioms 单词短语注解

1. **embarrassed** [ɪmˋbærəst] *a.* 困窘的，不好意思的
   I am embarrassed to wear dirty clothes.
   穿脏衣服让我觉得很不好意思。

2. **many** [ˋmɛnɪ] *a.* 许多的（之后接复数名词）
   Mr. Lee has many children. 李先生有许多孩子。

3. **little** [ˋlɪtḷ] *a.* 很少的（之后接不可数名词）
   I have very little homework tonight. 我今晚的功课很少。

4. **food** [fud] *n.* 食物（不可数）

5. **meat** [mit] *n.* 肉（不可数）

6. **much** [mʌtʃ] *a.* 许多的（之后接不可数名词）

7. **rice** [raɪs] *n.* 米，饭（不可数）

8. **few** [fju] *a.* 很少的，没几个（之后接复数名词）
   only a few 只有几个
   Only a few of my friends smoke cigarettes.
   我的朋友中只有少数人抽烟。

9. **can** [kæn] *n.* 罐头

10. **coke** [kok] *n.* 可乐（Coca-Cola 可口可乐的缩写形式）

11. **orange** [ˋɔrɪndʒ] *n.* 橙子

12. **juice** [dʒus] *n.* 果汁

13. **plenty** [ˋplɛntɪ] *pron.* 充分，够多
    plenty of... 很多的……，不少的……
    （之后可接复数名词或不可数名词）
    There's plenty of coffee and tea in the kitchen.
    厨房里有很多的咖啡和茶。

14. **beer** [bɪr] *n.* 啤酒

3 Grammar Points 语法重点

本课介绍表示数量的形容词(如 many、few、little、much 等)的用法。这些形容词亦称不定代词,有的之后要接复数名词,有的只能接不可数名词,有的则两者皆可。兹列述如下:

1. 之后须接复数名词者:

   few 有少数,没几个

   a few 有几个

   several 数个(意思接近 a few,但可能数目较 a few 多。)

   many 许多个

   例 He has few friends. 他没几个朋友——他的朋友很少。

   I have a few friends. 我有几个朋友。

   She has many friends. 她有许多朋友。

   注意

   a. few 表示"没几个",有否定意味;a few 表示"有几个",有肯定意味。

   b. quite a few 不少的,相当多的(= many)

   例 He has quite a few friends. 他朋友不少。

   c. only a few 只有几个(= few 没几个)

   例 Mary has only few friends. (×)

   → Mary has only a few friends. (√) 玛丽只有几位朋友。

2. 之后须接不可数名词者:

   little 很少,没多少

   a little 有一点

   much 许多

   例 He has little money. 他没多少钱——他几乎没钱。

   He has a little money. 他有一点钱。

   He doesn't have much money. 他的钱不多。

   注意

   a. little 表示"没多少",有否定意味;a little 表示"有一点",有肯定意味。

b. quite a little 不少的，相当多的

例 He has quite a little money.

他的钱不少。

c. much 用于否定句中，而不用于肯定句中。肯定句应使用 a lot of 或 lots of。

例 He has much money. (×)

→ He doesn't have much money. (√) 他的钱不多。

He has | lots of / a lot of | money. (√) 他有许多钱。

d. a great deal of 亦表示"许多的、大量的"，之后须接不可数名词。

例 He has a great deal of money. 他有许多钱。

= He has a lot of money.

= He has lots of money.

3. 之后可接复数名词或不可数名词者：

some 一些

a lot of (=lots of) 许多的

plenty of 不少的，相当多的

例 He has some friends / money. 他有一些朋友 / 钱。

He has a lot of (lots of) friends / money. 他有许多朋友 / 钱。

He has plenty of friends / money. 他有不少朋友 / 钱。

4 Substitution 替换

1. There are many people at his party.

There are only a few people at his party.

There aren't a lot of people at his party.

他的宴会上有许多人。

他的宴会上只有少数几个人。

他的宴会上并没有很多人。

2. There are only a few cans of coke and a little orange juice.
There are a lot of vegetables, but there isn't much meat.
There is plenty of food, but there aren't many drinks.
只有几罐可乐和一些橙汁。
有许多蔬菜，但肉并不多。
有不少菜，但饮料并不多。

Lesson 36

A Lot of Bills

许多账单

1 *Dialogue* 实用会话

Al: Do you have any money with you?

Sue: Not much. Why?

Al: I need to borrow some.

Sue: What's the matter?

Al: I have a lot of bills to pay this month.

艾尔：你身上带钱了吗?

苏　：我带的不多。干嘛问这个?

艾尔：我需要借点钱。

苏　：怎么回事?

艾尔：这个月我有许多账单要付。

2 *Key Points* 重点提示

1. **need** [nid] *vt.* 需要

   need to + 动词原形　需要……

   例 You need to be more patient. 你需要耐心一点。

2. **borrow** [ˋbɑro] *vt.* 借

   borrow + 物 + from + 人　向某人借某物

   例 Can I borrow a pen from you? 我可以向你借一支笔吗?

3. **matter** [ˈmætɚ] *n.* 事情

What's the matter (with you) ?（你）怎么啦？

= What's wrong (with you) ?

3 请选择下列各句中正确的一项

1. There are ______ pencils on the table.
   (A) a few (B) much (C) little (D) a little
2. We need ______ food for the party.
   (A) many (B) several (C) a lot (D) lots of
3. How ______ students are in the room?
   (A) much (B) few (C) many (D) a few
4. There is ______ juice in the refrigerator.
   (A) lots (B) a little (C) a lots of (D) many
5. There are ______ children playing in the yard.
   (A) a little (B) much (C) several (D) severals
6. There is something ______ with Fred.
   (A) matter (B) the matter (C) the wrong (D) what's wrong

解答 1. (A) 2. (D) 3. (C) 4. (B) 5. (C) 6. (B)

♫怀念老歌园地♫

All I Have to Do Is Dream

我只能梦想

C4/4

By The Everly Brothers

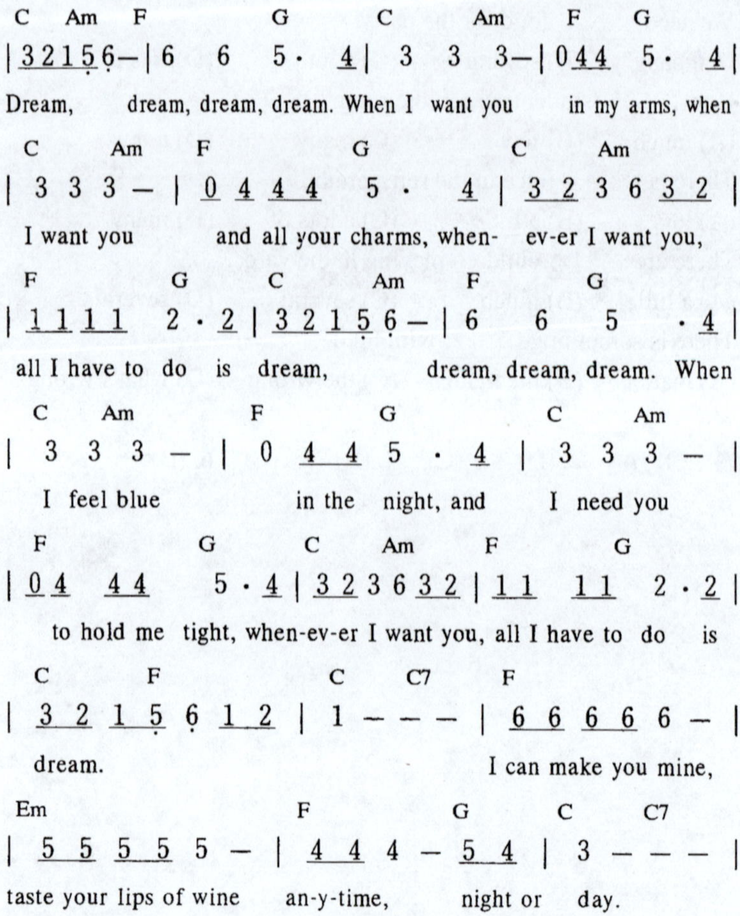

F　　　　　　　　　Em　　　　　　　D7

| 6 6 6 6 6 – | 0 7 5 · 5 | 6 6 6 6 5 · #4 |

On-ly trouble is, gee-whiz, I'm dreaming my life a-

G　　　G7　　C　Am　　F　　　　G

| 5 – 5 0 4 | 3 3 3 – | 0 4 4 4 5 · 4 |

-way. I need you so that I could die. I

C　Am　　F　　G　　　　C　　Am

| 3 3 3 – | 0 4 4 4 5 · 4 | 3 2 3 6 3 2 |

love you so and that is why when-ev - er I want you,

F　　　G　　　　C　　　F　　　C

| 1 1 1 1 2 · 2 | 3 2 1 5̣ 6̣ 1 2 | 1 – – – |

all I have to do is dream.

♫怀念老歌园地♫

All I Have to Do Is Dream

我只能梦想

1 *Lyrics* 歌词

Dream, dream, dream, dream. Dream, dream, dream, dream. When I want you in my arms, when I want you and all your charms, whenever I want you, all I have to do is dream, dream, dream, dream. When I feel blue in the night, and I need you to hold me tight, whenever I want you, all I have to do is dream, dream, dream, dream. I can make you mine, taste your lips of wine anytime, night or day. Only trouble is, gee whiz, I'm dreaming my life away. I need you so that I could die. I love you so and that is why whenever I want you, all I have to do is dream, dream, dream, dream.

梦啊……每当我想拥你入怀,每当我想要动人的你,每当我想要你时,我所能做的就是梦想……每当夜里我感到忧伤,每当我需要你紧紧拥抱我,每当我想要你时,我所能做的就是梦想……梦想我能让你完全属于我,不论白昼或夜晚,我都能亲吻你那醉人的双唇。唯一的困扰是，天啊，我的一生就在做白日梦中消逝了。我太需要你了，若得不到你的爱我将死去。我太爱你了，那也就是为何当我需要你时，我所能做的只是梦想。

2 Vocabulary & Idioms 单词短语注解

1. **All I have to do is dream.** 我所能做的就是梦想。

   注意

   凡以 all one has to do、all one does、what one has to do、what one does 等作主语，其后接 be 动词，再接不定式短语作补足语时，不定式中的 to 通常予以省略。

   All you have to do is to study hard. 你所必须做的就是用功读书。

   = All you have to do is study hard.

   What I will do is to take my book back. 我所要做的就是拿回我的书。

   = What I will do is take my book back.

2. **When I want you in my arms, when I want you and all your charms, whenever I want you, all I have to do is dream.**

   每当我想拥你入怀，每当我想要动人的你，每当我想要你时，我所能做的就是梦想。

   a. arms [ɑrmz] *n.* 怀抱

      in one's arms 在某人怀抱里

      The woman carried the crying baby in her arms.

      那个妇人将哭泣的宝宝抱在怀里。

   b. charm [tʃɑrm] *n.* 魅力 & *vt.* 吸引，使着迷

      Jack won Mary's heart with his charm.

      杰克以他的魅力赢得玛丽的芳心。

      Jack charmed Mary with his humor.

杰克的幽默吸引了玛丽。

c. whenever [hwɛnˋɛvɚ/wɛnˋɛvɚ] *conj.* 每当

注意

whenever 常引导状语从句，表示“每……必……”，此时亦可用“never / not...without + 动名词”的句型来表示。

Whenever she watches a sad movie, she will cry.

= She never watches a sad movie without crying.

= She will not watch a sad movie without crying.

她每次看悲伤的电影都会哭。

3. **When I feel blue in the night,** (a) **and I need you to hold me tight,** (b) **whenever I want you,** (c) **all I have to do is dream...** (d)

每当夜里我感到忧伤，每当我需要你紧紧拥抱我，每当我想要你时，我所能做的就是梦想。

句型分析：

a. 为 when 引导的状语从句；

b. 另一个 when 引导的状语从句，由 and 连接，而 and 与 I 之间的 when 已省略；

c. 为 whenever 引导的状语从句；

d. 为主句，被 a、b、c 三个状语从句修饰。

blue [blu] *a.* 忧伤的；蓝色的

That old love song makes me feel blue.

那首老式情歌令我感到忧伤。

in the night 晚上，夜里

= at night

He always does his homework in the night. / at night.

他总是在晚上做家庭作业。

tight [taɪt] *adv.* 紧紧地 & *a.* 紧紧的

hold + 人 + tight 紧紧地抱着某人

He held his wife tight as she cried in his arms.

当他太太在他怀里哭时，他紧紧地抱住她。

This shirt doesn't fit me. It's too tight.

我穿这件衬衫不合身，它太紧了。

4. **I can make you mine, taste your lips of wine anytime, night or day.**

= I can make you my sweetheart, and taste your warm, sweet lips anytime, whether it is night or day.

我能让你完全属于我，不论白昼或夜晚，我都能亲吻你那温暖甜蜜的双唇。

a. make you mine 使你成为我的甜心

= make you my sweetheart

注意

make 在此处作不完全及物动词，接宾语后，可用名词或形容词作补足语，表示"使……成为……"。

That war made him a hero. 那场战争使他成为英雄。

Her singing made everybody happy.

她的歌唱使每一个人都很快乐。

但 make 接宾语后，若以动词原形作补足语，则表"使……做……"。

My mother makes me clean my room every day.

母亲叫我每天都打扫我的房间。

b. taste [test] *vt.* 品尝 & *vi.* 尝起来 & *n.* 味道

As soon as my girlfriend tasted my cooking, she fell in love with me.

我女友一吃了我煮的菜之后就爱上我了。

This chicken curry tastes good. 这道咖喱鸡肉尝起来味道很好。

I don't like the taste of pineapples.

我不喜欢菠萝的味道。

c. lip [lɪp] *n.* 嘴唇

因为人都有两片嘴唇，故使用本单词时通常用复数。

Wally almost fainted when the girl kissed him on the lips.

当那个女孩亲沃利的嘴唇时，他差一点昏倒。

d. wine [waɪn] *n.* 酒，酒类

I like to have some wine with my dinner. 吃晚餐时我喜欢喝点酒。

e. whether [ˋhwɛðɚ/ˋwɛðɚ] *conj.* 不论……；是否

Whether she is rich or poor, I will marry her.

不论她是富有或贫穷，我都要娶她。

注意

whether 表示"是否"，引导名词性从句作及物动词的宾语时，whether 可用 if 取代。

I don't know whether he is still alive. 我不知道他是否还活着。

= I don't know if he is still alive.

5. **Only trouble is, gee whiz, I'm dreaming my life away.**

= The only trouble is that I'm dreaming my life away.

唯一的困扰是，天啊，我一生就在做白日梦中消逝。

a. trouble [ˋtrʌbl̩] *n.* 困扰，麻烦 & *vt.* 使困扰

troubled [ˋtrʌbl̩d] *a.* 困惑的

in times of trouble 在困难的时候

ask for trouble 自找麻烦，自讨苦吃

I hate to trouble people with my problems.

我讨厌用自己的问题来困扰别人。

You look troubled; what's the matter? 你看起来很困惑，怎么了？

In times of trouble, I always turn to my parents for advice.

有困难时，我总是去征询父母的意见。

If you always gamble, you're asking for trouble.

你若一直赌博的话，你就是在自找麻烦。

b. gee whiz [ˋdʒi ˋhwɪz] 是表叹息或惊讶的口语用法，可译为"哎呀！"或"哇！"

Gee whiz! I lost my car keys. 哎呀！我丢了车钥匙了。

c. dream one's life away 某人在梦想中虚度一生

The bum does nothing all day but dream his life away.

那个无业游民整天无所事事，只是虚度光阴。

Lesson 37

A Wonderful Time

美好时光

1 *Reading* 阅读

My girlfriend and I had a wonderful time last night. First, I took her to a cozy restaurant for dinner. Then, we went to a concert. Finally, we had some coffee at a nearby cafe. Just before we parted, she gave me a good-night kiss. At that moment, I was on top of the world. And now I'm in love.

我和女友昨晚共度了一段美好时光。首先我带她到一家舒适的餐厅吃晚饭。然后我们就去听演唱会。最后我们在附近的一家咖啡厅喝点咖啡。就在我们分手前,她给了我一个晚安之吻。就在那一刻,我飘飘欲仙。现在我恋爱了。

2 Vocabulary & Idioms 单词短语注解

1. **girlfriend** [ˋgɜlˏfrɛnd] *n.* 女朋友
   boyfriend [ˋbɔɪˏfrɛnd] *n.* 男朋友
2. **wonderful** [ˋwʌndɚfəl] *a.* 美妙的，棒的
   This is a wonderful party. 这是个很棒的宴会。
3. **last night** 昨晚
4. **first** [fɜst] *adv.* 首先
5. **took** [tʊk] *vt.* 带，载（take [tek] 的过去式）
   take + 人 + to + 地方　带（载）某人到某地
   Can you take me to school tomorrow? 你明天可以带我去学校吗？
6. **cozy** [ˋkozɪ] *a.* 舒适的
   Joe lives in a cozy little house in the countryside.
   乔住在乡下的一幢舒适小屋中。
7. **restaurant** [ˋrɛstərənt/ ˋrɛstəˏrɑnt] *n.* 餐厅
8. **went** [wɛnt] *vi.* 去（go [go] 的过去式）
   go to + 地方　到某地去
   We need to go to the supermarket. 我们需要到超市去一趟。
9. **concert** [ˋkɑnsɚt] *n.* 演唱会，音乐会
10. **finally** [ˋfaɪnəlɪ] *adv.* 最后
    After trying for an hour, Bill finally started the car.
    试了一个小时后，比尔终于把车子发动了。
11. **coffee** [ˋkɔfɪ] *n.* 咖啡
12. **nearby** [ˋnɪrˏbaɪ] *a.* 在附近的
    My brother lives in a nearby village. 我哥哥住在附近的一个村庄里。
13. **cafe** [kæˋfe/kəˋfe] *n.* 咖啡厅
14. **just** [dʒʌst] *adv.* 就在（强调用法）
    just before... 就在……之前

15. **before** [bɪˋfɔr] *conj.* 在……之前
Before I leave for work, I always kiss my wife goodbye.
上班前,我总是会和太太吻别。

16. **part** [pɑrt] *vi.* 分手
part from + 人　与某人分手
After saying goodbye, he parted from his parents and got on the train.
道别后,他就与父母分手并上了火车。

17. **kiss** [kɪs] *n.* 吻
a good-night kiss 晚上道别时之亲吻

18. **moment** [ˋmomənt] *n.* 片刻,时刻
at that moment 就在那时
At that moment, I had nothing to say. 就在那一刻,我无话可说。

19. **be on top of the world** 在世界的顶端,喻快乐得飘飘欲仙
top [tɑp] *n.* 顶端
world [wɜld] *n.* 世界
I got an "A" on my final exam. I am on top of the world.
期末考时我得了个"A",我真是高兴极了。

20. **love** [lʌv] *n.* 爱
be in love (with + 人) 爱上某人;(与某人)恋爱了
I think Carl is in love with Connie. 我想卡尔爱上康妮了。

3 Grammar Points 语法重点

本课介绍一般过去时的形式及其用法。课文中的动词如 had、took、went、parted、gave、was 等,分别为 have、take、go、part、give、am 的过去式。

1. 一般过去时的形式
主语 + 动词的过去式
例 I saw him yesterday. (saw 为 see 的过去式) 我昨天见到他。
He lived here ten years ago. (lived 为 live 的过去式)

他10年前住在这里。

They were angry when they heard the news. (were为are的过去式，heard为hear的过去式)

他们听到这消息时很生气。

注意

a. 动词的过去式均由动词原形变化而成，许多动词词尾加 -ed 即成过去式，如：

want → wanted 要

part → parted 分开

visit → visited 拜访

help → helped 帮助

但也有不少动词变成过去式时，呈不规则变化，如：

see → saw 看

tell → told 告诉

have → had 有

forget → forgot 忘记

属于不规则变化的动词过去式繁多，读者要在短时间内完全熟悉是不太可能的一件事。只有多读英文文章，勤查字典，持之以恒，不知不觉中就能运用自如了。

b. 由于 be 动词的过去式亦属不规则变化，且常用得到，故特列表如下，以利背诵：

	现在时	过去时
单数	I am ... You are ... He / She / It is ...	I was ... You were ... He / She / It was ...
复数	We are ... You are ... They are ...	We were ... You were ... They were ...

c. 一般过去时的否定句子结构如下：

主语 + did not / didn't + 动词原形

主语 + | was not / wasn't
were not / weren't | ……

例 肯定句：He left. 他离开了。
否定句：He didn't leave. 他没离开。
肯定句：We were happy. 我们很快乐。
否定句：We weren't happy. 我们不快乐。

2. 一般过去时使用的时机

一般过去时表示过去所发生的动作或状态。这种时态往往与表示过去的时间副词连用。

例 He came back at ten this morning. 他于今天早上 10 点回来。
He passed away last night. 他昨晚过世了。

4 Substitution 替换

1. My girlfriend and I | had a wonderful time last night.
saw a scary movie last night.
went to a French restaurant last night. |

我和我女友昨晚共度了一段美好时光。
我和我女友昨晚看了一部恐怖电影。
我和我女友昨晚去了一家法国餐厅。

---

2. We | had some coffee at a nearby cafe.
had dinner at a local restaurant.
had lunch at a cheap snack bar. |

我们到附近的一家咖啡厅喝点咖啡。
我们到本地的一家餐厅吃晚餐。
我们到一家便宜的小吃店吃午餐。

Lesson 38

Nobody Answered the Phone

没人接电话

1 Dialogue 实用会话

Jay and Rita are brother and sister.

Rita: Hi, Jay, where did you go last night?

Jay: I stayed home.

Rita: But I called you many times. Nobody answered the phone.

Jay: That's impossible.

Rita: Oh! Mom probably forgot to pay the phone bill again.

杰伊和丽塔是兄妹。

丽塔：嗨，杰伊，你昨晚到哪儿去了？

杰伊：我待在家里。

丽塔：但是我打了好几次电话给你。没人接电话。

杰伊：不可能。

丽塔：哦！妈可能又忘了付电话费了。

2 Key Points 重点提示

1. **stay** [ste] *vi.* 待在，留在

例 I stayed at Peter's house last night. 昨晚我留在彼得家。

2. **call** [kɔl] *vt.* 打电话（给某人）
例 I called my girlfriend on the phone last night.
昨晚我打电话给我女友。

3. **many times** 许多次
several times 几次
例 A baby eats many times a day. 宝宝一天要吃好几次。

4. **answer** [ˋænsɚ] *vt.* 回应，回答
answer the phone 接电话

5. **phone** [fon] *n.* 电话机（telephone [ˋtɛlə͵fon] 的缩写形式）

6. **impossible** [ɪmˋpɑsəbl̩] *a.* 不可能的

7. **probably** [ˋprɑbəblɪ] *adv.* 可能，或许
例 I will probably visit my grandmother tomorrow.
我明天或许会去探望我的祖母。

8. **forgot** [fɚˋgɑt] *vt.* 忘记（forget [fɚˋgɛt] 的过去式）
forget to + 动词原形　忘了要……
例 I forgot to tell you that your mother called.
我忘了告诉你，你母亲来过电话。

9. **pay** [pe] *vt.* 付（款）

10. **bill** [bɪl] *n.* 账单

11. **again** [əˋgɛn] *adv.* 再次，又
例 Fred is late for work again. 弗雷德上班又迟到了。

3 请选择下列各句中正确的一项

1. Fred ______ back at three o'clock last night.
(A) comes　(B) came　(C) come　(D) is coming

2. His poor old father ______ away this morning.
(A) go　(B) goes　(C) pass　(D) passed

3. We ______ a good movie last Saturday.
   (A) went (B) liked (C) saw (D) visited
4. Sally is ______ love with Bob.
   (A) in (B) on (C) at (D) inside
5. I ______ my mother to the beach yesterday.
   (A) and (B) told (C) took (D) went
6. Where ______ last night?
   (A) you were (B) were you
   (C) did you be (D) did you went

解答 1. (B) 2. (D) 3. (C) 4. (A) 5. (C) 6. (B)

Lesson 39

Homesickness

乡愁

1 *Reading* 阅读

After my graduation, I went to Beijing to further my studies. I lived there for three years. At first, I was happy, but later, I was frustrated and depressed. I was homesick all the time. Although the people were friendly, I missed my family, my friends and the lifestyle in my hometown.

我毕业后便到北京深造。我在那儿住了3年。起先我很快乐,但后来我便感到泄气、沮丧。我一直都很想家。虽然那里的人们都很友善,但我还是想念在故乡的家人、朋友以及生活方式。

2 Vocabulary & Idioms 单词短语注解

1. **homesickness** [ˋhomˏsɪknɪs] *n.* 乡愁，思乡病

2. **after** [ˋæftɚ] *prep.*（指时间）在……之后
   After my test, I went home to sleep. 考完试后，我就回家睡觉。

3. **graduation** [ˏgrædʒʊˋeʃən] *n.* 毕业
   graduate [ˋgrædʒʊˏet] *vi.* 毕业
   graduate from... 从……毕业
   I graduated from Beijing University last year. 我去年从北大毕业。

4. **further** [ˋfɝðɚ] *vt.* 增进

5. **studies** [ˋstʌdɪz] *n.* 学业（study 的复数形式）
   further one's studies 深造，进修
   Bob went to Paris to further his studies in art. 鲍勃到巴黎去进修艺术。

6. **live** [lɪv] *vi.* 住
   Some turtles can live for hundreds of years.
   有些乌龟可以活上好几百年。

7. **first** [fɝst] *n.* 最先，第一
   at first 起初（作状语用，通常置于句首）
   At first I forgot his name, but later, I remembered it.
   起初我忘了他的名字，但后来我又想起来了。

8. **later** [ˋletɚ] *adv.* 之后，后来
   I will call you later in the day. 我今天晚点再打电话给你。

9. **frustrated** [ˋfrʌstretɪd] *a.* 受挫的
   Fred was very sad and frustrated when no one came to his party.
   没有人来参加弗雷德的宴会使得他感到伤心又泄气。

10. **depressed** [dɪˋprɛst] *a.* 沮丧的
    Sarah was very depressed when her dog died.
    当莎拉的狗儿死掉时她很沮丧。

11. **homesick** [ˋhomˏsɪk] *a.* 思乡的，想家的

Children get homesick at summer camp. 孩子们在夏令营时会想家。

12. **time** [taɪm] *n.* 时间

    all the time 始终,一直(作状语用,使用时置于句尾)

    Charles is a good student. He studies all the time.

    查尔斯是个好学生。他总是在念书。

13. **friendly** [ˋfrɛndlɪ] *a.* 友善的

14. **miss** [mɪs] *vt.* 想念

    When I went abroad, I missed my friends.

    出国时,我很想念我的朋友们。

15. **lifestyle** [ˋlaɪf͵staɪl] *n.* 生活方式

    City people and country people have very different lifestyles.

    都市人和乡下人的生活方式大不相同。

16. **hometown** [͵homˋtaʊn] *n.* 家乡

3 Grammar Points 语法重点

本课介绍 after、at first 的用法,并介绍可作形容词用的分词用法。

1. **After my graduation, I went to Beijing to further my studies.**

   我毕业后便到北京深造。

   本句中的 After 是介词,之后以名词 graduation 作其宾语。但 after 亦可作连词,引导状语从句,亦即 after 之后可接"主语 + 动词"。故上句亦可改写为:

   After I graduated, I went to Beijing to further my studies.

   例 After his resignation, he went abroad. 他辞职后便出国去了。
   (After: 介词)

   = After he resigned, he went abroad.
   (After: 连词)

   before (在……之前)与 after 一样,亦有上述两种词性。

   例 Before she left, she gave me a kiss. 她在离开前给了我一个吻。
   (Before: 连词)

= Before her departure, she gave me a kiss.
介词

2. at first 与 first 均可置于句首，作副词用，修饰之后的句子，但意思不同。

at first 起初（使用于一般过去时中）

first 第一，首先（用来陈述观点）

例 At first, she was very nice to John, but later, she left him.
起先，她对约翰很好，但后来她却离开他了。
David is great in many ways. First, he never lies. Second (ly) , he is helpful.
大卫很多方面都很棒。首先是，他从不说谎。其次是，他乐于助人。

3. **...I was frustrated and depressed.** ……我便感到泄气、沮丧。

frustrated 及 depressed 均为过去分词，在本文中作形容词用，分别表示“感到泄气的”及“感到沮丧的”。

英语中有一些现在分词或过去分词均可作形容词用。初学英语的人较不易判断使用这两种分词的时机。其实我们可掌握下列原则：现在分词多译为“令人……的”，过去分词则译为“感到……的”。

例 The question is confused. (×) 这个问题感到迷惑。——不合逻辑
The question is confusing. (√) 这个问题令人迷惑。
The result is depressed. (×) 这个结果感到沮丧。——不合逻辑
The result is depressing. (√) 这个结果令人沮丧。
The baby is tiring. (√)
这个婴儿真累人。——抱着他的时候，他扭来扭去，晚上又爱哭，令父母睡不着。
The baby is tired. (√)
这个婴儿已累了。——他哭个老半天，终于筋疲力尽而感到累了。

由以上各例得知，使用分词作形容词时，只要合乎逻辑，掌握翻译的原则，就不易出错。

4 Substitution 替换

1. After my graduation, I went to Beijing to further my studies.
   After dinner, I went to my room to do my homework.
   After I ate dinner, I went to the living room to watch TV.
   我毕业后便到北京深造。
   吃过晚饭后，我到房间做功课。
   吃过晚饭后，我到客厅去看电视。

---

2. At first, I was happy, but later, I was frustrated.
   At first, Bill was brave, but later, he was afraid.
   At first, they were hardworking, but later, they were lazy.
   起先我很快乐，但后来我便感到泄气。
   起先比尔很勇敢，但后来他就害怕了。
   起先他们很努力工作，后来就偷懒了。

Lesson 40

Everybody Spoke English

大家都说英语

1 *Dialogue* 实用会话

Eve: Welcome back! What was America like?

Adam: OK, I guess.

Eve: What do you mean by "I guess?"

Adam: Well, frankly speaking, it was terrible.

Eve: Why?

Adam: Everybody only spoke English.

夏娃：欢迎归来！美国是什么样子呀？

亚当：我想还可以。

夏娃：你说“我想”是什么意思？

亚当：呃，坦白说，美国糟透了。

夏娃：为什么？

亚当：大家只说英语嘛。

2 *Key Points* 重点提示

1. **welcome** [ˈwɛlkəm] *a.* 受欢迎的
   “Welcome back!” 由 “ (You're) welcome back!” 简化而成。

2. **guess** [gɛs] *vt.* 猜想

本文中之“OK, I guess.”即等于“I guess that America was OK.”。

3. **mean** [min] *vt.* 意即，意思是

例 Do you know what this word means?

你知道这个词是什么意思吗?

4. **frankly** [ˋfræŋklɪ] *adv.* 坦白地

frankly speaking 坦白说,老实说(使用时多置于句首,以逗号与主语相隔)

例 A: I failed my test. 我考试没通过。

B: Frankly speaking, I'm not surprised. You never study.

坦白说,我并不惊讶。你从不念书。

5. **terrible** [ˋtɛrəbl̩] *a.* 糟糕的

例 The food at that restaurant is terrible.

那家餐厅的食物真是糟透了。

6. **spoke** [spok] *vt.* 说，讲（语言）（speak 的过去式）

3 请选择下列各句中正确的一项

1. At first, I was sad, ______ later, I was happy.

(A) and (B) but (C) also (D) so

2. That movie was good in many ways. First, it was exciting. ______, it was funny.

(A) Then (B) But later

(C) Second (D) After

3. After I did my homework, I ______ TV.

(A) saw (B) look (C) looked (D) watched

4. This job is very ______.

(A) tired (B) helping (C) tiring (D) confused

5. Before I saw the movie, I ______ the book.

(A) read (B) readed (C) watched (D) looked

6. Able: Paul is a great dancer.

   Sue: ______, I'm not surprised. He dances every day.

   (A) Speaking frankly　　(B) Frankly speaking

   (C) Spoke frankly　　(D) Frankly spoke

解答　1. (B)　2. (C)　3. (D)　4. (C)　5. (A)　6. (B)

Lesson 41

Going Camping

露营

1 *Reading* 阅读

Last weekend, my classmates and I went camping. We found a grassy spot beside a river. We put up our tents and made a campfire. Then, we fished at the river. We had only one fishing rod, so we took turns. After a while, we caught a big trout. Finally, we sat around the fire, roasted the fish and sang songs. Camping is really fun!

上个周末我和同学去露营。我们在河边找到一块草地。我们架起帐篷、生了营火，然后就在河边钓鱼。我们只有一根钓竿，因此我们就轮流钓鱼。没多久，我们钓到一条大鳟鱼。最后，我们围坐在营火旁，边烤鱼边唱歌。露营真有趣！

2 Vocabulary & Idioms 单词短语注解

1. **classmate** [ˋklæs,met] *n.* 同班同学
schoolmate [ˋskul,met] *n.* 同校同学

2. **camp** [kæmp] *vi.* 露营(使用时,多采用现在分词形式,置于 go 之后)
go camping 露营去
Every summer my family and I go camping in the mountains.
每年夏天我和我的家人都会到山中去露营。

3. **found** [faʊnd] *vt.* 找到,发现(find 的过去式)
I lost my umbrella yesterday, but found it today.
昨天我的雨伞丢了,但今天我又找到了。

4. **grassy** [ˋgræsɪ] *a.* 多草的

5. **spot** [spɑt] *n.* 地点

6. **beside** [bɪˋsaɪd] *prep.* 在……之旁
I sit beside Carol in math class. 上数学课时我坐在卡罗尔旁边。

7. **river** [ˋrɪvɚ] *n.* 河流

8. **put** [pʊt] *vt.* 放置

9. **tent** [tɛnt] *n.* 帐篷
put up a / the tent 搭帐篷
We should put up the tent. It is getting dark.
我们应该把帐篷搭起来,天快黑了。

10. **campfire** [ˋkæmp,faɪr] *n.* 营火
make a campfire 生营火
make a fire 生火
Do you know how to make a fire? 你知道如何生火吗?

11. **fish** [fɪʃ] *vi.* 钓鱼

12. **fishing rod** [ˋfɪʃɪŋ ,rɑd] *n.* 钓竿

13. **took** [tʊk] *vt.* 采取（take [tek] 的过去式）

14. **turn** [tɜn] *n.* 轮流
take turns 轮流
Let's take turns playing with the toy. 咱们轮流玩玩具吧！

15. **while** [hwaɪl / waɪl] *n.* 一会儿（通常与介词 for 或 after 连用）
after a while 一会儿之后，没多久
for a while 有一会儿
After a while, I found my keys. 没多久我就找到了钥匙。
I worked at that store for a while. 我在那家商店工作过一阵子。

16. **caught** [kɔt] *vt.* 捕捉（catch [kætʃ] 的过去式）

17. **trout** [traʊt] *n.* 鳟鱼（单复数同形）
a trout 一条鳟鱼
two trout 两条鳟鱼

18. **sat** [sæt] *vi.* 坐（sit [sɪt] 的过去式）
I sat in the library and read all day.
我坐在图书馆里看了一整天的书。

19. **around** [əˋraʊnd] *prep.* 围绕，在……周围

20. **roast** [rost] *vt.* 烤

21. **fish** [fɪʃ] *n.* 鱼（单复数同形）
a fish 一条鱼
two fish 两条鱼

22. **sang** [sæŋ] *vt.* 唱（sing [sɪŋ] 的过去式）

23. **song** [sɔŋ] *n.* 歌曲

24. **fun** [fʌn] *n.* 乐趣

3 Grammar Points 语法重点

本课主要介绍 and 连接含有两个或两个以上的人称代词作主语的位

置，及动名词作主语的用法。

1. **Last weekend, my classmates and I went camping.**

上个周末我和同学去露营。

注意下列有两个主语并存的位置：

a. 主语若有代词"I"及其他人时，应以 and 连接，并将其他人置于"I"之前，以示尊重。

例 I and my father went fishing last weekend. (×)

→ My father and I went fishing last weekend. (√)

上个周末我和我爸爸钓鱼去了。

b. 但除"I"以外，he、she、they、you、we 等代词与其他人共同作主语时，这些代词应置于第一个位置。

例 His father and he went swimming last Friday. (×)

→ He and his father went swimming last Friday. (√)

他和他爸爸上星期五游泳去了。

Mary and we sang songs at the party. (×)

→ We and Mary sang songs at the party. (√)

我们和玛丽在宴会上高歌。

c. 代词并存时，注意下列次序：

例 He, you and I are good friends. (×)

→ You, he and I are good friends. (√)

你、我和他都是好朋友。

You, we and they are good friends. (×)

→ We, you and they are good friends. (√)

我们、你们和他们都是好朋友。

2. **...my classmates and I went camping.** ……我和同学去露营。

本句采用了"go + 现在分词"的短语，表示"从事某种短暂性的活动"之意。常用的此类短语如下：

go camping	去露营	go hunting	去打猎
go dancing	去跳舞	go golfing	去打高尔夫球
go shopping	去购物	go swimming	去游泳
go mountain climbing		去爬山	

例 My best friend and I often go shopping together.
我经常和我的好友一起去购物。

3. **take turns** 轮流

take turns (at) + 动名词　轮流……

例 The three boys took turns to look after their sick mother. (×)

→ The three boys took turns (at) looking after their sick mother. (√)
这三个孩子轮流照顾他们生病的母亲。

4. **Camping is really fun!** 露营真有趣！

此处作主语的 camping 是动名词，由动词原形 camp 变化而成。作主语的词类通常是名词或代词。

例 The boy lives near my house. 这男孩就住在我家附近。
（boy：名词）

He is a student. 他是学生。
（He：代词）

动词不能直接作主语，应将动词变成动名词方可作主语。

中文：跟他唱歌很愉快。

英文：Sing songs with him is fun. (×)

理由：Sing 是动词原形，不可作主语。

改正：Singing songs with him is fun. (√)

请再看下例：

中文：在河边露营很愉快。

英文：Camp by the river is fun. (×)

理由：Camp 是动词原形，不可作主语。

改正：Camping by the river is fun. (√)

4 Substitution 替换

1. Last weekend, my classmates and I went camping.
Last Monday, my brother and I went mountain climbing.
Last week, she and her mother went shopping.
上个周末，我和同学去露营。

上星期一，我和哥哥去爬山。
上个星期，她和她母亲去购物。

---

2. We took turns using the fishing rod.
   They took turns riding the bicycle.
   We took turns singing songs.
   我们轮流使用钓竿。
   他们轮流骑自行车。
   我们轮流唱歌。

Lesson 42

Are You Having Fun?

你玩得愉快吗？

1 *Dialogue* 实用会话

Sally: How often do you go camping?

Bert: This is my first time.

Sally: Really? Are you having fun?

Bert: Yes. I'm having a wonderful time.

萨莉：你多久露营一次？

伯特：这是我第一次露营。

萨莉：真的吗？你玩得愉快吗？

伯特：愉快。我愉快极了。

2 *Key Points* 重点提示

1. **How often do you + 动词原形**

   你多久……一次？

   例 How often do you visit your grandparents?

   你多久看你爷爷奶奶一次？

2. **have fun 玩得愉快**

   = have a good time

   have fun (in) + 动名词　做……很愉快

   例 We had fun <u>to sing songs</u> at the party. (×)

→ We had fun singing songs at the party. (√)
= We had a good time singing songs at the party.
我们在宴会上唱歌唱得很愉快。

3. **I'm having a wonderful time.** 我玩得愉快极了。
= I'm having a great time.
= I'm having a lot of fun.

3 请选择下列各句中正确的一项

1. ______ went swimming.
(A) My and my brother (B) My brother and me
(C) My brother and I (D) I and my brother

2. We took turns ______ the guitar.
(A) to play (B) playing
(C) play (D) to playing

3. ______, ______ and ______ are classmates.
(A) You, she, I (B) I, you, she
(C) she, I, you (D) She, you, I

4. ______ bicycles in the mountains is fun.
(A) Ride (B) Rides (C) Rode (D) Riding

5. We had a good time ______ in the river.
(A) swam (B) to swim
(C) swimming (D) swim

6. ______ does your brother play basketball?
(A) How far (B) How often
(C) How good (D) How nice

解答 1. (C) 2. (B) 3. (A) 4. (D) 5. (C) 6. (B)

Lesson 43

Killing Two Birds with One Stone

两全其美

1 *Reading* 阅读

Dan must take a day off tomorrow. He has to take care of his sick mother. He ought to talk to his boss, but he's afraid. His boss might get angry with him. What should Dan do? He can take the work home. This way, he can kill two birds with one stone.

丹明天必须请一天假，他得照顾他生病的母亲。他应当向他的老板说的，但他担心老板可能会生他的气。丹该怎么办呢？他可以把工作带回家去。这样他就能两全其美。

2 Vocabulary & Idioms 单词短语注解

1. **must** [mʌst] *v. aux.* 必须

   You must have a driver's license to drive a car.

   你必须要有驾驶执照才能开车。

2. **take** | **a day off** 请一天假 | two days off 请两天假 | … ……

   Last week I was sick, so I took two days off from work.

   上星期我病了,所以我请了两天假。

3. **tomorrow** [təˋmɑro] *adv.* 明天

   today [təˋde] *adv.* 今天

   yesterday [ˋjɛstɚˏde] *adv.* 昨天

   the day after tomorrow 后天

   the day before yesterday 前天

4. **have to + 动词原形**　必须……

   = must + 动词原形

   I have to work all weekend. 整个周末我都必须工作。

5. **take care of...** 照顾……

   = look after...

   care [kɛr] *n.* 关怀,照料

   Can you take care of my dog for a few days?

   你可以帮我照顾我的狗几天吗?

6. **sick** [sɪk] *a.* 生病的

7. **ought** [ɔt] *v. aux.* 应该(之后应接 to,再接动词原形)

   ought to + 动词原形　应该……

   = should + 动词原形

   You ought to be more polite. 你应该要更有礼貌些。

8. **talk** [tɔk] *vi.* 谈话

   talk to + 人　对某人说话

You have to talk to your parents about your marriage plans.
你应该将你结婚的计划告诉你的父母。

9. **boss** [bɔs] *n.* 老板，上司

10. **afraid** [əˋfred] *a.* 害怕的
be afraid to + 动词原形　害怕……
Don't be afraid to speak English. 别害怕开口说英文。

11. **might** [maɪt] *v. aux.* 也许，大概
Bill might go to the party. 比尔大概会去参加宴会。

12. **get angry with + 人**　生某人的气
angry [ˋæŋgrɪ] *a.* 生气的
注意
angry 之前可置 be 动词或动词 get，但意思略有区别。使用 get 时，强调动作刹那间的发生；使用 be 动词时，则强调持续的状态。
He got angry with me when I broke the window, and he is still angry now.
我把窗户打破时，他生我的气，而且到现在他还在气头上呢。

13. **should** [ʃʊd] *v. aux.* 应该
You should brush your teeth three times a day.
你一天应该刷三次牙。

14. **work** [wɜk] *n.* 工作（不可数）
I don't have much work to do this afternoon.
今天下午我没有许多工作要做。

15. **this way** 以这种方式，这样的话
way [we] *n.* 方式
Let's work together. This way, we can finish the project sooner.
我们一起工作吧。这样的话，我们就可以早一点将工作做完。

16. **can** [kæn/kən] *v. aux.* 能够
Ted can swim very fast. 泰德游泳可以游得很快。

17. **kill two birds with one stone** 一石二鸟；两全其美；一举两得

kill [kɪl] *vt.* 杀死
bird [bɝd] *n.* 鸟
stone [ston] *n.* 石头
Charlie can study and work at the same time. This way, he kills two birds with one stone.
查理可以一边读书一边工作。这样他就可以两全其美了。

3 Grammar Points 语法重点

1. 本课旨在协助读者熟悉常用的一些助动词(亦指情态动词)及其用法。这些助动词有一个共同特征:它们之后皆接动词原形。

a. **Dan must take a day off tomorrow.** 丹明天必须请假一天。
He has to take care of his sick mother.
他得照顾他生病的母亲。
以上两句中的 must 及 has to (have to 的第三人称单数用法)均表示“必须”,但有其同异处。

1) 表示道德或义务(如爱国、孝顺父母)的“必须”时,只能使用 must。have to 则表示有勉强意味(不得不去做)的“必须”,此时亦可使用 must。

例 You have to love your country. (×)
→ You must love your country. (√) 你必须热爱祖国。
You have to finish the work before you can go home.
= You must finish the work before you can go home.
你得做完工作才能回家。

2) must 通常只能用来表示现在或未来的状况,不能用于过去时中。而 have to 除可表示现在或未来的状况外,亦可改为过去式 had to,使用于过去时中。

例 He must stay here now. 他现在必须留下来。
= He has to stay here now.
He must come here tomorrow. 他明天必须来。
= He has to come here tomorrow.
He must stay here yesterday. (×)

→ He had to stay here yesterday. (√) 他昨天必须留下来。

b. **He ought to talk to his boss, but he's afraid.**
他应当向他的老板说的，但他怕。
What should Dan do? 丹该怎么办呢？
在“单词短语注解”中，我们已说明 ought to 与 should 均表“应该”，用法相同。故上两句的 ought to 与 should 可互换，而改为：
He should talk to his boss, but he's afraid.
What ought Dan to do?
（可别写成“What ought to Dan do?”之错误句子结构）

2. **His boss might get angry with him.** 他的老板也许会生他的气。
此处助动词 might 是 may [me] 的过去式，但却非表示过去的状态，而是表示较低的可能性，可译成“也许”、“大概”、“说不定”。而 may 则表示较高可能性，可译成“很可能”。
例 You may be right, so I will take your advice.
你很可能是对的，因此我会接受你的建议。
You might be right, but I think my way is better.
你或许是对的，但我想我的方法比较好。

3. **He can take the work home.** 他可以把工作带回家去。
本句使用了“take + 人或物 + to + 地方”（将某物带 / 运送到某地）的短语。
例 Please take me to the station. 请带我到车站去。
故“He can take the work home.”不应写成：
He can take the work to home. (×)
由于 home 是副词，相当于表示场所的副词 there（那里）、here（这里）等，置于句尾修饰动词时，这些副词之前不能置介词 to。
例 Let's go to home now. (×)
→ Let's go home now. (√) 咱们回家去吧！
He went to there with Mary. (×)
→ He went there with Mary. (√) 他跟玛丽到那儿去了。
但 home 之前若置所有格代词（如 my、your、his 等），则 home 是名词，在上列句子结构中，之前应置介词 to，以作其宾语。

例 Let's go my home. (×)
→ Let's go to my home. (√) 咱们到我家去。
home 亦可与介词 at 连用,形成下列固定用法:
be at home 在家中
例 He is at home most of the time. 他大部分时间都待在家中。

4. **This way, he can kill two birds with one stone.**
这样的话,他就能两全其美。
本句中的 This way 原为 In this way (以这种方式,这样的话),是作副词用的短语,但 way 之前有 this 或 that 时,介词 in 常予省略。
例 You must be modest. That way, you will be respected.
你必须谦虚待人。那样的话,你就会受人尊敬。

4 Substitution 替换

1. He has to take care of his sick mother.
Robert must take his sick mother to the hospital.
Jim should clean his room.
Chris ought to wash his clothes.
他得照顾他生病的母亲。
罗伯特必须带他生病的母亲到医院。
吉姆必须打扫他的房间。
克里斯必须洗他的衣服。

---

2. He can take the work home.
He should take his children home.
The teacher often takes his students to his home.
She often takes her friends to her grandmother's home.
他可以把工作带回家去。
他应当把他的孩子带回家去。
那位老师经常带学生到家里去。
她经常把她的朋友带到她祖母家去。

Lesson 44

She Had a Bad Cold

她患了重感冒

1 Dialogue 实用会话

Mary: Where were you yesterday?

Jack: I was at home. In fact, I was taking care of Sally.

Mary: What's wrong with her?

Jack: She had a bad cold.

Mary: Is she getting better?

Jack: Yes. Thanks.

玛丽：你昨天在哪里？

杰克：我在家里。事实上，我在照顾萨莉。

玛丽：她怎么了？

杰克：她患了重感冒。

玛丽：她好多了吗？

杰克：好多了。谢谢。

2 Key Points 重点提示

1. **in fact** 事实上

   fact [fækt] *n.* 事实

   本短语通常置于句首，之后置逗号，再接主句。

   例 Mike likes Jessica. In fact, I think he loves her.

迈克喜欢杰西卡。事实上，我认为他爱上她了。

2. **have a bad cold** 患重感冒

cold [kold] *n.* 感冒

例 You have a bad cold. You should take some medicine.

你患了重感冒，你应该吃些药。

3. **be getting better** （病）渐渐好起来

此处 better 是形容词 well（身体健康的）的比较级

例 A: Do you still feel sick? 你还是觉得不舒服吗？

B: Yes, but I'm getting better. 是的，但我好多了。

3 请选择下列各句中正确的一项

1. Take your dog ______.
   (A) to home (B) home (C) at home (D) in home
2. Bill is a little fat. He______ to go on a diet.
   (A) should (B) must (C) have (D) ought
3. Carlos has a big exam tomorrow. He ______ to study tonight.
   (A) have (B) should (C) has (D) must
4. I ______ work last Sunday.
   (A) have to (B) must (C) had to (D) has to
5. I don't know, but it ______ rain tomorrow.
   (A) might (B) must (C) has to (D) ought to
6. Peter can sing. ______, he is a good singer.
   (A) However (B) At first
   (C) This way (D) In fact

解答 1. (B) 2. (D) 3. (C) 4. (C) 5. (A) 6. (D)

Lesson 45

What a Nightmare!

真是一场噩梦啊！

1 *Reading* 阅读

Jeff had a terrible day. He missed the train to work. Moreover, he had to wait a long time for the next train. As a matter of fact, he waited for two hours. To make matters worse, he left his briefcase on the train. As a result, he had to go to the police station. Poor Jeff never got to work that day. What a nightmare!

杰夫过了很糟的一天。他上班没赶上火车。而且，他得久候下一班火车的到来。事实上，他等了两个小时。更糟的是，他把公文包落在火车上了。结果，他得到警察局走一趟。可怜的杰夫那一天根本上不了班。真是一场噩梦啊！

2 Vocabulary & Idioms 单词短语注解

1. **terrible** [ˋtɛrəbḷ] *a.* 糟糕的，可怕的
   That was a terrible movie. 那真是一部很糟糕的电影。

2. **miss** [mɪs] *vt.* 错过
   Why did you miss the meeting today? 你为什么错过今天的会议呢？

3. **moreover** [mɔrˋovɚ] *adv.* 此外，更有甚者
   Mike is very kind. Moreover, he is honest.
   迈克为人很好。而且，他还很诚实。

4. **wait** [wet] *vi.* 等候
   wait for + 人或事物　等候某人或某事物
   I am still waiting for my girlfriend to write to me.
   我还在等我女友写信给我。

5. **as a matter of fact** 事实上（常置于句首，之后置逗号）
   = in fact
   That car is not cheap. As a matter of fact, it's very expensive.
   那辆车不便宜，事实上，它很昂贵。

6. **to make matters worse, ...** 更糟的是，……
   worse [wɝs] *a.* 更坏的（bad 的比较级）
   It was raining. To make matters worse, I forgot to bring my umbrella.
   下雨了。更糟的是，我忘了带伞。

7. **left** [lɛft] *vt.* 将……留在……（leave 的过去式）
   I left my umbrella on the bus. 我把雨伞留在公共汽车上了。

8. **briefcase** [ˋbrifˏkes] *n.* 手提箱，公文包

9. **police station** [pəˋlis ˏsteʃən] *n.* 警察局

10. **nightmare** [ˋnaɪtˏmɛr] *n.* 噩梦（本文中指“可怕的经历”）
    City traffic is a real nightmare. 市区的交通真像是一场噩梦。

3 Grammar Points 语法重点

本课介绍不定式短语作副词的用法及感叹句的用法。

1. **He missed the train to work.** 他上班没赶上火车。

   本句中的 to work 是介词短语,作形容词用,修饰之前的名词 the train。to 是介词,表示“通往”之意。work 则为名词,作 to 之宾语,原指“工作”,此处笼统指“上班”之意。其他有关 work 的常用短语尚有:

   a. go to work 上班

   例 He goes to work at 8:00 a.m. every morning.
   他每天早上 8 点上班。

   b. after work 下班后

   例 What do you usually do after work? 下班后你通常做什么?

2. **To make matters worse, he left his briefcase on the train.**
   更糟的是,他把公文包落在火车上了。

   to make matters worse 为不定式短语。这种短语由 to 之后接动词原形所成,此处的 to 是虚词,而非介词。这种不定式短语通常置于句首,之后置逗号,有副词的功能,修饰全句。类似的短语尚有:

   to tell (you) the truth 老实(对你)说
   to be frank (with you) 坦白(跟你)说

   例 A: Did you like the movie? 你喜欢这部电影吗?
   B: To tell the truth, I fell asleep in the middle of it.
   老实说,我看到一半时就睡着了。
   A: Do you like Picasso's paintings? 你喜欢毕加索的画吗?
   B: To be frank, I don't know who Picasso is.
   坦白说,我不知道谁是毕加索。

3. **What a nightmare!** 真是一场噩梦啊!

   = What a nightmare it was!

   原句句尾省略了主语 it 及动词 was; it 是代词,指的是杰夫一天里种种倒霉遭遇。

   本句属 what 引导的感叹句。英文中的感叹句有两种,一种由 how

引导，一种由 what 引导，均置于句首。这种感叹句多译成“多么地”、“真地”。感叹句均由陈述句（即“主语 + 动词……”的句子结构）转变而成，形成的方式如下：

a. 以 how 引导的感叹句

由于 how 是副词，可修饰形容词、副词或动词，因此：

1) 陈述句有形容词，之后又无名词时，该形容词移至 how 之后即告完成。

陈述句：He is nice. 他人很好。
（nice：a.）

感叹句：How nice he is! 他多好啊！

2) 陈述句有副词时，该副词移至 how 之后即告完成。

陈述句：He worked hard. 他工作努力。
（hard：adv.）

感叹句：How hard he worked! 他工作多努力啊！

3) how 亦可修饰陈述句中的动词，此时将 how 置于原陈述句句首即告完成。

陈述句：I love that picture. 我喜欢那张画。

感叹句：How I love that picture! 我多喜欢那张画啊！

b. 以 what 引导的感叹句

此时 what 是形容词，之后须接名词或含有形容词修饰的名词，因此：

1) 陈述句有名词时，该名词移至 what 之后即告完成。

例 陈述句：It was a nightmare. 那是一个噩梦。
（a nightmare：n.）

感叹句：What a nightmare it was! 真是一场噩梦啊！

例 陈述句：They are nice boys. 他们是好孩子。
（nice：a.　boys：n.）

感叹句：How nice boys they are! (×)

→ What nice boys they are! (√) 他们真是好孩子！

例 陈述句：He did a stupid thing. 他干了件蠢事。
（a stupid thing：n.）

感叹句：What a stupid thing he did! 他干了多蠢的一件事！

2) what 引导的感叹句中，what 之后接名词，再接“主语 + be 动词”时，主语及 be 动词可省略。

例 What a nightmare it was!
主语 be 动词
→ What a nightmare! 真是一场噩梦啊！

例 What nice boys they are!
主语 be 动词
→ What nice boys! 多好的孩子们啊！

4 Substitution 替换

1. He had to wait a long time. As a matter of fact, he waited for two hours.
We had to work a long time. As a matter of fact, we worked all night.
I had to study a long time. As a matter of fact, I studied all day.
他必须等很久。事实上，他等了两个小时。
我们必须工作很久。事实上，我们一整晚都在工作。
我必须学习很久。事实上，我一整天都在学习。

---

2. What a nightmare!
What a terrible day that was!
What a noisy child she is!
What a stupid thing to say!
真是一场噩梦啊！
真是可怕的一天啊！
那女孩好吵哦！
说那样的话真蠢！

Lesson 46

A Terrible Headache

头痛得很厉害

1 *Dialogue* 实用会话

Frank: Do you have any aspirins?

Jane: In fact, I don't. Why?

Frank: I have a terrible headache.

Jane: Well, you should go see a doctor immediately.

弗兰克：你有阿斯匹林吗?

简　　：事实上，我没有。干嘛问这个?

弗兰克：我头痛得很厉害。

简　　：那么，你应当立刻去看医生。

2 *Key Points* 重点提示

1. **headache** [ˋhɛdˌek] *n.* 头痛

   have a headache 头痛

   例 Don't shout; I have a terrible headache. 别叫了，我头痛得很厉害。

2. **aspirin** [ˋæspərɪn] *n.* 阿斯匹林（一种头痛药）

3. **go see a doctor** 去看医生

   = go and see a doctor

   英文中 come 或 go 以原形出现，其后接 and 再接另一动词原形时，and 可予省略，而形成 come 或 go 直接加动词原形的情况。

例 Come and see me when you have time. 你有空时要来看我。
= Come see me when you have time.

4. **doctor** [ˋdaktɚ] *n.* 医生

5. **immediately** [ɪˋmidɪətlɪ] *adv.* 立刻，马上

3 请选择下列各句中正确的一项

1. ______ beautiful your house is!
   (A) What (B) How (C) So (D) What's
2. ______ a good time we had!
   (A) What (B) How (C) So (D) What's
3. I got up late for work today. ______, my car wouldn't start.
   (A) As a matter of fact
   (B) To make matters worse
   (C) As a result
   (D) To tell the truth
4. I had to work yesterday. ______, I worked all day.
   (A) As a result (B) However
   (C) As a matter of fact (D) Therefore
5. Carl took a taxi ______.
   (A) for work (B) to working
   (C) and work (D) to work
6. Let's ______.
   (A) go seeing a movie
   (B) go to and see a movie
   (C) go see a movie
   (D) see and go to a movie

解答 1. (B) 2. (A) 3. (B) 4. (C) 5. (D) 6. (C)

Lesson 47

Be Polite

要有礼貌

1 *Reading* 阅读

Everyone should be polite. Polite people show good manners. Moreover, they are popular. On the other hand, rude people are looked down upon. Rudeness shows poor education. Therefore, why not be polite? A simple "Please," "Thank you," or "You're welcome," can make a big difference.

每个人都应有礼貌。有礼貌的人展现出的是良好的风度。而且，他们受人欢迎。另一方面，无礼的人则遭人轻视。无礼表示教育差。因此，何不有礼貌一点呢？ "请"、"谢谢你"或"不客气" 这几个词虽很简单，却会使情况大不相同。

2 Vocabulary & Idioms 单词短语注解

1. **polite** [pəˋlaɪt] *a.* 有礼貌的
A gentleman is always polite. 绅士总是很有礼貌。

2. **show** [ʃo] *vt.* 展现
Her poor test score showed that she didn't study.
她差劲的考试分数显示出她根本没读书。

3. **manners** [ˋmænɚz] *n.* 风度，礼貌
注意
manner 表示做事的“方式”或“方法”，而其复数形成 manners 则表示“风度”或“礼貌”。表示“方式”或“方法”时，多与介词 in 连用。
in a (n) ...manner 以……的方式
She spoke to us in an impolite manner. 她跟我们说话时很不礼貌。
It is bad manners to point at people. 对人指指点点是很不礼貌的。

4. **moreover** [mɔrˋovɚ] *adv.* 并且，此外

5. **popular** [ˋpɑpjəlɚ] *a.* 受人欢迎的
be popular with + 众人　受到一群人的欢迎
That teacher is very popular with her students.
那位老师非常受她学生的欢迎。

6. **on the other hand** 另一方面
on (the) one hand...on the other (hand)... 一方面……另一方面……
On the one hand, it's fun to have a dog. On the other hand, it's a big responsibility.
一方面来说，养狗很好玩。但另一方面来说，那是个很大的责任。

7. **rude** [rud] *a.* 粗鲁的，无礼的
rudeness [ˋrudnɪs] *n.* 粗鲁，无礼
Don't interrupt; it is very rude. 别打断别人的谈话，那是很无礼的。

8. **look down upon + 人**　轻视某人
look up to + 人　瞧得起 / 尊敬某人

People look down upon Barry, because he is a thief.
人们都瞧不起巴里，因为他是个贼。
People look up to a good leader. 人们都尊敬一位好的领导者。

9. **poor** [pʊr] *a.* 差劲的，不良的
注意
poor 亦可表示“可怜的”或“贫穷的”。本课中 poor 作“不良的”解。

10. **education** [ˌɛdʒəˋkeʃən] *n.* 教育
educate [ˋɛdʒəˌket] *vt.* 教育
Carl has a college education. 卡尔受过大学教育。
Chris was educated in England. 克里斯是在英国受教育的。

11. **therefore** [ˋðɛrˌfɔr] *adv.* 因此
We spent all our money; therefore, we had to go home.
我们把钱全花光了，因此，我们只得回家去。

12. **simple** [ˋsɪmpḷ] *a.* 简单的

13. **make a big difference** 产生很大的不同
difference [ˋdɪfərəns] *n.* 差异，不同
Your help can make a big difference. 你的帮忙可以使情况大为改观。

3 *Grammar Points* 语法重点

本课主要介绍被动语态的形成及用法。

1. **On the other hand, rude people are looked down upon.**
另一方面，无礼的人则遭人轻视。
本句中的“are looked down upon”（被轻视）乃短语动词“look down upon”的被动语态。

a. “被动语态”均由及物动词形成，句型如下：

主语 + 及物动词 + 宾语

主语 + be 动词 + 过去分词 + by + 宾语

例 They respect him.

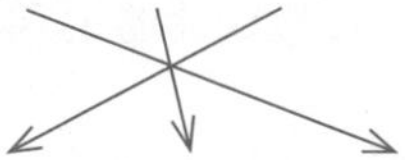

He is respected by them. 他受到他们的尊敬。

The teacher punished the naughty boy.

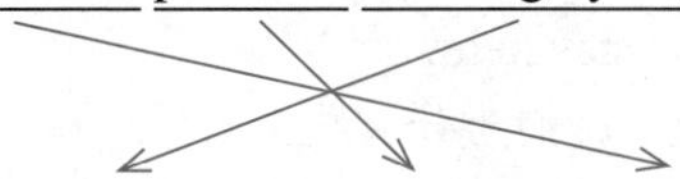

The naughty boy was punished by the teacher.

这顽皮的男孩被老师处罚了。

b. 及物动词变成被动语态时，除非绝对必要，否则“by + 宾语”往往省略。故以上二例均可写成：

He is respected. 他受到尊敬。

The naughty boy was punished. 这顽皮的男孩被处罚了。

c. 及物动词多是一个单词（如上例中的 respect 及 punish），但有时亦由两个或三个单词所构成，此时就称为短语动词，它们共同的特征就是最后一个单词一定是介词。现举一些常用的短语动词如下：

look at 凝视

point at 指着

rely on 依赖

pay attention to 注意

look down upon 轻视

take care of 照顾，注意

例 I cannot rely on him. 我不能依赖他。

Everyone looks down upon him. 每个人都轻视他。

以上两个例句中的短语动词均视为及物动词，之后皆有宾语，故可使用被动语态。原则和一般及物动词一样。但初学英文的人，将短语动词变成被动语态时，往往漏了介词。

例 He cannot be relied. (×)

→ He cannot be relied on. (√) 他不能被依赖。

A liar is looked down. (×)

→ A liar is looked down upon. (√) 说谎的人被人轻视。

2. **Therefore, why not be polite?** 因此，何不有礼貌一点呢？

why 或 why not 之后可直接用动词原形，形成简略的问句。

a. Why + 动词原形？

= Why should I / we + 动词原形？我 / 我们为何要……？

例 Why stay here? 我 / 我们为什么要待在这里？

= Why should I / we stay here?

Why be quiet? 我 / 我们为什么要安静？

= Why should I / we be quiet?

b. Why not + 动词原形？你 / 你们 / 我们为何不能……？

= Why can't you / we + 动词原形？

例 Why not be quiet? 你 / 你们 / 我们为何不能安静呢？

= Why can't you / we be quiet?

Why not stay here? 你 / 你们 / 我们为何不能待在这里？

= Why can't you / we stay here?

4 *Substitution* 替换

1. Rude people are looked down upon.
The patient is well taken care of.
Dishonest people can't be relied on.
无礼的人会遭人轻视。
这个病人被照顾得很好。
不诚实的人不可被信赖。

---

2. Why not be polite?
Why not eat at this restaurant?
Why get angry?
何不有礼貌一点呢？
何不在这家餐厅吃东西呢？
为何要生气呢？

Lesson 48

Don't Mention It

别客气

1 *Dialogue* 实用会话

Angel: Excuse me, Chris. Could you pass me the sugar, please?

Chris: Sure. Here you are.

Angel: Thanks.

Chris: Don't mention it.

安杰尔：对不起，克里斯。请你把糖递给我，好吗？

克里斯：没问题。给你。

安杰尔：谢谢。

克里斯：别客气。

2 *Key Points* 重点提示

1. **Excuse me.** 对不起。

   excuse [ɪkˋskjuz] *vt.* 原谅

   "Excuse me."是说话者用来表示要打扰对方的客气用语。而"I'm sorry."亦译成"对不起"或"抱歉"，但"I'm sorry."是说话者用来表示帮不上忙或未达到对方期望时的用语。

   例 A: Excuse me. Could you show me the way to the station?

   对不起。你能否告诉我车站怎么个走法？

B: I'm sorry. I'm new here. 抱歉。我刚到这儿来,路不熟。

2. **Could you pass me the sugar, please?**

= Could you pass the sugar to me, please?

请你把糖递给我好吗?

pass [pæs] *vt.* 传递

sugar [ˋʃʊgɚ] *n.* 砂糖

注意

本问句亦可说成:

Can you pass me the sugar, please?

但"Can you...?"有"你能不能……?"的意味,而"Could you...?"则有"您可否……?"的意味,故用 Could 形成的问句显然语气要客气得多。

3. **Don't mention it.** 别客气。

= You're welcome.

= Sure thing.

mention [ˋmɛnʃən] *vt.* 提及

3 请选择下列各句中正确的一项

1. Why ______ go to the movies tonight?
   (A) not we (B) do not we (C) not (D) don't
2. He is liked ______.
   (A) by we (B) us (C) by she (D) by us
3. Look ______ that man over there.
   (A) at (B) into (C) up (D) down
4. Why ______ I be honest?
   (A) not (B) shouldn't (C) be (D) not be
5. Bill is very honest. You can rely ______ him.
   (A) in (B) at (C) on (D) around

6. Can you please ______?
   (A) pass me the book
   (B) pass the book against me
   (C) pass me to the book
   (D) pass the book give me

解答 1. (C) 2. (D) 3. (A) 4. (B) 5. (C) 6. (A)

Lesson 49

Never Talk to Strangers

千万别跟陌生人说话

1 *Reading* 阅读

Something strange happened to me yesterday. On my way to school, I met a stranger. He stopped me and said, "You are Betty, aren't you?" "No," I replied. He asked, "You know me, don't you?" "I don't," I answered. Then he said, "You owe me $100, don't you?" I ran away. At that moment, I remembered my mother's words: "Never talk to strangers."

昨天有一件怪事发生在我身上。我在上学途中遇见一位陌生人。他将我拦住说:“你是贝蒂,对不对?”我回答说:“不是。”他又问:“你认识我,对不对?”我回答说:“我不认识。”然后他又说:“你欠我 100 美元,对不对?”我跑掉了。就在那个时候,我想起母亲对我说过的话:“千万别跟陌生人说话。”

2 Vocabulary & Idioms 单词短语注解

1. **stranger** [ˋstrendʒɚ] *n.* 陌生人

2. **strange** [strendʒ] *a.* 奇怪的

3. **happen** [ˋhæpən] *vi.* 发生
happen to + 人　发生在某人身上
Good things always happen to me. 好事总是会发生在我身上。

4. **on my way to + 地方名词**　在我往……的途中
* 此短语中的所有格代词可任意更换,如 your (你的)、his(他的)、her (她的)、their (他们的)等,形成不同的意思。
On my way to the grocery store, I saw an old friend.
我在往杂货店的途中看见一位老友。

5. **stop** [stɑp] *vt.* 阻止

6. **reply** [rɪˋplaɪ] *vt.* 回答
I asked Mary to go to the movies with me. She replied, "I'm too busy."
我找玛丽和我一起去看电影。她回答说:"我太忙了。"

7. **answer** [ˋænsɚ] *vt.* 回答
* 本单词在本文中即等于 reply。

8. **owe** [o] *vt.* 欠
owe + 人 + 钱　欠某人(多少)钱
You still owe me fifty dollars. 你还欠我 50 美元。

9. **run away** 跑走(ran 为 run 的过去式)

10. **at that moment** 在那一刻
moment [ˋmomənt] *n.* 片刻,瞬间

11. **remember** [rɪˋmɛmbɚ] *vt.* 记得
I'm sorry. I don't remember your name.
很抱歉。我不记得你的大名了。

3 Grammar Points 语法重点

本课主要介绍反意疑问句的句型及用法。

1. **You are Betty, aren't you?** 你是贝蒂，对不对？
   You know me, don't you? 你认识我，对不对？
   以上两句均为反意疑问句。反意疑问句形成的基本原则是：肯定句应以否定反问，否定句则以肯定反问。句型通常有下列五种：
   a. 句中有 be 动词时，以该 be 动词形成反问。
   例 肯定句：He is polite, isn't he? 他很有礼貌，对不对？
   否定句：You aren't happy, are you? 你不快乐，对不对？
   b. 句中有助动词时，以该助动词形成反问。
   例 肯定句：He can do it, can't he? 他能做这件事，对不对？
   否定句：He won't come, will he? 他不会来，对不对？
   c. 肯定句中有一般动词时，应按时态及人称，以 do、does 或 did 形成反问；否定句中因已有 do、does 或 did，反问部分则仍使用 do、does 或 did。
   例 肯定句：He studies hard, doesn't he? 他很用功，对不对？
   否定句：They didn't like it, did they? 他们不喜欢它，对不对？
   d. 以 Let's（Let us 的缩写形式）引导的祈使句，其反问部分固定为 shall we。
   例 Let's go, shall we? 咱们走吧，好不好？
   Let's rest for a while, shall we? 咱们休息一下，好不好？
   e. 以动词原形起首的祈使句，其反问部分固定为 will you。
   例 Come here, will you? 到这里来，好不好？
   Be quiet, will you? 安静点，好不好？

2. 使用反意疑问句时，注意下列事项：
   a. 反问部分的主语始终为人称代词。
   例 John is angry with me, isn't John? (×)
   → John is angry with me, isn't he? (√)
   约翰生我的气，对不对？
   You, John and I are good friends, aren't we?

你、约翰和我都是好朋友，对不对？

b. 句中主语若为指示代词 this、that、these、those 时，反问部分则一律使用 it 或 they。

例 That is good, isn't that? (×)

→ That is good, isn't it? (√) 那个东西不错，对不对？

These are beautiful, aren't these? (×)

→ These are beautiful, aren't they? (√) 这些很美，对不对？

c. 句子以 There is / There are 引导时，反问部分仍使用 isn't there / aren't there。

例 There is a man there, isn't it? (×)

→ There is a man there, isn't there? (√) 那里有个人，对不对？

4 *Substitution* 替换

1. You are Betty, aren't you?
   He is your brother, isn't he?
   You are a teacher, aren't you?
   That's not your basketball, is it?
   你是贝蒂，对不对？
   他是你兄弟，对不对？
   你是老师，对不对？
   那不是你的篮球，对不对？

---

2. You know me, don't you?
   Carl likes Chinese opera, doesn't he?
   You didn't clean your room, did you?
   Paul didn't study for the test, did he?
   你认识我，对不对？
   卡尔喜欢京剧，对不对？
   你没有打扫房间，对不对？
   保罗没有念书准备考试，对不对？

Lesson 50

You're Sally, Aren't You?

你是萨莉，对不对？

1 *Dialogue* 实用会话

George: Excuse me. You're Sally, aren't you?

Sally: Yes.

George: Hi! I'm George. You remember me, don't you?

Sally: No.

George: We met at Bill's party.

Sally: Now I remember. Nice to see you again.

乔治：对不起。你是萨莉，对不对?

萨莉：对的。

乔治：嗨！我是乔治。你还记得我吧，对不对?

萨莉：不记得了。

乔治：我们在比尔的宴会上见过面啊。

萨莉：现在我想起来了。很高兴再次见到你。

2 *Key Points* 重点提示

1. **remember** [rɪˋmɛmbɚ] *vt.* 记得，想起

例 I can't remember her telephone number. 我记不得她的电话号码。

2. **Nice to see you again.** 很高兴再次见到你。

= It's nice to see you again.

例 A: Nice to see you again, Joe. 很高兴能再次见到你,乔。

B: Nice to see you again, too, Mary.

我也很高兴能再次见到你,玛丽。

3 请选择下列各句中正确的一项

1. Bob is a hard worker, ______ he?
   (A) aren't (B) is (C) isn't (D) doesn't
2. They swim very fast, ______ they?
   (A) don't (B) doesn't (C) can't (D) do
3. You didn't read that book, ______ you?
   (A) didn't (B) did (C) do (D) don't
4. Do it, ______ you?
   (A) don't (B) do (C) didn't (D) will
5. Let's go eat, ______ we?
   (A) will (B) won't (C) shall (D) shall not

解答 1. (C) 2. (A) 3. (B) 4. (D) 5. (C)

Lesson 51

My Girlfriend

我的女友

1 *Reading* 阅读

My girlfriend always complains. According to her, I should be more ambitious. I should work harder and earn more money. She also thinks I should live in a bigger and nicer apartment. In a way, she's right. However, she should be more considerate and less critical. After all, I am trying my best. Besides, money isn't everything.

我的女友老爱发牢骚。根据她的说法，我应当更有进取心。我应当更卖力地工作，挣更多的钱。她也认为我应当住更大更好的公寓。就某方面来说，她的话是对的。不过，她也应当多体谅少批评。毕竟，我正尽力而为。而且，金钱并非万能呀。

2 Vocabulary & Idioms 单词短语注解

1. **complain** [kəm`plen] *vi.* 抱怨

   complain about + 名词 / 动名词　抱怨……

   Bob often complains about his work. 鲍勃经常抱怨他的工作。

   Mack complained about working seven days a week.

   麦克抱怨说他一星期 7 天都在工作。

2. **according to + 人**　根据某人的说法

   according [ə`kɔrdɪŋ] *adv.* 依照

   注意

   不要写成下列中式的英文：

   according to his words (×)

   → according to him (√)（根据他的说法）

   According to Judy, this is a good book. 根据朱迪的说法，这是本好书。

3. **ambitious** [æm`bɪʃəs] *a.* 有上进心的，野心勃勃的

   Peter is more successful than Bob because he is more ambitious.

   彼得比鲍勃成功，因为他比鲍勃更有上进心。

4. **harder** [`hɑrdɚ] *adv.* 更努力地（hard 的比较级）

5. **earn** [ɝn] *vt.* 赚得，挣得

   Cathy earns a lot more money than I. 凯茜挣的钱比我多。

6. **bigger** [`bɪgɚ] *a.* 更大的（big 的比较级）

7. **nicer** [`naɪsɚ] *a.* 更好的（nice 的比较级）

8. **apartment** [ə`pɑrtmənt] *n.* 公寓

9. **in a way** 就某方面而言

   Mother thinks I'm lazy. In a way, she's right.

   我的母亲认为我很懒。就某方面而言，她是对的。

10. **right** [raɪt] *a.* 正确的

    No, Johnny. That is not the right answer.

    不对，约翰尼。那不是正确答案。

11. **considerate** [kən`sɪdərɪt] *a.* 体谅的
Connie is the most considerate person (that) I know.
康妮是我所认识的人里面最体谅人的一个。

12. **critical** [`krɪtɪkḷ] *a.* 批评的
be critical of + 名词　批评……，挑剔……
You shouldn't be so critical of others. 你不应该对他人这么挑剔。

13. **after all** 毕竟
Don't be mad at him. After all, he was only trying to help.
别生他的气。毕竟，他只是想帮忙而已。

14. **try one's best** 某人尽全力
You should try your best to help her. 你应该尽全力帮她。

15. **besides** [bɪ`saɪdz] *adv.* 此外
I don't want to see that movie. Besides, I have work to do.
我不想去看那部电影。此外，我有工作要做。

16. **Money isn't everything.** 金钱并非万能。（谚语）
Money talks. 有钱能使鬼推磨。（谚语）

3 *Grammar Points* 语法重点

本课旨在说明比较等级的形态及其用法。比较等级乃由形容词或副词变化而成。由于副词的比较等级变化与形容词相同，故本单元不予讨论，仅就形容词的比较等级加以说明。

请先看下例：

It's hot today, but it was hotter yesterday. 今天固然热，但是昨天更热。
She is beautiful, but her younger sister is even more beautiful.
她很美，但她妹妹更美。
He is good, but John is even better. 他不错，但约翰更好。
以上句中的 hotter、more beautiful 及 better 均属形容词的比较级。
再请看下列例句：
Today is the hottest day of the year. 今天是今年最热的一天。

She is the most beautiful girl in her class. 她是班上最美的女孩子。
He is the best student of all. 他是所有学生里最棒的一位。
以上句中的 hottest、most beautiful、best 均属形容词的最高级，与定冠词 the 连用。由上得知，形容词的比较等级有两种：一为比较级，一为最高级。现列表如下：

原级	比较级	最高级
beautiful 美丽的	more beautiful 比较美丽的	most beautiful 最美丽的
hot 热的	hotter 比较热的	hottest 最热的
good 好的	better 比较好的	best 最好的

我们看了上面的表格后，不禁要问："hot 的比较级为何不可写成 more hot? good 的比较级为何不是 gooder，而是 better? beautiful 的比较级为何是 more beautiful，而非 beautifuler?"

1. 一般而言，形容词的比较等级变化有下列原则：

a. 原级是双音节或三音节以上的形容词

比较级：more + 原级

最高级：most + 原级

原级	比较级	最高级
beautiful 美丽的	more beautiful	most beautiful
considerate 体谅的	more considerate	most considerate

b. 原级是单音节的形容词

比较级：原级 + -er

最高级：原级 + -est

原级	比较级	最高级
tall 高的	taller	tallest
fast 快速的	faster	fastest

c. 原级是以辅音结尾同时亦是闭音节的单音节形容词

比较级：重复该辅音字母 + -er

最高级：重复该辅音字母 + -est

原级	比较级	最高级
hot 热的	hotter	hottest
fat 肥胖的	fatter	fattest

d. 原级是以 -e 结尾的单音节形容词，或以 -le 结尾的双音节形容词

比较级：原级 + -r

最高级：原级 + -st

原级	比较级	最高级
wise 有智慧的	wiser	wisest
gentle 温和的	gentler	gentlest

e. 形容词结尾为“辅音 + -y”时

比较级：将 y 改成 i + -er

最高级：将 y 改成 i + -est

原级	比较级	最高级
pretty 美丽的	prettier	prettiest
easy 容易的	easier	easiest

以上的比较等级变化称作规则变化。但亦有些形容词则呈不规则变化，如：

原级	比较级	最高级
good 好的	better，非 more good	best，非 most good
bad 坏的	worse，非 more bad	worst，非 most bad

所幸这些不规则变化的形容词并不多。限于篇幅，我们无法一一列出。读者唯有多读英文文章，见到一个就熟记一个。所有精通英语的人士都曾经过这个过程。

2. 在原级的形容词之前冠以副词 less 或 least，则分别表示“较不……”或“最不……”之意。

原级	比较级	最高级
beautiful 美丽的	less beautiful 较不美丽的	least beautiful 最不美丽的
cute 可爱的	less cute，非 less cuter 较不可爱的	least cute，非 least cutest 最不可爱的

4 Substitution 替换

1. She should be more considerate.
   They should be more polite.
   You ought to be more generous.

I should be less lazy.

You ought to be less stingy.

她应当多体谅些。

他们应当更有礼貌些。

你应当更慷慨些。

我应当少懒惰些。

你应当少小气些。

---

2. I live in a bigger apartment.

He lives in a smaller apartment.

She lives in a more expensive apartment.

我住在一间较大的公寓里。

他住在一间较小的公寓里。

她住在一间较昂贵的公寓里。

Lesson 52

Sam's OK

山姆不错

1 *Dialogue* 实用会话

Father: Do you like Ray or Sam?

Daughter: I like Ray.

Father: Why?

Daughter: Sam's OK, but Ray's taller, cuter and more interesting. What about you?

Father: I like Sam better.

Daughter: Why?

Father: He's less proud. Besides, he's richer!

父亲：你喜欢雷还是山姆？

女儿：我喜欢雷。

父亲：为什么？

女儿：山姆固然不错，但雷个儿更高、更可爱，也更风趣。您觉得呢？

父亲：我比较喜欢山姆。

女儿：为什么？

父亲：他比较不骄傲。而且，他比较有钱！

2 *Key Points* 重点提示

1. **OK** [ˌoˋke] *a.* 不错的（亦可写成 okay）
2. **cute** [kjut] *a.* 可爱的
   例 Sally is the cutest child in the kindergarten.
   萨莉是幼儿园里最可爱的孩子。
3. **interesting** [ˋɪntrɪstɪŋ] *a.* 令人觉得有趣的，风趣的
   interested [ˋɪntrɪstɪd] *a.* 感到有兴趣的
   例 Grace is a very interesting woman. 格雷斯是位非常风趣的女士。
   What are you interested in? 你对什么有兴趣呢？
4. **proud** [praʊd] *a.* 骄傲的
   例 Although you are successful, you should be less proud.
   虽然你很成功，但你不应该这么骄傲。
5. **rich** [rɪtʃ] *a.* 有钱的
   例 The king is the richest man in the city, but not the happiest.
   国王是城里最有钱的人，但却不是最快乐的人。

3 请选择下列各句中正确的一项

1. I am good at basketball, but Peter is ______.
   (A) more good　　(B) better
   (C) best　　(D) most good
2. Fred is the ______ student in the class.
   (A) worst　　(B) bad　　(C) most bad　　(D) more bad
3. They are all beautiful, but Betty is the ______.
   (A) beautifulest　　(B) prettier
   (C) more beautiful　　(D) most beautiful
4. Yesterday was cold, but today is ______.
   (A) coldest　　(B) colder　　(C) most cold　　(D) cold

5. These dogs are not cute, and this one is the ______.

(A) less cute (B) less cuter

(C) least cute (D) least cutest

6. I like this book. It is very ______.

(A) interested (B) interest

(C) interests (D) interesting

解答 1. (B) 2. (A) 3. (D) 4. (B) 5. (C) 6. (D)

Lesson 53

Country Life

乡间生活

1 *Reading* 阅读

My parents prefer to live in the country. The streets there are cleaner. The air is fresher and the people are nicer and friendlier. Besides, it is busier and noisier in the city. But above all, it is safer to live in the country. My parents believe in the saying, "Safety first."

我爸妈比较喜欢住在乡下。那儿的街道比较干净。空气较新鲜，人也比较好、比较友善。而且，城市里比较忙碌，也比较吵。不过最重要的是，住在乡下较安全。我爸妈都相信这句格言："安全至上。"

2 Vocabulary & Idioms 单词短语注解

1. **parent** [ˋpɛrənt] *n.* 父或母
2. **prefer** [prɪˋfɝ] *vt.* 比较喜欢
   prefer to + 动词原形　比较喜欢……；宁愿……
   I prefer to stay in and rest tonight. 今晚我宁愿待在家里休息。
3. **country** [ˋkʌntrɪ] *n.* 乡下(与定冠词 the 连用)
4. **street** [strit] *n.* 街
5. **clean** [klin] *a.* 干净的
6. **air** [ɛr] *n.* 空气
7. **fresh** [frɛʃ] *a.* 新鲜的
8. **friendly** [ˋfrɛndlɪ] *a.* 友善的
   be friendly with + 人　对某人友善
   I am friendly with my neighbors. 我对我的邻居很友善。
9. **busy** [ˋbɪzɪ] *a.* 忙碌的
   be busy (in) + 动名词　忙着从事……
   He is busy to write a letter. (×)
   → He is busy writing a letter. (√) 他正忙着写信。
10. **noisy** [ˋnɔɪzɪ] *a.* 吵闹的
   The television is too noisy; turn it down. 电视声音太大了,关小声点。
11. **city** [ˋsɪtɪ] *n.* 城市
12. **above all** 最重要的是
   = most important of all
   above all 是作副词用的介词短语,使用时置于句首,之后置逗号,修饰全句。
   The doctor told my father to go on a diet. Above all, he told him to stop smoking.
   医生叫我父亲节食。最重要的是,他要戒烟。

13. **safe** [sef] *a.* 安全的
 safety [ˋseftɪ] *n.* 安全

14. **believe in...** 笃信……
 believe [bɪˋliv] *vi.* & *vt.* 相信
 I believe in working hard. 我深信辛勤工作是对的。

15. **saying** [ˋseɪŋ] *n.* 格言

3 *Grammar Points* 语法重点

1. 本课仍侧重于形容词比较级的变化。如 clean 变成 cleaner(更清洁的)、busy 变成 busier(更忙碌的)、noisy 变成 noisier(更吵闹的)、safe 变成 safer(更安全的)等。有关变化的原则,请参考 Lesson 51 的语法重点。

2. **prefer** 的用法
 a. prefer to + 动词原形　比较喜欢……
  例 I prefer to listen to music. 我比较喜欢听音乐。
 b. prefer to + 动词原形 + rather than + 动词原形
  喜欢……胜于……
  此处 rather than 视为并列连词,表示"而非"之意,连接两个动词原形。
  例 I prefer to listen to music rather than watch TV.
  我喜欢听音乐胜于看电视。
 c. prefer + 名词 + to + 名词　喜欢……胜于……
  此处 to 是介词,有"针对"的意味,"prefer A to B"表示"就 A 和 B 而言,比较喜欢 A"。
  例 I prefer music to movies. 我喜欢音乐胜于电影。

3. **Besides, it is busier and noisier in the city.**
 而且,城市里比较忙碌,也比较吵。
 此处的 it 是代词,泛指某地的环境。使用这个 it 时,句尾一定有一个表示场所的介词短语。
 中文:房间里很闷。(stuffy [ˋstʌfɪ] *a.* 闷热的)

英文：In the room is stuffy. (×)
理由：in the room 是介词短语，不能作主语。只有名词或代词方可作主语。
改正：It is stuffy in the room. (√)
说明：此处 It 指房间里的环境。

4. **...it is safer to live in the country.**……住在乡下较安全。
初学英文的人容易将这句中文译成：
Live in the country is safer. (×)
这当然是错误的句子，因为动词不可以直接作主语。动词应变成不定式(即 to + 动词原形)或动名词(即动词字尾加 -ing)方可作主语。故上句中的动词应变成 To live 或 Living 才合语法。即：
To live in the country is safer. (√) 住在乡下较安全。
= Living in the country is safer.
但这种不定式或动名词短语所形成的主语往往过大，故写作的人经常用 it 代替这些过大的主语，不定式或动名词短语则移至句尾，此时动名词亦常改为不定式。即：
To live in the country is safer. (√)
= It is safer to live in the country. (佳)
Living in the country is safer. (√)
= It is safer living in the country. (佳)
= It is safer to live in the country. (佳)
了解上面的说明后，我们不妨试译下列中文句子：
中文：学英文很有趣。
英文：Learn English is interesting. (×)
→ Learning English is interesting. (√)
= It is interesting to learn English. (佳)

5. **believe** 可作及物或不及物动词。believe 作及物动词时，之后直接接宾语。believe 若作不及物动词时，须接介词 in 之后，方可接宾语。区别如下：
believe + 宾语　相信某人 / 某人的话
believe in + 宾语　坚信某格言 / 信仰某宗教 / 相信某种神的存在

（强调信仰或信念）

例 I believe him. 我相信他。

I believe what he says. 我相信他的话。

He believes in Buddhism. 他信奉佛教。

Do you believe in God? 你相信上帝的存在吗？

I believe in the saying, "Live and learn."

我认为："活到老，学到老。"这句格言很有道理。

4 Substitution 替换

1. My parents prefer to live in the country.

He prefers to eat in a restaurant.

We prefer to swim in a swimming pool.

Sarah prefers to drink black tea.

I prefer reading history novels.

我父母比较喜欢住在乡下。

他比较喜欢在餐厅吃饭。

我们比较喜欢在游泳池游泳。

萨拉比较喜欢喝红茶。

我比较喜欢看历史小说。

---

2. It is busier and noisier in the city.

It is quieter and more relaxing in the country.

It is hotter in the south.

It is colder in the north.

城市里比较忙碌，也比较吵。

乡下比较安静，也比较悠闲。

南方比较热。

北方比较冷。

Lesson 54

I Like Brighter Colors 我喜欢较明亮的颜色

1 *Dialogue* 实用会话

Tracy: Do you like my new dress, Mike?

Mike: Frankly, I like brighter colors better. They make you look younger.

Tracy: Do darker colors make me look older?

Mike: Well...yes.

Tracy: Then, buy me another dress.

特蕾西：迈克，你喜欢我这件新的连衣裙吗？

迈　克：坦白说，我比较喜欢明亮一点的颜色。它们会使你看起来年轻些。

特蕾西：深一点的颜色会使我看起来年纪大一点吗？

迈　克：呃……是的。

特蕾西：那么，给我另外买一件吧！

2 *Key Points* 重点提示

1. **bright** [braɪt] *a.* 明亮的
2. **frankly** [ˋfræŋklɪ] *adv.* 坦白地说

   此副词常置于句首，之后置逗号，修饰全句。相当于 to be frank with you（坦白地对你说）。

例 Frankly, I don't like your idea. 坦白地说，我不喜欢你的构想。
= To be frank with you, I don't like your idea.

3. **young** [jʌŋ] *a.* 年轻的

4. **dark** [dɑrk] *a.* 暗的

3 请选择下列各句中正确的一项

1. ______ a bicycle in the mountains is fun.
   (A) Ride (B) Riding (C) Rides (D) Rode
2. It is more relaxing ______ in the country.
   (A) to live (B) to living (C) lived (D) to lives
3. I prefer Chinese food ______ American food.
   (A) or (B) than (C) to (D) but
4. David prefers to watch TV rather than ______.
   (A) go to movie (B) going to movie
   (C) going to see movie (D) go to the movies
5. Joe is friendly, but Kathy is ______.
   (A) friendlier (B) friendlyer
   (C) friendly (D) more friendlier
6. ______, you should work harder.
   (A) To be frankly
   (B) Being frankly
   (C) I am frank with you
   (D) To be frank with you

解答 1. (B) 2. (A) 3. (C) 4. (D) 5. (A) 6. (D)

♫怀念老歌园地♫

Stoney

史东妮

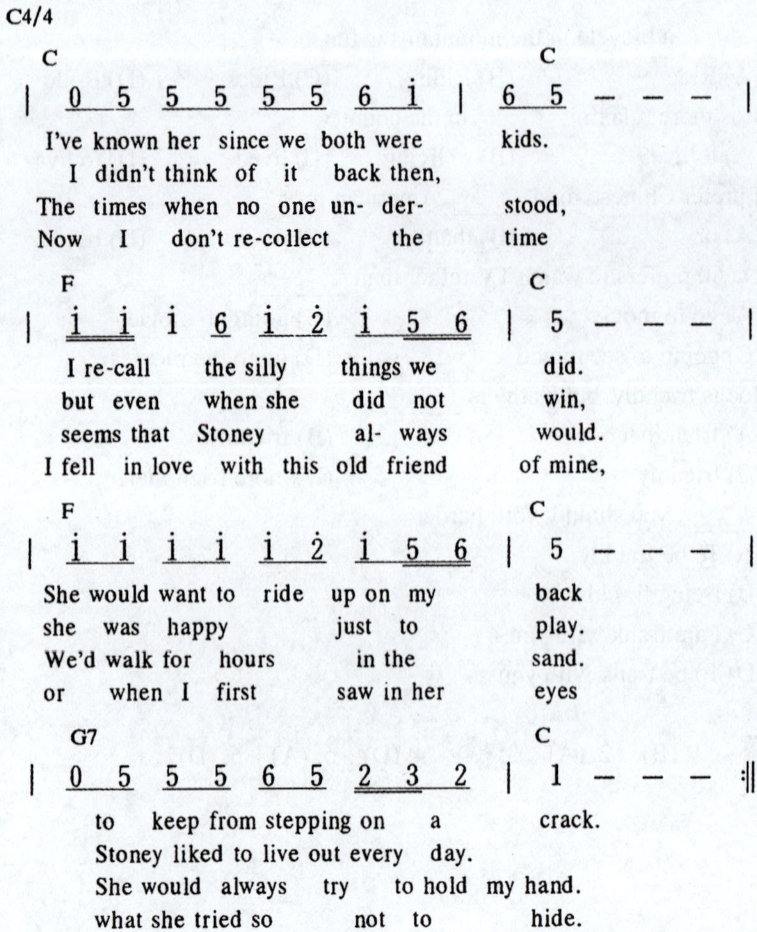

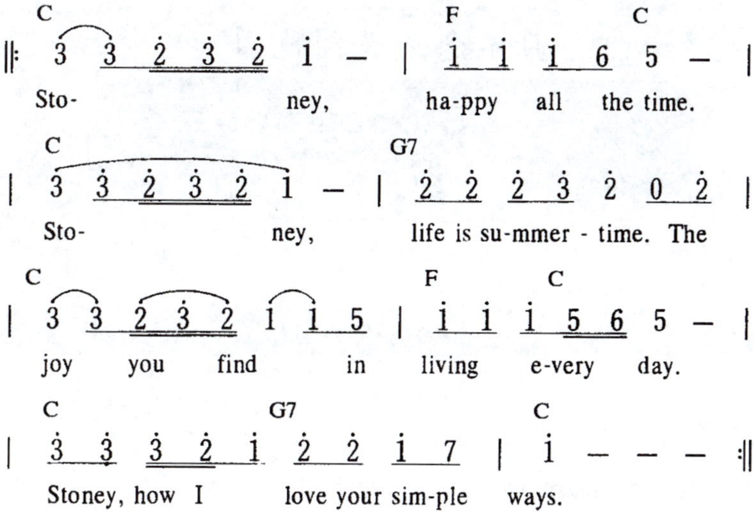
C F C
Sto- ney, ha-ppy all the time.
C G7
Sto- ney, life is su-mmer - time. The
C F C
joy you find in living e-very day.
C G7 C
Stoney, how I love your sim-ple ways.

♫怀念老歌园地♫

Stoney

史东妮

1 *Lyrics* 歌词 ☺

I've known her since we both were kids. I recall the silly things we did. She would want to ride up on my back to keep from stepping on a crack. I didn't think of it back then, but even when she did not win, she was happy just to play. Stoney liked to live out every day.

Stoney, happy all the time. Stoney, life is summertime. The joy you find in living every day. Stoney, how I love your simple ways. The times when no one understood, seems that Stoney always would. We'd walk for hours in the sand. She would always try to hold my hand.

Now I don't recollect the time I fell in love with this old friend of mine, or when I first saw in her eyes what she tried so not to hide.

我和史东妮自孩提时代就相识了。我还记得那时我们常做的一些傻事。她总是想要骑在我背上，以免踩在路砖之间的裂缝。当时我根本没有想到她骑在我背上的事情。但是，即使她游戏玩输了，她也不会介意，只要能够参加她就很高兴了。史东妮希望每天都过得非常愉快。

史东妮，你始终很快乐。你的人生犹如夏日时光般的美好。你每天都能在生活中找到乐趣。史东妮，我真的好喜欢你那单纯的个性。我常常觉得没有人了解我，但史东妮似乎总能了解我。我们在沙滩上经常一走就是好几个小时，她总是想要握我的手。

我不记得何时已爱上我这位儿时玩伴，也想不起何时我第一次在她眼里看见她不想隐藏的感情。

2 Vocabulary & Idioms 单词短语注解

1. **I've known her since we both were kids.**
   = Ever since we were little kids, I have known Stoney.
   我和史东妮自孩提时代就相识了。

2. **recall** [rɪˋkɔl] *vt.* 想起，忆起 & *n.* 回想，回忆
   be beyond one's recall 某人不能忆起；某人不记得
   I cannot recall the words I said at that time.
   我记不得当时我说了些什么。
   The name of that guy I liked in junior high school is beyond my recall.
   我已记不得初中时我所喜欢的那个男孩的名字了。

3. **silly** [ˋsɪlɪ] *a.* 愚蠢的；傻的
   It is very silly of you to trust such a bad person.

你信赖如此坏的人真是愚蠢。

4. **crack** [kræk] *n.* 裂缝；缝隙
此处乃指小孩走在路砖上比赛不要踩在路砖之间裂缝，谁踩到谁输的一种游戏。
Be careful. There's a crack in that glass you're drinking from.
小心，你喝水的玻璃杯上有裂缝。
歌词中的 Stoney 喜欢骑在作者的背上，以免踩着砖与砖之间的裂缝。这种 on my back 的游戏称为 piggyback。piggyback [ˋpɪgɪˏbæk] *a.* & *adv.* 在肩（背）上，骑在肩（背）上地
Children who are carried piggyback all the time will become bow-legged.
经常一直被背在肩上的小孩，其两腿将会变成外八字。
The babysitter carried the children piggyback to their rooms.
这保姆肩上背着小孩进入房间。

5. **I didn't think of it back then.**
那时我甚至没有想过她骑在我背上的事情。
it 指 Stoney 骑在我背上的事情。

6. **Stoney liked to live out every day.**
= Stoney liked to get the most enjoyment out of every day.
史东妮希望每天都过得非常愉快。

7. **Stoney, happy all the time.** 史东妮始终很快乐。
= Stoney is happy all the time.

8. **Stoney, life is summertime.**
= For Stoney, life is always like summertime.
对史东妮而言，人生犹如夏日时光一样美好。

9. **The joy you find in living every day.**
= Stoney, it seems to me that you find joy in living every day.
史东妮，对我而言，你好像每天都能从生活中找到乐趣。

10. **Stoney, how I love your simple ways.**

= Stoney, I really love you because of your simple manner of doing things.

史东妮，我真的好喜欢你，因为你的个性很随和，很容易与人相处。

11. **The times when no one understood, seems that Stoney always would.**

= There were times when no one understood me, and it seems that Stoney would always understand me.

常常没有人了解我，而似乎史东妮总能了解我。

12. **We'd walk for hours in the sand.**

= We would walk for hours along the beach.

我们在沙滩上经常一走就是好几个小时。

13. **recollect** [ˌrɛkəˈlɛkt] *vt.* 记起；忆起

I don't recollect making that mistake. 我不记得犯了那个错误。

14. (1) **Now I don't recollect the time I fell in love with this old friend of mine...**

= Now I don't recollect the time when I fell in love with this childhood friend of mine...

(a = I; b = don't recollect; c = the time; d = when I fell in love with this childhood friend of mine)

我不记得我何时爱上我这位儿时玩伴。

句型分析：

a. 为主语

b. 为及物动词

c. 为宾语

d. 为关系副词 when 所引导的定语从句，修饰前面的 the time。when 此处等于 in which，但在歌词中因省略音节关系，故把关系副词 when 省略掉。

(2) **...or when I first saw in her eyes what she tried so not to hide.**

(e = or; f = when; g = I; h = first saw; i = in her eyes; j = what she tried so not to hide)

= ...or I don't recollect the time when I first saw in her eyes the feelings that she didn't want to hide.

我也想不起何时第一次在她眼里看见她不想隐藏的感情。

句型分析：

e. 为并列连词

f. 为另一个关系副词 when 所引导的定语从句，与 (1) 中 d 的 when 从句对等，此处 when 也等于 in which，均引导定语从句，修饰前面的 the time。

g. 为主语

h. 为及物动词

i. 介词短语，当副词，修饰 saw

j. 为一个名词性从句，作 saw 的宾语

Lesson 55

More Is Not Always Better

多未必佳

1 *Reading* 阅读

Some people have more money than others. However, they're not necessarily happier. On the other hand, some people are as poor as church mice, but they are happy. In a way, these poor people are as rich as kings. Therefore, I always remember my father's words, "More is not always better."

有些人比别人有钱。不过，他们未必就比较快乐。相反地，有些人穷得要命，可他们却很快乐。就某方面而言，这些穷人却像国王一样富有。因此，我始终记得父亲的话："多未必佳。"

2 Vocabulary & Idioms 单词短语注解

1. **than** [ðæn] *conj.* 比……
   He is more knowledgeable than his father. 他比他父亲更有学问。

2. **however** [haʊˋɛvɚ] *adv.* 不过
   John is neither handsome nor rich. However, he is nice.
   约翰既不英俊又不富有，不过他人很好。

3. **not necessarily** 未必
   necessarily [ˏnɛsəˋsɛrəlɪ] *adv.* 必然地
   The boss isn't necessarily always right. 老板未必永远是对的。

4. **as poor as a church mouse**（与单数主语连用）
   as poor as church mice（与复数主语连用）
   * 穷得像教堂里的老鼠一样，比喻“穷得要命”。
   church [tʃɝtʃ] *n.* 教堂
   The businessman lost everything he had and is now as poor as a church mouse.
   那个商人失去了一切，现在穷得要命。

5. **king** [kɪŋ] *n.* 国王

6. **remember** [rɪˋmɛmbɚ] *vt.* 记住
   Mary remembered my birthday. 玛丽记得我的生日。

7. **words** [wɝdz] *n.*（某人所说的）话（word 的复数）
   I don't believe his words. He is a liar. 我不相信他的话，他是个骗子。

8. **more** [mɔr] *a.* 更多的（much 的比较级）& *adv.* 更加 & *pron.* 更多的分量
   I have more friends than you. 我的朋友比你多。
   * 本句中的 more 是形容词。
   She is more beautiful than Mary. 她比玛丽更漂亮。
   * 本句中的 more 是副词。
   He has a lot of money, but she has more.

他固然钱很多，但她的钱却更多。

* 本句中的 more 是代词，等于 more money。

3 Grammar Points 语法重点

本课主要介绍"more...than..."（比……更……）及"as...as..."（和……一样……）的用法。

1. **Some people have more money than others.**

   有些人比别人有钱。

   此处的 than 为从属连词，引导状语从句，修饰之前的比较级形容词或副词。

   本句中的状语从句 than others 修饰其前的比较级形容词 more。than others 原本应为 than others do，do 为助动词，代替之前主句中相同的动词 have，此处 do 已省略。兹将 than 引导的状语从句中动词省略的法则陈述如下：

   a. 主句有 be 动词时，从句亦应使用 be 动词，该 be 动词通常予以省略。

   例 She is more beautiful than you do. (×)
   → She is more beautiful than you are. (√)
   = She is more beautiful than you. 她比你美。

   b. 主句有一般动词时，从句理应使用相同的动词，但为了避免重复，该动词应按时态及人称改为 do、does 或 did；而 do、does 或 did 通常亦予以省略。

   例 He studies harder than I study.（劣，study 与 studies 重复。）
   → He studies harder than I do.（佳，由于 study 是现在式，故改用 do 取代。）
   = He studies harder than I. 他比我用功。
   He came back earlier than I came back.（劣，came back 重复。）
   → He came back earlier than I did.（佳，由于 came 是过去式，故改用 did。）
   = He came back earlier than I. 他比我早回来。

   由上得知：

Some people have more money than others have.（劣，have 重复。）
动词 动词

→ Some people have more money than others do.（佳）

= Some people have more money than others.

2. **Some people have more money than others.**

有些人比别人有钱。

本句中的 others [ˋʌðəz] 是代词，等于 other people。some 亦可作代词，等于 some people。

some...others... 有些人……有些人……

例 People have different hobbies. Some like to go swimming, and others are fond of dancing.

人的爱好各有不同。有些人喜欢游泳，有些人则喜欢跳舞。

3. **Some people are as poor as church mice.**

有些人穷得像教堂里的老鼠一样——穷得要命。

In a way, these poor people are as rich as kings.

就某方面而言，这些穷人像国王一样富有。

以上两句均使用“as...as...”（和……一样地……）。这种“as...as...”的句子结构一定要有形容词或副词方可使用。因为第一个 as 是副词，译成“一样地”，之后须接形容词或副词以供该 as 修饰，第二个 as 则为从属连词，译成“和”，之后接主语及动词，形成状语从句，修饰第一个 as。但和 than 引导的状语从句一样，第二个 as 之后的动词为避免与主句的动词重复而省略。省略的原则与 than 引导的状语从句完全一样。

a. 主句有 be 动词时，从句亦应使用 be 动词，该 be 动词通常予以省略。

例 She is as beautiful as you do. (×)

→ She is as beautiful as you are. (√)

= She is as beautiful as you. 她跟你一样美。

b. 主句有一般动词时，状语从句里理应使用相同的动词，但为了避免重复，该动词应按时态及人称改为 do、does 或 did；而 do、does 或 did 通常亦予以省略。

例 He studies as hard as I study.（劣，study 与 studies 重复。）
→ He studies as hard as I do.
（佳，由于 study 是现在时，故改由 do 取代。）
= He studies as hard as I. 他跟我一样用功。
He came back as early as I came back.（劣，came back 重复。）
→ He came back as early as I did.
（佳，由于 came 是过去时，故用 did 取代。）
= He came back as early as I. 他和我一样早回来。

4 *Substitution* 替换

1. Some people have more money than others (do).
Paul has more friends than I (do).
My sister is fatter than I (am).
Jim finished his test earlier than Mary (did).
有些人比别人有钱。
保罗的朋友比我的多。
我妹妹比我胖。
吉姆比玛丽早做完考卷。

---

2. These poor people are as rich as kings (are).
I have as much money as my brother (does).
Today is as cold as yesterday (was).
A horse isn't as big as an elephant (is).
这些穷人像国王一样富有。
我的钱和我哥哥一样多。
今天和昨天一样冷。
马不像大象那样大。

Lesson 56

I Want the Cheaper One 我要买那块便宜的手表

1 *Dialogue* 实用会话

Customer: Why is this watch more expensive than that one?

Salesgirl: Because its brand name is more famous.

Customer: Is it more reliable?

Salesgirl: No. Not really.

Customer: Then, I want the cheaper one.

顾　客：这块手表为什么比那块贵？

女店员：因为它的牌子比较出名。

顾　客：它比较可靠吗？

女店员：不。不见得。

顾　客：那么，我要买那块便宜的手表。

2 *Key Points* 重点提示

1. **customer** [ˈkʌstəmɚ] *n.* 顾客
2. **salesgirl** [ˈselzˌgɝl] *n.* 女售货员，女店员
3. **brand name** [ˈbrænd ˌnem] *n.* 商标名称，牌子
4. **famous** [ˈfeməs] *a.* 有名的

   例 My sister is a famous singer. 我妹妹是个著名歌手。

5. **reliable** [rɪˋlaɪəbl̩] *a.* 值得信赖的

例 Our postman is a reliable person. 我们的邮递员是个值得信赖的人。

6. **cheap** [tʃip] *a.* 便宜的

例 Cheap perfume smells terrible. 廉价香水闻起来很糟糕。

3 请选择下列各句中正确的一项

1. Peter is taller than Harry ______.
   (A) is (B) does (C) is tall (D) are
2. Bobby writes better than I ______.
   (A) does (B) am (C) do (D) is
3. Joe did better on the test than we ______.
   (A) do (B) have (C) did (D) are
4. Sue's hair isn't ______ Mary's.
   (A) curly as (B) as curly as
   (C) as curly than (D) as curly
5. We worked as hard as they ______.
   (A) did (B) are (C) have (D) does
6. Kim's car is not as reliable as Peter's because it is ______.
   (A) less cheap (B) more cheap
   (C) the most cheap (D) cheaper

解答 1. (A) 2. (C) 3. (C) 4. (B) 5. (A) 6. (D)

Lesson 57

The Elephant and the Whale
大象与鲸鱼

1 *Reading* 阅读

The biggest and strongest animal on land is the elephant. The largest and heaviest animal in the sea is the whale. It's also the biggest eater in the world. It eats a ton of food a day. It looks like a fish, but it is really a mammal. Although the elephant and the whale are both mammals, they are indeed very different.

陆地上最大、最壮的动物就是大象。海中最大、最重的动物则是鲸鱼,它也是世界上吃得最多的动物,它每天要吃一吨的食物。它看起来像鱼,但它实际上是哺乳动物。虽然大象和鲸鱼都是哺乳动物,它们却大不相同。

2 Vocabulary & Idioms 单词短语注解

1. **elephant** [ˋɛləfənt] *n.* 大象

2. **whale** [wel] *n.* 鲸

3. **biggest** [ˋbɪgɪst] *a.* 最大的（为 big 的最高级）

4. **strongest** [ˋstrɔŋgɪst] *a.* 最强壮的（为 strong 的最高级）

5. **animal** [ˋænəml̩] *n.* 动物

6. **on land** 在陆地上
   land [lænd] *n.* 陆地
   Some mammals live on land, and some live in the sea.
   有些哺乳动物居住在陆地上，而有些则居住在海里。

7. **largest** [ˋlɑrdʒɪst] *a.* 最大的（为 large 的最高级）
   * 此处 largest 即等于 biggest，皆表体积最大的。

8. **heaviest** [ˋhɛvɪst] *a.* 最重的（为 heavy 的最高级）
   heavy [ˋhɛvɪ] *a.* 重的
   Can you help me lift this heavy box?
   你可以帮我抬这个很重的箱子吗？

9. **sea** [si] *n.* 海洋

10. **eater** [ˋitɚ] *n.* 食者，食客

11. **in the world** 世界上
    world [wɝld] *n.* 世界
    My son, Mike, is the cutest boy in the world.
    我儿子迈克是全世界最可爱的男孩。

12. **ton** [tʌn] *n.* 吨
    a ton of... 一吨的……

13. **fish** [fɪʃ] *n.* 鱼
    注意
    此单词单复数同形，亦即 a fish、two fish、three fish...many fish。

14. **mammal** [ˋmæml̩] *n.* 哺乳动物

15. **indeed** [ɪnˋdid] *adv.* 实在

My teacher is indeed very knowledgeable. 我的老师实在是很有学问。

3 *Grammar Points* 语法重点

本课主要介绍比较等级中形容词的最高级及其用法。

1. **The biggest and strongest animal on land is the elephant.**

陆地上最大、最壮的动物就是大象。

以上句中的 biggest 及 strongest 均为形容词的最高级。

在前面的课文中我们已提到形容词的比较级及最高级的变化。本课则就形容词的最高级使用时应注意事项提出说明如下：

a. 形容词的最高级应与定冠词 the 连用：

例 She is a most beautiful girl in her class. (×)

→ She is the most beautiful girl in her class. (√)

她是她班上最美丽的女孩子。

David is a best student in his school. (×)

→ David is the best student in his school. (√)

大卫是他学校中最好的学生。

b. 含有比较等级的句子结构中，有三个或三个以上的比较对象时，方可使用最高级；若只有两个对象相互比较时，只能使用比较级。

例 Of the three girls, she is the most beautiful.

这三个女孩子中，她是最美的。

Of the ten students, David is the best.

这十个学生中，大卫是最好的一个。

Of the two books, this one is the more interesting.

这两本书中，这一本比较有趣。

Of the two teachers, John is the kinder.

这两位老师中，约翰是比较仁慈的一位。

c. 在 b 项的例句中，均含有“of the + 数字 + 名词”的介词短语，句中的形容词不论是最高级或比较级,其前均冠以定冠词 the。且由于介词短语已有名词出现,形容词的最高级或比较级之后相同的名词就应省略。

例 Of the two boys, John is better. (×)

Of the two boys, John is the better boy. (劣, boy 与 boys 重复)

→ Of the two boys, John is the better. (√)

这两个男孩中,约翰比较好。

d. 上列 of 引导的介词短语中,数字为 three (三)或以上时, of 可由 among [əˈmʌŋ] (在……之中)取代,但若为 two (二)时,只能使用 of,而不可使用 among。

例 Of the five cars, the red one is the prettiest.

= Among the five cars, the red one is the prettiest.

这五辆汽车中,红色的那一辆最漂亮。

Among the two cars, the red one is the prettier. (×)

→ Of the two cars, the red one is the prettier. (√)

这两辆汽车中,红色的那一辆比较漂亮。

e. 形容词的最高级与 the 之间可置数字(如 two、three 等),与复数名词连用。

例 John and Mary are two best students in our class.(×)

→ John and Mary are the two best students in our class. (√)

约翰和玛丽是我们班上最好的两个学生。

4 *Substitution* 替换

1. The biggest animal on land is the elephant.

February is the shortest month of the year.

The Sears Building in the United States is the tallest building in the world.

陆地上最大的动物是大象。

二月是一年之中最短的一个月。

美国的西尔斯大楼是世上最高的建筑物。

2. The heaviest animal in the sea is the whale.
Of all the animals in the sea, the whale is the biggest.
Of the five continents, Asia is the largest.
海中最重的动物是鲸鱼。
海中所有的动物中，鲸鱼是最大的。
在五大洲中，亚洲是最大的。

Lesson 58

The Smartest Teacher 最聪明的老师

1 *Dialogue* 实用会话

Teacher: Which country is the biggest in the world?

Student: Russia.

Teacher: Which country has the most people in the world?

Student: China.

Teacher: Who is the smartest teacher in the school?

Student: But...you are the only teacher in the school.

Teacher: I know.

老师：世界上哪个国家最大？

学生：俄罗斯。

老师：世界上哪个国家的人最多？

学生：中国。

老师：本校中哪一位老师最聪明？

学生：但是……你是本校唯一的老师啊。

老师：我知道。

2 Key Points 重点提示

1. **Russia** [ˋrʌʃə] *n.* 俄罗斯

2. **Which country has the most people in the world?**

世界上哪个国家的人最多?

比较:

She is the most beautiful girl in her class.

她是她班上最美的女孩子。

在第二句中, most 是副词,译成“最”,修饰后面的形容词 beautiful。而在第一句中, most 是形容词,译成“最多的”,修饰后面的名词 people。

由上得知,第一句中的 most 乃形容词 many 的最高级, 后面接复数名词,变化如下:

原级	比较级	最高级
many	more	most

例 He has many friends. 他朋友很多。

I have more friends. 我朋友比较多。

She has the most friends. 她朋友最多。

most 亦可作形容词 much 的最高级,后面接不可数名词, 变化如下:

原级	比较级	最高级
much	more	most

注意

much 多用于否定句中,肯定句中则使用 a lot of 取代 much。

例 He has much money. (劣)

→ He doesn't have much money. (√) 他钱不多。

He has a lot of money. (√) 他钱很多。

I have more money. 我的钱比较多。

She has the most money. 她的钱最多。

3. **smart** [smɑrt] *a.* 聪明的

例 My wife is very smart. She married me, didn't she?

我太太很聪明，她嫁给我了，不是吗？

3 请选择下列各句中正确的一项

1. Among the ten boys in the room, Bill is ______.
   (A) the oldest (B) older
   (C) more old (D) most old
2. _____ two bicycles, this one is the more expensive.
   (A) Among (B) Among the
   (C) Of (D) Of the
3. Miss Lee is ______ patient teacher in the school.
   (A) most (B) a most (C) the most (D) more
4. Of the four kids, Little Johnny has the ______ toys.
   (A) many (B) most (C) much (D) mostest
5. Of the two men, my dad is ______.
   (A) stronger (B) strongest
   (C) the strongest (D) the stronger
6. My brother has ______ toys, but I have ______ toys.
   (A) many, many (B) more, many
   (C) many, more (D) more, most

解答 1. (A) 2. (D) 3. (C) 4. (B) 5. (D) 6. (C)

Lesson 59

My Best Friend

我最好的朋友

1 *Reading* 阅读

My best friend is the most thoughtful person in the world. When I'm sad, he is the most sympathetic. When I'm sick, he is the most concerned. When I'm in trouble, he is the most helpful. In fact, he is the most dependable person in the world. He is the closest person to me. He is my father.

我最好的朋友是世界上最体贴我的人。当我难过时，他最富有同情心了。我生病时，他最为关心。我有困难时，他最能帮我了。事实上，他是世界上最值得信赖的人。他是我最亲的人。他就是我父亲。

2 Vocabulary & Idioms 单词短语注解

1. **thoughtful** [ˈθɔtfəl] *a.* 体贴的
   It was very thoughtful of you to send me a birthday card.
   你寄给我生日卡片真是体贴。

2. **person** [ˈpɝsn̩] *n.* 人(男性、女性皆可)
   The mayor is the most important person in the city.
   市长是一个城市中最重要的人。

3. **sympathetic** [ˌsɪmpəˈθɛtɪk] *a.* 同情的

4. **sick** [sɪk] *a.* 生病的
   I was very sick yesterday, so I stayed home from work.
   昨天我病得很重,所以我待在家里没有去上班。

5. **concerned** [kənˈsɝnd] *a.* 关切的
   be concerned about + 人 / 事物　关心某人 / 某事物
   I'm very concerned about Bill. He looks sick.
   我很关心比尔,他看起来像生病了。

6. **be in trouble** 处于困难 / 麻烦中
   trouble [ˈtrʌbl̩] *n.* 困难
   Mary is in trouble because she cheated on a test.
   玛丽有麻烦了,因为她考试作弊。

7. **helpful** [ˈhɛlpfəl] *a.* 有帮助的;乐于助人的
   Bob's advice was very helpful. 鲍勃的建议非常有帮助。

8. **dependable** [dɪˈpɛndəbl̩] *a.* 可信赖的
   My car always breaks down. It is not dependable.
   我的车子老是出故障,它真是不可靠。

9. **closest** [ˈklosɪst] *a.* 最亲的(为 close 的最高级)

3 Grammar Points 语法重点

本课复习形容词最高级的用法。

1. **When I'm sad, he is the most sympathetic. When I'm sick, he is the most concerned. When I'm in trouble, he is the most helpful.**
当我难过时，他最有同情心了。我生病时，他最为关心。我有困难时，他最能帮我。
以上句中划线部分均省略了 person in the world，以免与本文中第一个句子 "My best friend is the most thoughtful person in the world." 的划线部分重复。

2. 本文中的形容词 sympathetic 是不及物动词 sympathize [ˋsɪmpəˏθaɪz] 的衍生词，名词则为 sympathy [ˋsɪmpəθɪ]。注意下列的相关用法：
be sympathetic to + 人　同情某人
= sympathize with + 人
= feel sympathy for + 人
例 Jane was sympathetic to the starving puppy, so she took it home and fed it.
简很同情那只挨饿的小狗，所以她就把它带回家喂它。
Connie sympathizes with those orphans and their problems.
康妮很同情那些孤儿以及他们的问题。
I felt sympathy for the poor beggar, so I gave him some money.
我很同情那位可怜的乞丐，所以我给了他一些钱。

4 Substitution 替换

1. My best friend is the most thoughtful person in the world.
Your brother is the most stupid person in the world.
My professor is the smartest man in the school.
Our house is the biggest in the neighborhood.
我最好的朋友是世界上最体贴的人。
你弟弟是世界上最笨的人。
我的教授是学校中最聪明的人。
我们的房子是附近最大的。

2. He is the closest person to me.
   She was the kindest person to me.
   You were the nicest person to him.
   I was the cruelest person to them.
   他是我最亲近的人。
   对我来说她是最好的人。
   对他来说你是最好的人。
   对他们来说我是最残忍的人。

Lesson 60

The Longest River in the World 世界上最长的河流

1 *Dialogue* 实用会话

Teacher: Which is the longest river in the world?

Student: The Nile.

Teacher: Which is the biggest ocean in the world?

Student: The Pacific Ocean.

Teacher: Which is the best school in the village?

Student: But...this is the only school in the village, sir.

Teacher: I know.

老师：世界上最长的河流是哪一条？

学生：尼罗河。

老师：世界上最大的海洋是哪一个？

学生：太平洋。

老师：本村最好的学校是哪一所？

学生：但是……老师，本校是村里唯一的一所学校啊。

老师：我知道。

2 *Key Points* 重点提示

1. **river** [ˈrɪvɚ] *n.* 河

2. **the Nile** 尼罗河（Nile [naɪl]）

3. **ocean** [ˈoʃən] *n.* 海洋

4. **the Pacific Ocean** 太平洋（Pacific [pəˈsɪfɪk]）

   *表示河川、山脉、海洋等专有名词，在英文中均与定冠词 the 连用，如：

   the Yellow River 黄河

   the Yangtze River 长江

   the Himalayas 喜玛拉雅山脉

   the Atlantic Ocean 大西洋

   the South China Sea（中国）南海

   这些专有名词中有些经常使用，原有的 River、Ocean 或 Sea 均可省略，如：

   the Nile River → the Nile 尼罗河

   the Mediterranean Sea → the Mediterranean

   [ˌmɛdətəˈrenɪən] 地中海

   the Pacific Ocean → the Pacific 太平洋

5. **village** [ˈvɪlɪdʒ] *n.* 村庄

3 请选择下列各句中正确的一项

1. Andrew thinks he's the strongest person ______ the world.
   (A) on (B) above (C) in (D) under
2. That is the ______ restaurant in the city.
   (A) worst (B) most bad
   (C) baddest (D) most worse
3. Jessica is the ______ dancer in our class.
   (A) better (B) best
   (C) most good (D) most best
4. This question is the ______ one in the book.
   (A) easyest (B) most easy
   (C) easier (D) easiest

5. The red book is ______ the blue one, but the brown book is the ______.

(A) cheapest, cheaper

(B) more cheap, most cheap

(C) cheaper, cheapest

(D) cheaper than, cheapest

6. ______ is bigger than ______.

(A) Pacific Ocean, Atlantic Ocean

(B) The Pacific Ocean, Atlantic

(C) The Pacific Ocean, the Atlantic Ocean

(D) The Pacific, Atlantic

解答 1. (C) 2. (A) 3. (B) 4. (D) 5. (D) 6. (C)

Lesson 61

The Hare and the Turtle 兔子与乌龟

1 *Reading* 阅读

The hare can run very fast, but the turtle can only walk slowly. One day the hare proudly challenged the turtle to a race. The hare started quickly but stopped to take a nap every now and then. The turtle walked slowly but surely. While the hare was sleeping, the turtle passed him. Finally, the turtle won the race. In the end, he was rewarded for his perseverance. We can all learn a lesson from the turtle.

兔子可以跑得很快，但乌龟只能慢慢地走。有一天兔子骄傲地向乌龟挑战赛跑。兔子开始时跑得很快，但它偶尔会停下来小睡片刻。乌龟走得很慢但却走得很稳。当兔子在睡觉时，乌龟超过了兔子，终于赢了比赛。最后乌龟因坚韧不拔的精神而获得回报。我们全都可以从乌龟那里得到一点启示。

2 Vocabulary & Idioms 单词短语注解

1. **hare** [hɛr] *n.* 野兔

2. **turtle** [ˋtɝtḷ] *n.* 乌龟

3. **walk** [wɔk] *vi.* 步行,散步
I love walking in the forest. 我喜欢在森林里散步。

4. **slowly** [ˋslolɪ] *adv.* 缓慢地
Please speak slowly. My English isn't very good.
请说慢一点。我的英文不是很好。

5. **proudly** [ˋpraudlɪ] *adv.* 骄傲地
Betty smiled proudly when the teacher praised her.
当老师称赞贝蒂时,她很骄傲地微笑着。

6. **challenge + 人 + to a race** 向某人挑战赛跑 / 比赛
challenge [ˋtʃælɪndʒ] *vt.* 向……挑战
race [res] *n.* 赛跑;比赛
Bob challenged Peter to a bicycle race and lost.
鲍勃向彼得挑战骑自行车比赛,结果输了。

7. **start** [stɑrt] *vi.* 开始
The movie will start in five minutes. 电影再过 5 分钟就要开始了。

8. **quickly** [ˋkwɪklɪ] *adv.* 迅速地
You're driving too quickly; slow down. 你开得太快了,开慢一点。

9. **take a nap** 小睡片刻
nap [næp] *n.* 小睡
I'm feeling tired. I'm going to take a nap.
我觉得很累,我要去小睡一下。

10. **every now and then** 偶尔
A: How often do you visit your grandmother?
B: Every now and then.
A: 你多久去看望一次你的祖母?

B: 偶尔去一次。

11. **surely** [ˈʃurlɪ] *adv.* 稳定地

12. **pass** [pæs] *vt.* 经过,通过

After you pass the library, turn left. 你经过图书馆后就向左转。

13. **won** [wʌn] *vt.* 赢得(win [wɪn] 的过去式)

14. **in the end** 最后

James always smoked cigarettes. In the end, he died of cancer.

詹姆斯总是在抽烟。最后,他死于癌症。

15. **reward** [rɪˈwɔrd] *vt.* 报酬,奖赏

The boss rewarded me for doing a good job.

老板因我工作表现良好而奖赏我。

16. **perseverance** [ˌpɜsəˈvɪrəns] *n.* 毅力

If you have perseverance, you can learn anything.

如果你有毅力,你就可以学会任何一件事。

17. **learn a lesson** 得到一个教训

learn [lɜn] *vt.* 学习

lesson [ˈlɛsn̩] *n.* 教训

I learned a lesson from my older brother's failures.

我从我哥哥的失败中吸取教训。

3 Grammar Points 语法重点

本课主要介绍副词的功能及用法。

1. **One day the hare proudly challenged the turtle to a race.**

有一天兔子骄傲地向乌龟挑战赛跑。

one day 是表示时间的状语,可指过去或将来的某一天。换言之,one day 可使用于过去时或将来时的句子中。

例 One day I had dinner with her at that restaurant.(过去时)

有一天我曾和她在那家餐厅吃晚饭。

One day the little boy will be a great man.（将来时）
有一天这个小男孩会成为伟人。

注意

a. someday 将来有一天(用于将来时)

例 Someday the little boy will be a great man.
= One day the little boy will be a great man.
有一天这个小男孩会成为伟人。

b. the other day 前几天(用于过去时)

例 The other day I met him at the train station.
前几天我曾在火车站遇见他。

以上这些副词或状语可置于句首或句尾。故上列各例句均可改写为：

I had dinner with her at that restaurant one day.
The little boy will be a great man one day.
The little boy will be a great man someday.
I met him at the train station the other day.

2. **In the end, he was rewarded for his perseverance.**

最后它因坚韧不拔的精神而获得回报。

in the end 到最后
= at last
in the beginning 起初
= at first

例 In the beginning of the race I was energetic, but in the end, I was exhausted.
比赛开始时我精力充沛,但到最后,我精疲力尽。

3. 本文中的诸多动词均有副词修饰。如：

a. The hare can run very fast, but the turtle can only walk slowly.

b. The turtle walked slowly but surely.

一般而言，副词有下列几个主要功能：

a. 修饰形容词，此时置于该形容词之前：

例 She is very beautiful. 她很美。

adv. a.

b. 修饰副词，此时置于该副词之前：

例 He worked quite hard. 他工作相当努力。

adv. adv.

c. 修饰动词，此时多置于该动词之后：

例 He walked slowly. 他走得很慢。

vi. adv.

John speaks English well. 约翰英语说得很好。

vt. adv.

注意

very 虽是副词，却无法修饰动词，只能修饰形容词或副词；但 very much 却可修饰动词，使用时置于句尾。

例 He is very polite. 他很有礼貌。

adv. a.

He speaks Japanese very well. 他日语说得很好。

adv. adv.

I very like him. (×)

adv. vt.

→ I like him very much. (√) 我很喜欢他。

vt. adv.

4 Substitution 替换

1. One day the hare proudly challenged the turtle to a race.
One day Paul will be successful.
Someday Betty will be a famous singer.
The other day I treated my parents to dinner.
有一天兔子骄傲地向乌龟挑战赛跑。
有一天保罗会成功。
有一天贝蒂将会成为著名歌手。
前几天我请我父母吃晚餐。

---

2. The turtle can only walk slowly.
That man is extremely rude.
Sally works very efficiently.
乌龟只能慢慢走。
那个男人真的很粗鲁。
萨莉工作很有效率。

---

3. In the end, he was rewarded for his perseverance.
In the end, you will benefit from your hard work.
Carl will do well in the end.
Fred didn't want to go in the beginning.
最后他因坚韧不拔的精神而获得回报。
最后你会因努力工作而获益的。
卡尔最后会做得很好的。
起初弗雷德不想去。

Lesson 62

Practice Makes Perfect 熟能生巧

1 *Dialogue* 实用会话

Customer: Can you help me gift-wrap this, please?
Salesgirl: Sure. (after a while)
Customer: Wow! You did that beautifully.
Salesgirl: Well, I practice daily.
Customer: Practice makes perfect, right?
Salesgirl: Certainly!

顾　客：请你帮我把这个东西用礼品纸包起来好吗？
女店员：好啊。（过了一会儿）
顾　客：哇！你包得好美啊。
女店员：嗯，我每天都在练习嘛。
顾　客：熟能生巧，对吗？
女店员：那当然！

2 *Key Points* 重点提示

1. **Can you help me gift-wrap this, please?**
   请你帮我把这个东西用礼品纸包起来好吗？
   a. gift-wrap [ˋgɪftˏræp] *vt.* 将……包装成礼品
   例 My wife and I gift-wrapped our children's Christmas gifts last

night.

昨晚我和太太把要给孩子们的圣诞礼物包起来。

b. Can you help me gift-wrap this, please?

= Can you help me to gift-wrap this, please?

本句 help 为及物动词，之后接“人”为宾语，可再接虚词 to 引导的动词不定式作宾语补足语，但 to 往往予以省略。即：

help + 人 + to + 动词原形

= help + 人 + 动词原形

例 I helped him to write the letter. 我帮他写这封信。

= I helped him write the letter.

2. **wow** [waʊ] *int.* 哇！

3. **practice** [ˋpræktɪs] *n.* & *vi.* 练习

4. **daily** [ˋdelɪ] *adv.* 每天（=every day）

例 Dave jogs daily at 6:30 in the morning.

戴夫每天早上 6 点半都去慢跑。

5. **Practice makes perfect.** 熟能生巧。(谚语)

perfect [ˋpɝfɪkt] *a.* 完美的

6. **certainly** [ˋsɝtn̩lɪ] *adv.* 当然（=sure）

3 请选择下列各句中正确的一项

1. The other day I ______ a very good movie.
   (A) will see (B) saw (C) watch (D) see
2. Roger believes that someday he ______ an English professor.
   (A) will be (B) will (C) was (D) is
3. Steve ______ fast.
   (A) very read (B) reading very
   (C) read much (D) reads very
4. My father works slowly and ______.
   (A) very happy (B) happy

(C) happily (D) is happily

5. In the beginning, Chris was very sad; ______ in the end, he was happy.
   (A) so (B) but
   (C) moreover (D) as a result
6. He helped me ______ the problem.
   (A) handle (B) handled
   (C) handling (D) to handled

解答 1. (B) 2. (A) 3. (D) 4. (C) 5. (B) 6. (A)

Lesson 63

Saving a Drowning Boy

救难记

1 *Reading* 阅读

Ray was walking on the beach one summer day when he heard a little boy shout, "Help! Help!" The boy was drowning. Without thinking, Ray dove into the water. Soon he was swimming back to shore with the boy. Crowds of people were watching eagerly. After a while the boy was breathing again. Then the boy sat up and said to Ray, "You are my hero."

某个夏日雷正在海滩上散步,这时他听到一个小男孩大叫:“救命啊!救命啊!”这个男孩快要淹死了。雷不假思索地就跳进了水里。不久他便带着小男孩游回岸上。成群的人们正焦急地注视着。过了一会儿这个男孩又开始呼吸了。接着这个男孩坐了起来,对雷说:“你是我的英雄。”

2 Vocabulary & Idioms 单词短语注解

1. **save** [sev] *vt.* 拯救

   The fireman saved the child from the burning building.

   那个消防队员将这个小孩从起火的大楼中救出。

2. **drowning** [ˋdraunɪŋ] *a.* 溺水的

   drown [draun] *vi.* 溺水

   Last year, ten people drowned in this lake.

   去年有十个人淹死在这湖里。

3. **walk** [wɔk] *vi.* 散步

   I love walking through the city at night. 我喜欢晚上在城市里散步。

4. **on the beach** 在海滩上

   beach [bitʃ] *n.* 海滩，海边

5. **shout** [ʃaut] *vt.* & *vi.* 喊叫，大叫

   shout at + 人 对着某人大叫

   The teacher entered the noisy classroom and shouted, "Shut up!"

   老师走进闹哄哄的教室大叫："闭嘴！"

   The angry mother shouted at her son. 那愤怒的母亲对着她儿子大叫。

6. **help** [hɛlp] *vi.* 救命

   A: Help! There's a cockroach in my room!

   B: Well, just step on it and kill it.

   A: 救命啊！我的房间里有只蟑螂！

   B: 呃，把它踩死就好了。

7. **dive** [daɪv] *vi.* 跳水

   动词三态：dive、dove / dived、dove / dived。

   I can swim, but I'm afraid to dive. 我会游泳，但我不敢跳水。

8. **shore** [ʃɔr] *n.* （海）岸

   There is a place by the shore that is great for fishing.

   岸边有一处钓鱼的好地方。

9. **crowd** [kraʊd] *n.* 群

crowds of... 成群的……

a crowd of... 一群的……

Crowds of fans waited at the airport for the singer to arrive.

成群的歌迷在机场等候该歌手抵达。

10. **watch** [wɑtʃ] *vi.* & *vt.* 注视，看

I seldom watch TV. 我很少看电视。

11. **eagerly** [ˋigɚlɪ] *adv.* 焦急地；渴望地

The children eagerly jumped into the swimming pool.

那些孩子迫不及待地跳入游泳池里。

12. **after a while** 一会儿之后（介词短语，作副词）

while [waɪl] *n.* 一段时间

A: The child is crying again.

B: Don't worry. After a while he will stop.

A: 那孩子又哭了。

B: 别担心，过一会儿他就不哭了。

13. **breathe** [brið] *vi.* & *vt.* 呼吸

breathe the fresh air 呼吸新鲜空气

There's too much cigarette smoke in here; I can't breathe.

这里的烟味太重了，我无法呼吸。

14. **hero** [ˋhɪro] *n.* 英雄

3 *Grammar Points* 语法重点

本课强调过去进行时的形态及其功能。

1. **Ray was walking on the beach...** 雷正在海滩上散步……

The boy was drowning. 这个男孩快要淹死了。

以上两句的划线部分均为过去进行时。过去进行时与现在进行时的形态与功能大致相同，只不过，过去进行时强调过去进行的状态。

a. 形态

主语 + was / were + 现在分词

例 I was sleeping at five. 5 点钟时我正在睡觉。

They were watching TV when I called.

我打电话时，他们正在看电视。

b. 功能

1) 表示过去某个时刻正在发生的动作。

例 What was he doing then? 他那时正在做什么？

When I walked in, he was eating. 我进来时，他正在吃东西。

2) leave（离开）、come（来）、go（去）等表示“来”或“去”的动词可用于过去进行时的句中，表示过去即将发生的事情。

例 He told me that he was leaving soon.

= He told me that he would leave soon.

= He told me that he would be leaving soon.

他告诉我他很快就要离开了。

He said that he was coming this afternoon.

= He said that he would come this afternoon.

= He said that he would be coming this afternoon.

他说他今天下午要来。

本课阅读原文中“The boy was drowning.”亦属此用法。

比较

The boy was drowning. 这男孩快要淹死了。

The boy was drowned. 这男孩已经淹死了。

2. **Ray was walking on the beach one summer day when he heard a little boy shout, "Help! Help!"**

某个夏日雷正在海滩上散步，这时他听到一个小男孩大叫：“救命啊！救命啊！”

a. 本句使用了下列句型：

主语 + was / were + 现在分词 + when 所引导的过去时状语从句

……正在……这时……就……

例 I was having dinner when he came.

我正在吃晚饭,这时他就来了。

I was taking a shower when the phone rang.

我正在淋浴,这时电话铃就响了。

b. ...he heard a little boy shout, "Help! Help!"

……他听到一个小男孩大叫:“救命啊!救命啊!”

注意

本句中,及物动词 heard(听到)接了宾语 a little boy,另接动词原形 shout 作宾语补足语。英语中,表“看”(如 see)、“听”(如 hear)、“感觉”(如 feel)等三类及物动词,接了宾语之后,可用动词原形、现在分词或过去分词作宾语补足语。现分项说明如下:

1) 以动词原形作补足语旨在强调确有事情发生。

例 I saw him steal my money. 我看到他偷了我的钱。

I heard him sing. 我听到他唱歌。

I felt him touch my hand. 我感觉他碰了我的手。

“...he heard a little boy shout...”即属此用法。

2) 以现在分词作补足语旨在强调事情正在发生。

例 I saw him stealing my money. 我看到他正在偷我的钱。

I heard him singing. 我听到他正在唱歌。

I felt him touching my hand. 我感觉他正在碰我的手。

3) 以过去分词作补足语旨在强调被动语态。

例 I saw him punished. 我看到他被处罚了。

I heard him dragged away. 我听到他被拖走的声音。

I felt my hand lifted. 我感觉我的手被抬了起来。

4 *Substitution* 替换

1. Ray was walking on the beach when he heard a boy shout.

They were playing outside when they heard their mother call.

I was watching TV when the doorbell rang.

We were playing volleyball in the yard when it started to rain.

雷正在海滩上散步，这时他听到一个小男孩大叫。
他们正在外面玩时，听到他们的妈妈在叫他们。
我正在看电视，这时门铃响了。
我们正在院子里打排球，这时开始下起雨来了。

---

2. He heard a little boy shout. 他听到一个小男孩在大叫。
I saw a woman dancing. 我看到一位女士在跳舞。
We saw a man robbed. 我们看见一个男人被抢了。
I felt my arm bitten. 我感觉我的手臂被咬了。

Lesson 64

Dan's a Good Swimmer 丹很会游泳

1 *Dialogue* 实用会话

Lucy: Dan's a good swimmer, isn't he?

Lewis: Yes. In fact, he's a lifeguard.

Lucy: Wow! Can he teach me the butterfly and the backstroke?

Lewis: Yes. He can also teach you the free style and the breaststroke.

Lucy: Great!

露　西：丹很会游泳，是不是？

刘易斯：是啊。事实上，他是个救生员。

露　西：哇！他能教我蝶泳和仰泳吗？

刘易斯：能。他还能教你自由泳和蛙泳。

露　西：太棒了！

2 *Key Points* 重点提示

1. **swimmer** [ˋswɪmɚ] *n.* 游泳者
2. **lifeguard** [ˋlaɪfˏgɑrd] *n.* 救生员
3. **butterfly** [ˋbʌtɚˏflaɪ] *n.* 本词原指“蝴蝶”，此处指“蝶泳”（游泳的一种姿势）

4. **backstroke** [ˈbæk,strok] *n.* 仰泳（游泳）

5. **free style** [ˈfri ,staɪl] *n.* 自由泳

6. **breaststroke** [ˈbrɛst,strok] *n.* 蛙泳

3 请选择下列各句中正确的一项

1. Sally and Mike ______ comic books last night.
   (A) was seeing (B) was reading
   (C) were reading (D) were seeing
2. I ______ on the computer when my wife called me on the phone.
   (A) were typing (B) typed
   (C) was typed (D) was typing
3. I ______ a child ______ off his bicycle.
   (A) see, fell (B) saw, fall
   (C) saw, fell (D) see, fall
4. The students were talking when the teacher ______ into the room.
   (A) coming (B) comes (C) came (D) comed
5. I thought you ______ soon.
   (A) leaving (B) would leaving
   (C) would be leave (D) would be leaving
6. She isn't as beautiful as Mary, ______?
   (A) is she (B) isn't she
   (C) is he (D) does she

解答 1. (C) 2. (D) 3. (B) 4. (C) 5. (D) 6. (A)

Lesson 65

The Fortune-teller

算命师

1 *Reading* 阅读

My friend Mike is a fortune-teller. He often tells me many things about my future. First, I will become a father next year. Then, I will get a promotion and earn a lot of money. Two years later, I will buy a new car. Soon after that, I will be able to afford a new house. I'm not superstitious, but I hope he's right.

我的朋友迈克是个算命师。他经常会告诉我许多有关我前途的事。首先，我明年就要当爸爸了。然后，我会升职并且挣大钱。两年后，我会买部新车。之后没多久，我就会有能力买幢新房子。我并不迷信，但我希望他说的是真的。

2 Vocabulary & Idioms 单词短语注解

1. **fortune-teller** [ˈfɔrtʃənˌtɛlɚ] *n.* 算命师，算命先生

2. **tell** [tɛl] *vt.* 告诉

3. **about** [əˈbaʊt] *prep.* 有关
   Chris told me about a dream he had last night.
   克里斯告诉我有关他昨晚做的梦。

4. **future** [ˈfjutʃɚ] *n.* 前途，未来
   What will you do in the future? 你将来想做什么？

5. **become** [bɪˈkʌm] *vt.* 成为
   Eventually, Sally and Susie became good friends.
   萨莉和苏西终成好友。

6. **get a promotion** （职位上的）晋升
   promotion [prəˈmoʃən] *n.* 晋升
   After this project Ted and Carl will get a promotion.
   这项计划完成后，泰德和卡尔将会获得晋升。

7. **earn** [ɝn] *vt.* 挣（钱）
   My wife earns more money than I. 我太太挣的钱比我多。

8. **later** [ˈletɚ] *adv.* 稍后，后来
   此单词使用时，通常置于时间名词之后，如：
   five years later 5 年后
   two days later 2 天后
   I started to attend university when I was eighteen. Four years later I graduated.
   我 18 岁时开始念大学，4 年后我毕业了。

9. **be able to + 动词原形** 能够……
   = can + 动词原形
   I'm sorry. I won't be able to go to your birthday party.
   很抱歉，我无法参加你的生日宴会。

10. **afford** [ə'fɔrd] *vt.* 买得起

注意

使用 afford 时，通常与 can 或 be able to 连用，即：

can be able to	afford + 名词　有能力买得起……

I can't afford that shirt. It's too expensive.

我买不起那件衬衫，它太贵了。

11. **superstitious** [ˌsupɚ'stɪʃəs] *a.* 迷信的

A: If you break a mirror, you will have seven years of bad luck.

B: Oh, you're just superstitious.

A: 如果你打破镜子，你将会有连续七年的恶运。

B: 哦，你真是迷信。

3 Grammar Points 语法重点

本课主要介绍一般将来时的形式及用法。

1. **First, I will become a father next year.**

首先，我明年就要当爸爸了。

Then, I will get a promotion and earn a lot of money.

然后，我会获得晋升并且挣大钱。

以上两句均为一般将来时的句子结构。这里就这种句子结构及其使用时机叙述如下：

a. 句子结构：

主语 + will / shall + 动词原形

例 He will come this afternoon. 他今天下午会来。

We will / shall call on our teacher tomorrow.

我们明天会去拜访我们的老师。

英式的习惯用法为：主语若为第一人称代词（I、we）时，之后使用 shall，其余第二人称或第三人称的主语一律使用 will，但美式用法则为不论第几人称的主语一律使用 will。即：

英式：I shall do it. 我将会做这件事。

We shall do it. 我们将会做这件事。

You will do it. 你 / 你们将会做这件事。

He will do it. 他将会做这件事。

She will do it. 她将会做这件事。

It will do it. 它将会做这件事。

They will do it. 他们将会做这件事。

美式 : I will do it. 我将会做这件事。

We will do it. 我们将会做这件事。

You will do it. 你 / 你们将会做这件事。

由于美式的用法较英式统一,因此现今的趋势多偏向美式用法。

b. 一般将来时使用的时机 :

一般将来时表示未来会发生的动作或状态。这个动作或状态可能会在最近或很久以后才会发生,均须借助动词 will 来表现。这个 will 就相当中文的“将要”或“会”之意。

例 中文 : 我 10 年后会娶你。

英文 : I will marry you ten years later.

中文 : 他很快就会来。

英文 : He will come soon.

c. 其他注意事项 :

1) will 与作主语的代词连用时,可采用下列的缩写形式 :

I will → I'll

He will → He'll

They will → They'll

2) will 与 not 连用时,可缩写成 won't [wont]

例 I will not → I won't

2. **Soon after that, I will be able to afford a new house.**

后来没多久,我就有能力买幢新房子。

a. afford 是及物动词,表示“买得起”、“负担得起”,之后可用名词或虚词 to 引导的不定式短语作其宾语。而 afford 之前一定要有助动词 can。

例 I afford that car. (×)
→ I can afford that car. (√) 我买得起那辆车。
I don't afford to take the trip with you. (×)
→ I can't afford to take the trip with you. (√)
我没有钱和你一起去旅游。

b. afford 若使用于一般将来时，理应说成：
I will can afford that car. (×)
因 will 与 can 均为助动词不能并存，此时应将 can 改成 be able to，即成：
I will be able to afford that car someday. (√)
有一天我会买得起那辆车。

4 *Substitution* 替换

1. Two years later, I will buy a new car.
She'll finish high school three years later.
We shall meet you in a couple of hours.
2 年后，我会买辆新车。
3 年后，她将完成高中学业。
几个小时后，我们将与你碰面。

---

2. Soon after that, I will be able to afford a new house.
Shortly after I show him how, he will be able to fix a car.
Soon after they meet, I'm sure they will fall in love.
之后没多久，我就有能力买幢新房子。
我教他后不用多久，他就能够修车了。
我相信他们见面后很快就会坠入爱河。

Lesson 66

Will It Leave on Time? 它会准时开吗?

1 *Dialogue* 实用会话

Girl: Excuse me. When will the next train leave?

Man: In ten minutes.

Girl: Will it leave on time?

Man: It always does.

Girl: Thank you.

女孩：抱歉。请问下一班火车何时开?

男士：10 分钟后。

女孩：它会准时开吗?

男士：它总是很准时的。

女孩：谢谢你。

2 *Key Points* 重点提示

1. **in ten minutes** 10 分钟后

例 The next train will leave in ten minutes.

下班火车 10 分钟后会离开。

in + 一段时间　一段时间之后(用于一般将来时)

= 一段时间 + later

例 I'll be there in five minutes. / five minutes later. 我5分钟后会到那儿。

I'll finish it in two hours. / two hours later. 我两个小时后会做完这件事。

注意

咱们很容易将上列句子写成：

I'll be there after five minutes. (×)

I'll finish it after two hours. (×)

after five minutes 表示“过了5分钟以后再说”。因此，“I'll be there after five minutes.”暗示“5分钟过了之后，我才会考虑到那里，至于何时会去，我尚未决定。”而“I'll be there in five minutes.”则暗示“5分钟一过我就会在那里出现。”after two hours 与 after five minutes 所犯的毛病一样，在此就不再赘述。within 则表示“在……以内”。

比较

I'll be there in five minutes. 我5分钟后会到那里。

I'll be there within five minutes. 我5分钟内会到那里。

2. **on time** 准时

例 Carl always comes to work on time. 卡尔总是准时来上班。

3. **It always does.** 它总是很准时。

= It always leaves on time.

此处 does 是助动词，代替前句出现过的相同动词及其他词类。

例 A: You went to Nanjing the other day, didn't you?

B: Yes, I did.

A: 你前几天到南京去了，对不对？

B: 对，我是到南京去了。

* 此处 did 代替前面提过的 went to Nanjing the other day。

3 请选择下列各句中正确的一项

1. Three years later, I ______ to America.
   (A) will go (B) go
   (C) will going (D) will
2. Peter will be here ______.
   (A) after ten minute (B) after ten minutes
   (C) in ten minute (D) in ten minutes
3. I know the party ______ be a success.
   (A) is (B) will (C) can will (D) was
4. I hate Bobby. I ______ go to dinner with him.
   (A) will (B) won't (C) not (D) willn't
5. ______ you go to a movie with me tonight?
   (A) Want (B) Have (C) Does (D) Will
6. Class will ______.
   (A) on five minutes
   (B) starting in five minutes
   (C) start in ten minutes
   (D) start on ten minutes

解答 1. (A) 2. (D) 3. (B) 4 (B) 5. (D) 6. (C)

Lesson 67

Getting Married

结婚

1 *Reading* 阅读

My girlfriend and I are going to get married this year. We are going to have a big wedding party. All our friends and relatives are going to come. We are going to have a traditional wedding. After the wedding we are going to live with my parents. We are going to be one big happy family.

我和女友今年将结婚。我们将举行盛大的婚宴。我们所有的亲朋好友都会来参加。我们将要举行传统的婚礼。婚礼后我们要和我的父母亲一起住。我们将成为一个快乐的大家庭。

2 Vocabulary & Idioms 单词短语注解

1. **girlfriend** [ˈgɜlˌfrɛnd] *n.* 女朋友
   boyfriend [ˈbɔɪˌfrɛnd] *n.* 男朋友
2. **get married** 结婚
   married [ˈmærɪd] *a.* 结婚的
   Susie and Roger are getting married next summer.
   苏西和罗杰将在明年夏天结婚。
3. **wedding party** [ˈwɛdɪŋ ˌpɑrtɪ] *n.* 婚宴
4. **relative** [ˈrɛlətɪv] *n.* 亲戚
5. **traditional** [trəˈdɪʃənl̩] *a.* 传统的
   It's traditional in America to eat turkey on Christmas Day.
   在美国圣诞节时吃火鸡是项传统。

3 Grammar Points 语法重点

本课介绍"be going to + 动词原形"作一般将来时的用法。

1. **My girlfriend and I are going to get married this year.**
   我和女友今年将结婚。
   We are going to have a big wedding party.
   我们将举行盛大的婚宴。
   以上两句为一般将来时的句子结构,其中 are going to 就等于 will。即:
   主语 + will + 动词原形
   = 主语 + be going to + 动词原形
   例 I will leave soon. 我很快就会离开。
   = I am going to leave soon.
   He will be there in five minutes. 他 5 分钟后就会到那儿。
   = He is going to be there in five minutes.

注意

will 与 be going to 虽然意思相同，可相互取代，不过 be going to 多指短期内会发生的动作或状态，而 will 则可指短期内或长期以后会发生的动作或状态。

短期内：

例 He is going to climb mountains with us this weekend.

= He will climb mountains with us this weekend.

这个周末他会跟我们爬山去。

长期以后：

例 He is going to marry the girl ten years later. (劣)

→ He will marry the girl ten years later. (佳)

10 年后他会娶那个女孩。

2. 句中若有表示某种条件下会产生某种现象时，宜使用 will，而非 be going to。

例 He is going to lose everything without your help. (劣)

→ He will lose everything without your help. (佳)

若没有你的帮忙，他会失去一切。

I am going to get angry if you don't come. (劣)

→ I will get angry if you don't come. (佳) 你若不来，我会生气的。

4 Substitution 替换

1. My girlfriend and I are going to get married this year.

   My girlfriend and I will get engaged this year.

   My girlfriend and I are going to a play tonight.

   My girlfriend and I are going to travel to the south this weekend.

   我和女友今年将结婚。

   我和女友今年将订婚。

   我和女友今晚要去看一出戏。

   我和女友这个周末要到南方去旅行。

2. We are going to be one big happy family.
We are going to have a great time.
Bill's team is going to win the game.
I'm going to take a break.
我们将成为一个快乐的大家庭。
我们将会玩得很愉快。
比尔的球队将会赢得比赛。
我要休息一下。

Lesson 68

Are You Going to Come? 你会来吗？

1 Dialogue 实用会话

Candy: Are you going to come to my wedding?

Joe: Of course.

Candy: Good. Are you going to bring your girlfriend?

Joe: Yes. She likes weddings.

Candy: So when are you going to get married?

Joe: We haven't decided yet.

凯蒂：你会来参加我的婚礼吗?

乔：当然。

凯蒂：太好了。你会带女朋友一起来吗?

乔：会的。她喜欢参加婚礼。

凯蒂：那么，你们什么时候要结婚呢?

乔：我们尚未决定。

2 Key Points 重点提示

decide [dɪˋsaɪd] *vt.* & *vi.* 决定

例 Have you decided where you will go for your vacation ?

你已经决定要去哪里度假了吗?

Let me know what you have decided by tomorrow.
明天以前让我知道你的决定。

3 请选择下列各句中正确的一项

1. If you study, you ______ well on the test.
   (A) will do (B) going to
   (C) will (D) will doing
2. They ______ have a party tonight.
   (A) going to (B) are will
   (C) are going (D) are going to
3. Mary is very sick. She ______ attend class today.
   (A) going to (B) is going to
   (C) isn't going to (D) isn't
4. Paul should come today, but maybe he ______.
   (A) will (B) won't
   (C) willn't (D) is going to
5. What time ______ they arrive?
   (A) going to (B) won't (C) are (D) will

解答 1. (A) 2. (D) 3. (C) 4. (B) 5. (D)

Lesson 69

Running a Bookstore

经营书店

1 *Reading* 阅读

Tom will be retiring next year. He will be opening a small bookstore. His wife will be helping him run the store. It will be a small family business, so they won't be needing too much money. He won't be making a lot of money, but it'll be enough.

汤姆明年将要退休。他将开一家小书店。他太太将会帮他经营这家店。这将是一个小型的家庭事业,所以他们并不需要太多资金。他将不会挣很多钱,但那样就够用了。

2 Vocabulary & Idioms 单词短语注解

1. **retire** [rɪˋtaɪr] *vi.* 退休
   When I'm sixty, I'll retire. 60 岁时，我将要退休。
2. **open** [ˋopən] *vt.* 开业
   Peter opened a small English class for beginners.
   彼得为初学者开了一个小型的英文班。
3. **bookstore** [ˋbʊkˏstɔr] *n.* 书店
4. **help** [hɛlp] *vt.* 帮助
   Help your brother wash the car. 去帮你哥哥洗车。
5. **run** [rʌn] *vt.* 经营
   It's my dream to run my own business someday.
   我的梦想是将来有一天自己创业。
6. **family business** [ˋfæməlɪ ˏbɪznɪs] *n.* 家庭事业
7. **need** [nid] *vt.* 需要
   The poor boy needs some clothes. 那可怜的男孩需要一些衣服。
8. **make a lot of money** 挣很多钱
   = earn a lot of money
   make [mek] *vt.* 挣(钱)
   Bob got a new job in a big bank and is making a lot of money.
   鲍勃在一家大银行找到新工作，并且正在挣大钱。

3 Grammar Points 语法重点

本课介绍将来进行时的形态及用法。

Tom will be retiring next year. 汤姆明年将要退休。

He will be opening a small bookstore. 他将开一家小书店。

以上两句使用了将来进行时。这里就其句子结构及使用时机叙述如下：

1. 句子结构：
   主语 + will be + 现在分词

例 He will be leaving soon. 他很快就会离开。

We will be coming tomorrow. 我们明天会来。

2. 使用时机：

a. 表示短期内即将发生的动作：

此时 will be 译成“将要”或“将会”。将来进行时亦可用一般将来时(will + 动词原形或 be going to + 动词原形)来取代；只不过是将来进行时更强调短期内即将发生的动作。

例 He will be visiting us tomorrow. 他明天会来看我们。

= He is going to visit us tomorrow.

= He will visit us tomorrow.

b. 表示在将来某一时刻将会进行的动作：

此时宜使用将来进行时，will be 译成“会在”。

例 I'll be watching TV this time tomorrow.

我明天这个时候会在看电视。

He'll be studying in the library this afternoon.

今天下午他会在图书馆看书。

4 Substitution 替换

1. Tom will be retiring next year.

My sister will be arriving at two o'clock this afternoon.

She'll be getting ready for bed at ten o'clock.

汤姆明年将要退休。

我妹妹今天下午两点将会抵达。

她将在 10 点钟时准备上床睡觉。

---

2. He won't be making a lot of money.

I won't be attending Fred's party.

I won't be studying accounting; I'll be studying English.

I won't be going to work tomorrow.

他将不会挣很多钱。
我将不会去参加弗雷德的宴会。
我将不会学会计，我要学英语。
我明天将不会去上班。

Lesson 70

When Will You Be Moving? 你什么时候搬家？

1 Dialogue 实用会话

Tina: When will you be moving?

Chuck: Next week.

Tina: When will we be seeing you again?

Chuck: Maybe next year.

Tina: Don't forget to write.

Chuck: I won't. Goodbye, Tina.

蒂娜：你什么时候搬家？

查克：下星期。

蒂娜：我们什么时候会再见到你呢？

查克：也许明年吧。

蒂娜：别忘了写信啊。

查克：我不会忘记的。再见了，蒂娜。

2 Key Points 重点提示

1. **move** [muv] *vi.* 搬家

   (= move house, 非 move the house)

   例 Irene moved back to the country to be with her family.

艾琳搬回乡下和她的家人一起住。

The Lee family is moving house. 李家正在搬家。

2. **maybe** [ˈmebɪ] *adv.* 也许

注意

maybe 与 may be 完全不一样。maybe 是副词,相当于 perhaps [pəˈhæps],使用时通常置于句首,修饰全句。而 may be 是 be 动词之前加了助动词 may,译成"也许是"。

例 May be he'll be coming tomorrow. (×)

→ Maybe he'll be coming tomorrow. (√)

= Perhaps he'll be coming tomorrow.

也许他明天会来。

May be you are right. (×)

→ Maybe you are right. (√)

= Perhaps you are right.

也许你是对的。

You maybe right. (×)

→ You may be right. (√)

你也许是对的。

3 请选择下列各句中正确的一项

1. ______ we'll be playing basketball tomorrow.
   (A) Maybe (B) May be
   (C) Might (D) Perhaps be
2. She ______ the winner of the race.
   (A) maybe (B) may be
   (C) might (D) perhaps be
3. Bobby ______ his homework tonight.
   (A) will be (B) is going to
   (C) doing (D) will be doing

4. Paul ______ to travel this summer.
   (A) is going (B) will be
   (C) will (D) will being
5. I ______ tonight.
   (A) not will work (B) will work not
   (C) will to not work (D) won't be working
6. ______ Sally and Joe are girlfriend and boyfriend.
   (A) Could be (B) Perhaps be
   (C) Perhaps (D) May be

解答 1. (A) 2. (B) 3. (D) 4. (A) 5. (D) 6. (C)

Lesson 71

Working Hard

努力用功

1 *Reading* 阅读

My best friend Billy and I decided to learn English last year. We promised each other to work hard. We never failed to attend class. Billy always remembered to do his homework. I never forgot to do mine, either. Our English is pretty good now. It only proves that there's no gain without pain.

我和挚友比利去年决心要学英文。我们彼此允诺要努力用功，我们从不缺课。比利总是会记得做功课，而我也从未忘记做自己的功课。我们的英文现在很不错了。这就证明了一分耕耘，一分收获的道理。

2 Vocabulary & Idioms 单词短语注解

1. **promise** [ˋprɑmɪs] *vt.* 允诺，答应
   promise + 人 + to + 动词原形　允诺某人做……
   I promised my teacher to do my homework. 我答应老师会做功课。

2. **each other** 彼此（指两者之间）
   one another 彼此（指三者或三者以上）
   * one another 只能用于指三者或三者以上，而就严谨语法而言，each other 只能用于指两者之间。但现今美语口语用法里，也常用 each other 来指三者或三者以上。
   We helped each other study for the test. 我们互相帮忙准备考试。
   We must help one another in times of trouble.
   有困难时我们必须互相帮助。

3. **fail** [fel] *vt.* 无法做到，失败
   fail to + 动词原形　未能……
   never fail to + 动词原形　一定会……

4. **attend** [əˋtɛnd] *vt.* 参加
   attend class 上课
   = go to class
   attend school 上学
   = go to school
   Frank will be attending high school in Beijing next fall.
   明年秋天弗兰克将要去北京念高中。

5. **remember** [rɪˋmɛmbɚ] *vt.* 记得
   remember to + 动词原形　记得要……

6. **homework** [ˋhom,wɝk] *n.* 家庭作业（不可数）

7. **forgot** [fɚˋgɑt] *vt.* 忘记（为 forget [fɚˋgɛt] 的过去式）
   forget to + 动词原形　忘了要……

8. **pretty** [ˋprɪtɪ] *adv.* 颇，相当
   The new student in my class is pretty smart.

我班上的新同学相当聪明。

9. **prove** [pruv] *vt.* 证明

The clever lawyer proved the man was a thief.

那聪明的律师证明这男子是小偷。

10. **gain** [gen] *n.* 收获

11. **pain** [pen] *n.* 劳苦

12. **There is no gain without pain.**

一分耕耘，一分收获。（谚语）

3 Grammar Points 语法重点

本课介绍动词不定式的用法。

1. **My best friend Billy and I decided to learn English last year.**

我和挚友比利去年决心要学英文。

We promised each other to work hard.

我们彼此允诺要努力用功。

以上两句的划线部分是动词不定式。动词不定式由虚词 to 加动词原形形成，具有名词、形容词及副词的功能。

a. 名词：

1) 作主语

例 To work with him is pleasant. 与他共事很愉快。

= It is pleasant to work with him.

2) 作宾语

此时所使用的动词均有“愿望”、“决心”等含义，如 decide（决心要……）、wish（希望……）、want（要……）、desire（想要……）、promise（允诺……）、plan（计划……）等。

例 I decided to visit him tomorrow. 我决定明天去看他。

He is planning to study abroad. 他正计划要出国念书。

He promised (me) to write the letter.

他答应（我）要写这封信。

3) 置于 be 动词之后，作表语

此时主语亦多为表示“愿望、决心”等名词。

例 My only wish before I leave is to see her one more time.
我离开前，唯一的愿望就是再见她一面。
His plan is to marry her soon. 他的计划就是要很快娶到她。

b. 形容词

此时动词不定式置于被修饰的名词之后，修饰该名词。

例 I have some work to do. 我有一些工作要做。
n.

That's not the right way to learn English.
n.

那并不是学英文的正确方法。

c. 副词

此时动词不定式可置于完整的句子之前或之后，表示目的。

例 完整句

He worked hard. 他用功。

加入动词不定式

To pass the exam, he worked hard. 为了考试能及格，他很用功。

= He worked hard to pass the exam.

2. **never fail to + 动词原形** 一定会……

例 My son never fails to call me up on Sunday mornings.
我儿子总会在星期天早上打电话给我。

fail to + 动词原形 未能……

例 Paul failed to get into medical school. 保罗未能进入医学院就读。

3. **remember to + 动词原形** 记得要……

例 Son, remember to turn off the light. 儿子，记得把电灯关掉。

remember + 动名词 记得曾经……

例 Do you remember losing this ring many years ago?
你记得多年前曾遗失这枚戒指吗？

4. **forget to + 动词原形** 忘了要……

例 Don't forget to meet Sally after school.
别忘了下课后与萨莉碰面。

forget + 动名词　忘了曾经……

例 I'll never forget seeing my son graduate.
我永远不会忘记看到我儿子毕业。

5. **Our English is pretty good now.**
我们的英文现在很不错了。
pretty 可作形容词或副词。作形容词时，表示"美丽的"；作副词时，则表示"颇"、"相当"的意思，比 very 语气稍弱些。

例 Who's that pretty girl over there? 那里那位漂亮女孩是谁？
(pretty: a.　girl: n.)

It's pretty hot today. 今天天气相当热。
(pretty: adv.　hot: a.)

4 Substitution 替换

1. My best friend and I decided to learn English.
We decided to go home.
They want to take a break.
Do you want to see a movie?
我和挚友决心要学英文。
我们决定回家。
他们想要休息一会儿。
你想看电影吗？

---

2. Billy always remembered to do his homework.
Paul never forgot to write.
My youngest boy never wants to go to school.
I usually like to take a rest at lunch time.
比利总是会记得做功课。
保罗从未忘记要写信。
我的小儿子从来就不想去上学。
我通常喜欢在午餐时间休息一下。

Lesson 72

Remember to Wash

别忘了漱洗

1 *Dialogue* 实用会话

Mother: Don't forget to brush your teeth before you go to bed!

Micky: Yes, Mom.

Mother: And remember to wash your hands before meals.

Micky: Yes, Mom. Anything else?

Mother: Yes, remind me to tell your sister the same thing.

母亲：睡觉前别忘了要刷牙！

米奇：是的，妈妈。

母亲：而且吃饭前要记得洗手。

米奇：是的，妈妈。还有其他的事吗？

母亲：有的，要提醒我告诉你妹妹同样的事。

2 *Key Points* 重点提示

1. **meal** [mil] *n.* 一餐

   例 I usually eat three meals a day. 我一天通常吃三餐。

2. **remind** [rɪˋmaɪnd] *vt.* 提醒

remind + 人 + to + 动词原形　提醒某人去做……

例 Please remind me to call him tomorrow. 请提醒我明天打电话给他。

3 请选择下列各句中正确的一项

1. Vivian ______ love stories.
   (A) likes to read　(B) likes to reading
   (C) is like to read　(D) is like reading
2. Billy lives ______ far away from here.
   (A) pretty　(B) smart
   (C) cute　(D) ugly
3. Todd's dream ______ a novel.
   (A) wants to write　(B) wants writing
   (C) is to write　(D) enjoys to write
4. I'm sorry. I don't ______ your name.
   (A) forget　(B) remember
   (C) hear　(D) look
5. Please ______ clean your room when you get home.
   (A) remember　(B) remember to
   (C) don't forget　(D) to remember to
6. I might ______, so please remind me to call Roger.
   (A) remember　(B) not forget
   (C) forgot　(D) forget

解答　1. (A)　2. (A)　3. (C)　4. (B)　5. (B)　6. (D)

Lesson 73

Joe's Restaurant

乔的餐厅

1 *Reading* 阅读

Joe is learning how to cook. He has to learn because he wants to start a small restaurant. His mother is teaching him. She used to be a chef at a big restaurant. With her help, he ought to have no problem. I'm sure Joe's restaurant is going to be the best restaurant in town.

乔正在学习如何烹饪。他必须要学,因为他想要开一家小餐厅。他母亲正在教他。她曾在一家大餐厅当过厨师。有了她的帮助,他应当不会有什么问题。我确信乔的餐厅将成为镇上最好的餐厅。

2 Vocabulary & Idioms 单词短语注解

1. **learn** [lɜːn] *vt.* & *vi.* 学习
   Sam learned three foreign languages in university.
   山姆在大学里学了三门外语。
   The smart young boy learns very fast.
   那个聪明的年轻男孩学东西很快。
2. **cook** [kʊk] *vi.* 烹饪
   My mother is cooking in the kitchen. 妈妈正在厨房煮饭。
3. **start** [stɑrt] *vt.* 开始(本文中指"设立")
4. **teach** [titʃ] *vt.* 教
   I need someone to teach me English composition.
   我需要有人能教我英文作文。
5. **主语 + used to + 动词原形** 以前曾经……
   used [just] *vi.* 惯常,向来(恒用过去式)
   I used to run five kilometers every morning.
   我以前每天早上都跑 5 公里。
6. **chef** [ʃɛf] *n.* 主厨,厨师
7. **ought to + 动词原形** 应当……
   ought [ɔt] *v. aux.* 应当
   Don't get so angry; you ought to be more patient.
   别这么生气,你应当更有耐心。
8. **problem** [ˋprɑbləm] *n.* 问题
   Fred's computer has a problem, so he's using a typewriter.
   弗雷德的计算机出了问题,因此他正在用打字机。
9. **be sure + that 引导的从句** 确定……
   Kate, be sure (that) you turn off the radio before going to sleep.
   凯特,你在上床前一定要把收音机关掉。
10. **in town** 在城镇中

town [taʊn] *n.* 城镇

Is this the only shoe store in town? 这是镇上唯一的一家鞋店吗?

3 *Grammar Points* 语法重点

本课继续介绍动词不定式的用法。

1. 以下是有关动词不定式的两个重要用法:

a. **Joe is learning how to cook.**

乔正在学习如何烹饪。

此处 how to cook 称作名词短语,由"疑问词 + 动词不定式"形成。如:

where to go 到哪儿去

when to do it 什么时候做这件事

how to do it 如何做这件事

what to do 做什么

whom to talk to 要跟谁说话

which to buy 要买哪一个

注意

1) 以上这些名词短语中,where、when、how 均为疑问副词,修饰之后的动词不定式。而 what、whom、which 则为疑问代词,要作动词不定式中及物动词的宾语,如上列名词短语中:what 作 do 的宾语,which 作 buy 的宾语。但疑问代词之后的动词不定式是不及物动词时,则该名词短语之后应有介词,使该疑问代词作该介词之宾语,如"whom to talk to"中 whom 即作介词 to 的宾语。

2) 名词短语具有名词的功能,在句中通常作及物动词的宾语。在"Joe is learning how to cook."一句中,how to cook 即作及物动词 learn 的现在进行时 is learning 的宾语。

例 He knows how to handle the problem.

vt. 名词短语

他懂得如何处理这个问题。

I don't know whom to work with. 我不知道要跟谁工作。
vt. 名词短语

b. **She used to be a chef at a big restaurant.**
她曾在一家大餐厅当过厨师。
此处 used to 表示“过去曾经……”的意思。句型如下：
主语 + used to + 动词原形
例 They used to live there. 他们以前曾在那里住过。
I used to study Japanese. 我以前曾经学过日文。
He used to be my student, but he is my colleague now.
他以前是我的学生，但现在却成了我的同事。

2. **I'm sure Joe's restaurant is going to be the best restaurant in town.**
我确信乔的餐厅将成为镇上最好的餐厅。
本句原为“I'm sure that Joe's restaurant is going to be the best restaurant in town.”。that 是连词，引导的从句修饰之前的形容词 sure，that 经常予以省略。
例 I am sure (that) he will be coming this afternoon.
我相信今天下午他会来。
= I believe (that) he will be coming this afternoon.

注意

在“I believe”之后由 that 引导的从句，因作及物动词 believe 的宾语，故称名词性从句，that 亦可省略。

4 Substitution 替换

1. Joe is learning how to cook.
Paul is wondering where to go on his vacation.
I don't know what to say.
I can't decide which restaurant to eat at.
乔正在学习如何烹饪。
保罗正在想要去哪里度假。

我不知道该说什么。

我无法决定去哪一家餐厅吃饭。

---

2. I'm sure (that) Joe's restaurant is going to be the best restaurant in town.

I think (that) our baseball team is the best team in the city.

Carl believes (that) his girlfriend is the prettiest girl in the school.

We're sure (that) we have the most caring parents in the world.

我确信乔的餐厅将成为镇上最好的餐厅。

我认为我们的棒球队是本市最好的队伍。

卡尔相信他的女友是学校里最漂亮的一个。

我们深信自己拥有世上最关心我们的父母。

Lesson 74

You Ought to Learn to Swim 你应当学习游泳

1 *Dialogue* 实用会话

Adam: Do you know how to swim?

Eva: No, I don't.

Adam: You ought to learn.

Eva: Why?

Adam: Well, maybe you'll have to save me one day.

亚当：你知道怎么游泳吗?

夏娃：不，我不知道。

亚当：你应当学习。

夏娃：为什么?

亚当：嗯，也许有一天你将必须救我。

2 *Key Points* 重点提示

1. **maybe** [ˋmebɪ] *adv.* 也许
   a. 使用本单词时应置于句首。
   例 He maybe can do it. (×)
   → Maybe he can do it. (√) 也许他能做这件事。
   b. maybe 与 may be 不一样,前者是副词,后者则为“助动词 may (也许) + be 动词 (是)”。

比较下列各句：

例 Maybe you are right. 也许你是对的。

You maybe right. (×)

→ You may be right. (√) 你也许是对的。

2. **save** [sev] *vt.* 拯救

例 In the movie, the hero saved the woman from drowning.

在这部电影中，那位英雄救了溺水的女士。

3 请选择下列各句中正确的一项

1. I don't know ______ to speak with.
   (A) where (B) how (C) when (D) whom
2. We haven't decided ______ to go for lunch yet.
   (A) whom (B) where (C) what (D) which
3. ______ it will rain today.
   (A) May be (B) Maybe
   (C) Might be (D) Could be
4. I'm ______ we'll have a good time.
   (A) think that (B) believe
   (C) sure (D) believe that
5. This ______ the best restaurant in town.
   (A) may be (B) maybe
   (C) perhaps (D) might

解答 1. (D) 2. (B) 3. (B) 4. (C) 5. (A)

Lesson 75

Michael's Dream

迈克尔的梦想

1 *Reading* 阅读

Michael wanted to be a musician, but his mother wanted him to be a doctor. Michael didn't want to make his mother feel sad, so he decided to obey her. Rather than play music, he studied medicine. Unfortunately, Michael failed to graduate from medical school. However, he isn't sad because he is now a famous musician.

迈克尔想要当音乐家,但他的母亲却希望他成为一名医生。迈克尔不想使他的母亲感到难过,因此他决定听她的话。他没有演奏音乐而改学医去了。不幸的是,迈克尔未能从医学院毕业。然而,他并不难过,因为他现在成了一位知名的音乐家。

2 Vocabulary & Idioms 单词短语注解

1. **musician** [mjuˋzɪʃən] *n.* 音乐家
2. **doctor** [ˋdɑktɚ] *n.* 医生
3. **decide** [dɪˋsaɪd] *vt.* 决定
   Joe had a sore throat, so he decided to stay home from school.
   乔喉咙痛,因此他决定待在家里而不去学校。
4. **obey** [əˋbe] *vt.* 服从
   When driving, you must obey the traffic regulations.
   开车时,你必须遵守交通规则。
5. **rather than...** 而不……,而非……
   Rather than play pool, we went bowling.
   我们没去打台球而去打保龄球。
6. **medicine** [ˋmɛdəsn̩] *n.* 医学
7. **unfortunately** [ʌnˋfɔrtʃənɪtlɪ] *adv.* 不幸地
   We wanted to go to the beach; unfortunately, it was raining.
   我们想去海边,不幸的是天空正在下雨。
8. **graduate from...** 毕业于……
   graduate [ˋgrædʒʊˏet] *vi.* 毕业
   After I graduated from university, I got a job in a trading company.
   大学毕业后,我在一家贸易公司找到一份工作。
9. **medical** [ˋmɛdɪkl̩] *a.* 医学的
   medical school 医学院
10. **famous** [ˋfeməs] *a.* 有名的
    This restaurant is famous for its steamed dumplings.
    这家餐厅以其蒸饺而闻名。

3 *Grammar Points* 语法重点

本课继续介绍有关动词不定式的其他重要用法,并介绍感官动词的用法。

1. **Michael wanted to be a musician, ...**
   迈克尔想要当音乐家……。
   ...so he decided to obey her. ……因此他决定听她的话。
   以上两句的动词 wanted(想要)及 decided (决定)均为表示意愿的及物动词过去式,之后须接动词不定式(即 to + 动词原形)作其宾语。
   常用的此类表示意愿的动词有:want、decide、expect (期望)、desire (渴望)、plan(计划)、wish (希望)、hope (希望)、try (设法)、attempt (企图)等。
   例 I wish to jog with him tomorrow morning.
   我希望明天早上跟他慢跑去。
   When do you plan to take the trip? 你计划什么时候去旅行?
   注意
   think 表示"想"或"认为",应使用 that 引导的名词性从句作宾语,不可使用动词不定式作宾语。
   例 I think to buy a bike for my son. (×)
   → I think (that) I'll buy a bike for my son. (√)
   我想我会买一辆自行车给我儿子。
   比较
   I want to buy a bike for my son. (√)
   我想要买一辆自行车给我儿子。

2. **Michael didn't want to make his mother feel sad ...**
   迈克尔不想使他的母亲感到难过……。
   a. 此处 make 表示"使/令……从事……"的意思,之后接宾语 his mother,再以动词原形 feel 及形容词 sad 形成的短语作宾语补足语。此类句型如下:
   make + 人 + 动词原形

例 Mother made me clean the house. 妈妈叫我打扫房子。

make 接宾语时,之后亦可置名词或形容词作宾语补足语,此时 make 表示"使 / 令……变成 / 成为……"的意思,句型如下:

make + 人 / 物 + 名词 / 形容词

例 The music made me happy. 这音乐令我快乐。

The teacher has made John a good boy.

老师使约翰变成了好孩子。

His help has made our plan quite successful.

他的帮助使我们的计划相当成功。

b. feel sad 感到难过的

此处 feel 表示"感到"的意思,是一种意思不完全的不及物动词,之后须接形容词。此类感官动词一共有五个,句型如下:

feel(感到) smell(闻起来) taste(尝起来) look(看起来) sound(听起来)	+ 形容词

例 The food smells really good. 这食物闻起来真香。
　　　　　　　　　　　a.

Though he is sixty, he looks young.
　　　　　　　　　　　　　　a.

虽然他已 60 岁了,但他看起来很年轻。

The idea sounds good. 这个主意听起来不错。
　　　　　　　　a.

3. **Rather than play music, he studied medicine.**

他没有演奏音乐而改学医去了。

此处 rather than 为并列连词,表示"而非"的意思,用以连接彼此为并列关系的单词、短语或从句等。

例 He is lazy rather than diligent. 他是懒惰,而非勤奋。
　　　a.　　　　　　　a.

Mary is a student rather than a teacher. 玛丽是学生而非老师。

n. n.

He is interested in swimming rather than (in) dancing.

介词短语 介词短语

他对游泳而非舞蹈有兴趣。

He failed because he was lazy rather than because he was stupid.

状语从句 状语从句

他失败是因为他懒惰而不是因为他愚蠢。

注意

a. rather than 亦可连接两个有并列关系的动词，句型如下：

rather than + 动词原形，主语 + 动词……

非但不……反而……

例 Rather than work hard, he plays around all the time.

= Instead of working hard, he plays around all the time.

他非但不用功，反而一直都在鬼混。

本课阅读中的"Rather than play music, he studied medicine."即属此用法。

b. rather than 亦可连接两个有并列关系的主语，之后的动词则应按第一个主语作变化。

例 He rather than I am wrong. (×)

→ He rather than I is wrong. (√) 是他错，而非我错。

4 Substitution 替换

1. Michael didn't want to make his mother feel sad.

We tried to make Jane feel happy.

I tried to make the soup taste better by adding salt.

She decided to quit smoking.

迈克尔不想让他的母亲感到难过。

我们设法让简感到高兴。

我在这道汤里加盐以试着让它的味道尝起来好一点。

她决定戒烟。

---

2. Rather than play music, he studied medicine.

I stayed home and slept rather than go to work.

Mike likes jazz rather than classical music.

They like living in the mountains rather than near the ocean.

他没有演奏音乐而改学医去了。

我待在家里睡觉而没有去工作。

迈克喜欢爵士乐而非古典音乐。

他们喜欢住在山中而非海边附近。

Lesson 76

I Want to Be a Doctor 我想当医生

1 *Dialogue* 实用会话

Mother: What do you want to be when you grow up?
Child: I want to be a doctor.
Mother: Why?
Child: I want to help sick people.

母亲：你长大以后想要当什么？
孩子：我想当医生。
母亲：为什么？
孩子：我想要帮助生病的人。

2 *Key Points* 重点提示

grow up 长大成人

例 I want to be a scientist when I grow up. 我长大后要做科学家。

3 请选择下列各句中正确的一项

1. Billy expects ______ his grandparents soon.
   (A) visit (B) to visit
   (C) visiting (D) paying a visit to

2. My boss ______ me work all weekend.
   (A) made (B) make
   (C) wanted making (D) wanted
3. ______ eat at home, we ate in a restaurant.
   (A) To (B) Instead
   (C) To not (D) Rather than
4. I think ______ camping this weekend.
   (A) to go (B) going
   (C) I'll to (D) that I'll go
5. He rather than I ______ successful.
   (A) is (B) are
   (C) am (D) have been

解答 1. (B) 2. (A) 3. (D) 4. (D) 5. (A)

Lesson 77

Rome Wasn't Built in a Day

罗马不是一天建成的

1 *Reading* 阅读

Learning English is like building a house. Laying a strong foundation is the first and most important step. In other words, you should read and speak English every day. Memorizing new words and phrases is also helpful. Like building a house, learning English takes some time. So don't be impatient. Remember, "Rome wasn't built in a day."

学英文就像盖房子一样。奠定扎实的基础是第一步也是最重要的一步。换句话说，你应该每天读英文和说英文。记新的单词和短语也是很有帮助的。就像盖房子一样，学英文需要一些时间。因此不要没有耐心。记住："罗马不是一天建成的。"

2 Vocabulary & Idioms 单词短语注解

1. **build** [bɪld] *vt.* 建造

   动词三态：build、built、built。

   It is said that the house was built more than two hundred years ago.

   据说这幢房子是 200 多年前建的。

2. **lay a strong foundation** 奠定坚实的基础

   lay [le] *vt.* 安放

   动词三态：lay、laid、laid。

   foundation [faʊnˋdeʃən] *n.* 基础

   When you build a house, you need to lay a strong foundation.

   盖房子时你需要先打下稳固的基础。

3. **important** [ɪmˋpɔrtn̩t] *a.* 重要的

   I have an important exam in history class tomorrow.

   明天我的历史课有一场重要的考试。

4. **step** [stɛp] *n.* 步骤

5. **in other words** 换句话说

   I have to work late tonight; in other words, I can't go to the movies with you.

   今晚我必须工作到很晚，换句话说，我不能和你一起去看电影。

6. **memorize** [ˋmɛməˏraɪz] *vt.* 记，背

   I can memorize every single word he said.

   我可以背下他所说的每个单词。

7. **phrase** [frez] *n.* 短语

8. **helpful** [ˋhɛlpfəl] *a.* 有帮助的

   My teacher gave me many helpful suggestions on how to improve my English.

   我的老师就如何改进我的英文方面给了我很多有帮助的建议。

9. **impatient** [ɪmˋpeʃənt] *a.* 不耐烦的，没耐性的

Don't be so impatient with Johnny; he's just a child.
别对约翰尼这么没耐性,他只是个孩子。

3 Grammar Points 语法重点

本课介绍动名词的用法。

动名词与现在分词的形态完全一样,均由动词加 -ing 形成,但功能不同。现叙述如下:

1. 现在分词

   a. 与 be 动词连用,形成进行时,表示"正在……"的意思。

   例 He is swimming now. 他现在正在游泳。

   b. 作形容词,表示"令人……的"的意思。

   例 Who is that charming girl over there?
   那边那位迷人的女孩子是谁?
   The question is confusing. 这个问题令人迷惑。

2. 动名词

   动名词可视为名词,功能与名词一样,有下列用法:

   a. 作主语

   名词:
   The boy is his son. 那男孩是他的儿子。
   动名词:
   Swimming is my hobby. 游泳是我的爱好。

   b. 作及物动词或介词的宾语

   名词:
   No one enjoyed that movie. 没人喜欢那部电影。
   He is interested in music. 他对音乐有兴趣。
   动名词:
   I enjoy listening to music. 我喜欢听音乐。
   I am sick of talking to him. 我讨厌跟他说话。

   c. 作表语(置于 be 动词之后,作表语)

   名词:

He is my teacher. 他是我的老师。

动名词：

My hobby is swimming. 我的爱好是游泳。

d. 作定语(置于名词之前作形容词,修饰该名词)

名词：

Can I borrow your chemistry book?

n. n.

你的化学书可不可以借给我？

动名词：

I lost my walking stick. 我把我的拐杖弄丢了。

动名词 n.

3. 动名词与现在分词的分辨：

初学英语的读者见到 be 动词之后或名词之前有词尾为 -ing 的单词时,不易分辨该单词是现在分词或动名词。其实我们可通过中文的翻译来破解这个迷惑。

a. "be 动词 + 词尾为 -ing 的单词"若可译成"正在……"时,则该单词是现在分词,形成进行时的句子结构。

例 英文：He is swimming.

中译：他正在游泳。

说明：swimming 是现在分词。

b. "be 动词 + 词尾为 -ing 的单词"若译成"令人……的"时,则该单词仍是现在分词,作形容词,在句中作表语。

例 英文：The question is confusing.

中译：这问题令人迷惑。

说明：此处 confusing 是现在分词。

c. "be 动词 + 词尾为 -ing 的单词"若译成"是……"时,则该单词是动名词,且该动名词可与主语互换位置。

例 英文：His hobby is swimming.

中译：他的爱好是游泳。

说明：swimming 是动名词。

His hobby is swimming.

= Swimming is his hobby. 游泳是他的爱好。

d. 在"词尾为 -ing 的单词 + 名词"中,若该单词译成"令人……的"时,或"主动会……的"时,则该单词是现在分词作形容词,修饰之后的名词。

例 英文 : He asked a confusing question.
a. n.

中译 : 他问了一个令人迷惑的问题。

英文 : He knows many words, so we call him a walking dictionary.
a. n.

中译 : 他认识许多字,因此我们称他为"活字典"。

说明 : 此处 confusing 表示"令人迷惑的", walking 则表示"会走路的",即"活的"之意。confusing 与 walking 均为现在分词。

e. 在"词尾为 -ing 的单词 + 名词"中,若该单词译成"供……之用的"时,则该单词是动名词,仍作形容词,修饰之后的名词。

例 英文 : I lost my walking stick.
a. n.

中译 : 我把我那供来走路用的棍子弄丢了。

即 : 我把我的拐杖弄丢了。

说明 : 此处 walking 是动名词。

现在我们且来自我测验一下,通过译文分辨下列各句中词尾为 -ing 的单词,何者是动名词,何者是现在分词。

1) He is smoking.
2) His bad habit is smoking.
3) There is a swimming pool near my house.
4) I enjoy swimming with them.
5) Mary is swimming with us.
6) The news is exciting.

1) 他正在抽烟。(smoking 是现在分词)
2) 他的不良爱好是抽烟。(smoking 是动名词)
3) 我家附近有一座游泳池。(swimming 是动名词,译成"供来游泳的")

4) 我喜欢跟他们游泳。（swimming 是动名词，作及物动词 enjoy 的宾语）
5) 玛丽正在跟我们游泳。（swimming 是现在分词）
6) 这消息令人兴奋。（exciting 是现在分词）

4. 及物动词变成动名词时，之后仍应接宾语，该动名词作主语时，不论其宾语是单数、复数或不可数名词，之后应接单数动词。

例 Writing English is easy for him. 对他来说，写英文很容易。
(Writing: 动名词; English: n.)

Climbing mountains is my hobby. 爬山是我的爱好。
(Climbing: 动名词; mountains: n.)

4 Substitution 替换

1. Learning English is like building a house.
I love learning new things.
That university has a foreign language learning center.
Harry is tired of learning how to play the guitar.
学英文就像盖房子一样。
我喜欢学习新的东西。
那所大学有一个外语学习中心。
哈里厌烦了学弹吉他。

---

2. Memorizing new words and phrases is also helpful.
Reading these books is a good idea.
Watching TV is a waste of time.
记新的单词和短语也是很有帮助的。
阅读这些书是个不错的主意。
看电视是浪费时间。

Lesson 78

Don't Be Discouraged 不要泄气

1 Dialogue 实用会话

Teacher : Your written English is fairly good, but your spoken English needs improvement.

Student : I know, but speaking English is difficult.

Teacher : Don't be discouraged. Practice makes perfect.

老师：你的书面英语还不错，但你的英文口语就需要加强了。

学生：我知道，但讲英文很难啊。

老师：不要泄气。熟能生巧嘛。

2 Key Points 重点提示

1. **written English** [ˌrɪtn̩ ˈɪŋglɪʃ] *n.* 书面英语
2. **spoken English** [ˌspokən ˈɪŋglɪʃ] *n.* 英语口语
3. **improvement** [ɪmˈpruvmənt] *n.* 改善

   例 "I don't see any improvement in your work," the boss said.
   老板说："我看不出你的工作有任何改善。"
4. **discouraged** [dɪsˈkɝɪdʒd] *a.* 泄气的，沮丧的

   例 Jim was discouraged by his exam result.
   吉姆对他的考试成绩感到很沮丧。
5. **Practice makes perfect.** 熟能生巧。(谚语)

3 请选择下列各句中正确的一项

1. Frank really ______ to his pen pal.
   (A) enjoy writing (B) enjoy to write
   (C) enjoys writing (D) enjoys to write
2. I'm tired ______ you to clean your room.
   (A) of telling (B) to tell
   (C) of tell (D) for telling
3. ______ a bicycle is good exercise.
   (A) Riding (B) Driving
   (C) Sitting (D) Going on
4. I've been thinking ______ a computer.
   (A) to buy (B) buying
   (C) of buying (D) in buying
5. Playing basketball with my friends ______ a lot of fun.
   (A) are (B) is (C) am (D) were

解答 1. (C) 2. (A) 3. (A) 4. (C) 5. (B)

Lesson 79

Showing Off

炫耀

1 *Reading* 阅读

Many people are fond of showing off. They always insist on footing the bill when they are out with friends. They always think of impressing people with their wealth. They seem to think that money can buy friends. In fact, it can't. Instead of trying to show off, they should be themselves.

有很多人喜欢炫耀。当他们和朋友外出时总是争着付账。他们老是想用自己的财富给别人留下深刻的印象。他们似乎认为钱可以买到朋友。但事实上，钱无法买到朋友。他们不应炫耀，而应做真正的自我。

2 Vocabulary & Idioms 单词短语注解

1. **show off** 炫耀
   I think people who show off are silly. 我认为爱炫耀的人是很愚蠢的。
2. **be fond of...** 喜欢……
   fond [fɑnd] *a.* 喜欢的
   My mother is not only fond of cooking; she's also a wonderful cook.
   我母亲不只喜欢烹饪,她还是很棒的厨师。
3. **insist on + 动名词** 坚持要……
   insist [ɪnˋsɪst] *vi.* 坚持
   Whenever I take my son out to dinner, he insists on eating hamburgers.
   每当我带我儿子外出晚餐时,他总是坚持要吃汉堡。
4. **foot the bill** 付账
   He didn't have enough money to foot the bill. 他没有足够的钱付账。
5. **impress + 人 + with + 事物** 以某事物使人印象深刻
   impress [ɪmˋprɛs] *vt.* 使印象深刻
   Bob impressed us with his knowledge of world history.
   鲍勃对世界史的知识使我们印象深刻。
6. **wealth** [wɛlθ] *n.* 财富
   The king has great wealth. 这个国王拥有大笔的财富。
7. **seem to + 动词原形** 似乎……
   seem [sim] *vi.* 似乎
   John seems to be happy, but I can't be sure.
   约翰似乎很快乐,但我不能肯定。
8. **instead of + 动名词** ... 非但不……反而……
   instead [ɪnˋstɛd] *adv.* 代替
   Instead of riding bicycles, let's go for a walk.
   咱们不要骑自行车，改去散步吧。
9. **be oneself** 做真实的自我

Don't be nervous about your interview; just be yourself and you'll do fine.

别担心你的面试，你只要表现出真正的自我就会做得很好。

3 Grammar Points 语法重点

本课强调动名词可作介词的宾语之用法。

Many people are fond of showing off. 有很多人喜欢炫耀。

They always insist on footing the bill when they are out with friends.

他们与朋友外出时总是争着付账。

以上两句中 showing off 及 footing the bill 均为动名词短语，分别作介词 of 及 on 的宾语。

在前一课中，我们已说明动名词除可作及物动词的宾语外，亦可作介词的宾语。

例 I'm looking forward to seeing you again soon.

我期盼很快再与你见面。

* look forward to 期盼

（to 是介词，故之后应接动名词作其宾语。）

He's thinking about getting married this year. 他正考虑今年要结婚。

4 Substitution 替换

1. Many people are fond of showing off.

   Some people are good at singing, and some are good at dancing.

   Some people are afraid of watching horror movies.

   Turn off the lights before leaving the house.

   有很多人喜欢炫耀。

   有些人擅长唱歌，而有些人擅长跳舞。

   有些人害怕看恐怖电影。

离开屋子前要把灯关掉。

---

2. Instead of trying to show off, they should be themselves.
   Instead of waiting for his friends, he left by himself.
   Rather than wait for his friends, he left by himself.
   他们不应炫耀，而应做真正的自我。
   他没等他的朋友，而是自己离开了。
   他没等他的朋友，而是自己离开了。

Lesson 80

I'm Good at Cooking

我擅长烹饪

1 Dialogue 实用会话

Marty: Are you good at sewing?

Becky: No, but I'm good at cooking. What about you?

Marty: I'm not good at cooking, but I'm fond of eating.

马蒂：你对缝纫很在行吗?

贝基：不，但我对烹饪很在行。你呢?

马蒂：我对烹饪不在行，但我却很喜欢吃。

2 Key Points 重点提示

1. **cooking** [ˋkʊkɪŋ] *n.* 烹饪

   cook [kʊk] *vt.* & *vi.* 烹饪

   例 My sister's cooking is terrible. 我姐姐的烹饪很糟糕。

   Mother cooked some dumplings for lunch. 妈妈午餐时煮了些水饺。

2. **be good at...** 精通于……，擅长于……

   例 Frank is good at playing the piano but is terrible at singing.

   弗兰克擅长弹钢琴,但歌却唱得很难听。

3. **sewing** [ˋsoɪŋ] *n.* 缝纫

   sew [so] *vt.* 缝(衣服)

   例 Mother sewed the buttons onto one of my shirts.

   妈妈把纽扣缝在我的一件衬衫上面。

3 请选择下列各句中正确的一项

1. Bob is bad ______ baseball.
   (A) at play (B) playing
   (C) at playing (D) and plays
2. John is thinking ______ changing his major.
   (A) about (B) in (C) on (D) for
3. Instead of studying with his friends, he studied ______.
   (A) by himself (B) of his own
   (C) by hisself (D) on himself
4. Rather than ______ to work, Bill took a bus.
   (A) walking (B) to walk
   (C) of walking (D) walk
5. Are you afraid ______ him the truth?
   (A) to telling (B) of telling
   (C) of tell (D) telling
6. Charlie is ______ playing basketball. In fact, he's the best player in our school.
   (A) really good for (B) good really in
   (C) very good about (D) very good at

解答 1. (C) 2. (A) 3. (A) 4. (D) 5. (B) 6. (D)

♫怀念老歌园地♫

Tennessee Waltz

田纳西华尔兹

C3/4

by Patti Page

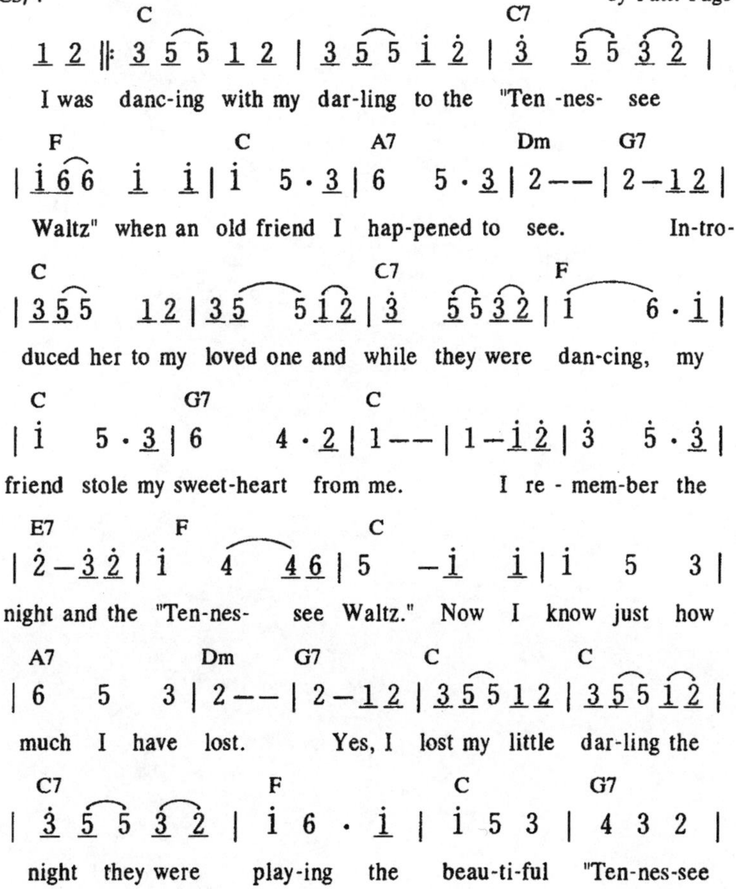

C　　　　　　　　　　C
| 1 – – | 1 – 1. 2 :‖ 1 – – | 1 – – ‖

Waltz."　　　　I was

♫怀念老歌园地♫

Tennessee Waltz

田纳西华尔兹

1 *Lyrics* 歌词

I was dancing with my darling to the "Tennessee Waltz" when an old friend I happened to see. Introduced her to my loved one and while they were dancing, my friend stole my sweetheart from me. I remember the night and the "Tennessee Waltz." Now I know just how much I have lost. Yes, I lost my little darling the night they were playing the beautiful "Tennessee Waltz."

我和爱人随着田纳西华尔兹起舞时，碰巧遇见一位老朋友。我把她介绍给我的爱人，当他们俩在跳舞时，我朋友偷走了我的爱人。我记得那一夜和那首田纳西华尔兹。现在我知道我的损失有多大。是的，就在那一夜他们播放那首动听的田纳西华尔兹时，我失去我的爱人。

2 Vocabulary & Idioms 单词短语注解

1. **Tennessee Waltz** 田纳西华尔兹(一首华尔兹舞曲)

   Tennessee [ˋtɛnəˏsi] *n.* (美国)田纳西州

   waltz [wɔlts] *n.* 华尔兹舞(曲) & *vi.* 跳华尔兹舞

   Most youngsters don't know how to waltz.

   大部分的年轻人都不会跳华尔兹舞。

2. **dance with + 人 + to...** 与某人随着……起舞

   My father danced with my mother to the music of Strauss.

   我父亲与母亲随着斯特劳斯的音乐起舞。

3. **happen to + 动词原形** 碰巧……,意外地……

   = 动词 + | by accident / accidentally |

   accident [ˋæksədənt] *n.* 意外,事故

   accidentally [ˏæksəˋdɛntḷɪ] *adv.* 意外地

   I happened to meet my old friend in the supermarket yesterday.

   = I met my old friend by accident in the supermarket yesterday.

   昨天我和老友在超级市场不期而遇。

   Jim broke a leg in a car accident last year.

   去年吉姆在一场车祸中断了条腿。

4. **I was dancing with my darling to the "Tennessee Waltz" when an old friend I happened to see.**

   我和我的爱人随着田纳西华尔兹起舞时,碰巧遇见了一位老友。

   主语 + | was / were | + 现在分词 + when 引导的过去时从句

   正在……就……

   I was enjoying my ice cream when Peter came in.

   我正在享受冰淇淋时,彼得就进来了。

   He was taking a bath when the telephone rang.

   他正在洗澡时,电话就响了。

   类似句型:

主语 + | was / were | + | going to / about to | + 动词原形 + when 引导的过去时从句

正要……,这时……

She was going to go out when it rained.

她正要出门,这时天空却下雨了。

They were about to eat dinner when the lights went out suddenly.

他们正要吃晚餐,这时灯光突然熄灭了。

5. **introduce** [ˌɪntrəˋdus] *vt.* 介绍

introduction [ˌɪntrəˋdʌkʃən] *n.* 介绍

introduce A to B　把 A 介绍给 B 认识

I will introduce my best friend to you at the party tonight.

今晚的聚会中我将介绍我最要好的朋友给你认识。

The actor is so famous that he doesn't need an introduction.

那位男演员太有名了,因此不需任何介绍。

6. **steal** [stil] *vt.* 偷窃 & *vi.* 偷偷行走,潜行

动词三态 : steal、stole、stolen。

The thief stole my gold watch. 那个小偷偷走了我的金表。

Simon came stealing out of the closet. 西蒙从衣橱中偷偷地走出来。

7. **sweetheart** [ˋswitˌhɑrt] *n.* 甜心,爱人

= honey [ˋhʌnɪ]

He bought his sweetheart a dozen roses on her birthday.

他在女友生日时买了 12 朵玫瑰送她。

8. **Introduced her to my loved one and while they were dancing, my friend stole my sweetheart from me.**

我把我的朋友介绍给我爱人认识,当他们俩在跳舞时,我的朋友偷走了我的爱人。

a. Introduced her to my loved one 为一不完整的句子,因为没有主语。事实上,依照语法和语意, Introduced 之前应该有主语 I (我), 但在歌曲中,为了迁就旋律的音节而省略了。

b. while [waɪl] *conj.* 当……时 ; 而 while 作副词连词,引导状语从

句时,句中动词常用进行时,表“当……时”。

While he was watching TV, he heard a strange sound.

在他看电视的时候,他听见一个奇怪的声音。

但 while 亦可作并列连词,连接两个主句,表示“而”。

He is tall while his brother is short. 他长得很高而他弟弟却很矮。

Some people are rich while others are poor.

有些人很有钱而有些却很穷。

9. **I remember the night and the "Tennessee Waltz."**

我记得那一夜和那首田纳西华尔兹。

remember [rɪˋmɛmbɚ] *vt.* 记得

forget [fɚˋgɛt] *vt.* 忘记

remember 和 forget 除了以名词作宾语外,还可用不定式或动名词作宾语,但意思稍有不同,这里分列如下:

remember to + 动词原形　记得去……

remember + 动名词　记得曾经……

forget to + 动词原形　忘记去……

forget + 动名词　忘记曾经……

I will remember to buy some flowers for you.

我会记得去买些花来送你。

I remember seeing this movie before.

我记得以前曾经看过这部电影。

She forgot to mail the letter this morning.

今天早上她忘了去寄这封信。

Did you forget swimming in the lake with me?

你是否忘记曾经和我在这个湖里游泳?

10. **lose** [luz] *vt.* 失去,失落

lost [lɔst] *a.* 迷路的

lose 的动词三态为 lose、lost、lost。

be lost 迷路

I lost my watch while swimming. 我游泳时丢了手表。

The farmer was lost in the streets of London.

那名农民在伦敦的街道上迷了路。

11. **I lost my little darling the night they were playing the beautiful "Tennessee Waltz."**

a b

我失去我的爱人,就在那一夜他们播放那首动听的田纳西华尔兹时。

句型分析:

a. 为主句

b. 为状语从句

上列 b 句原为 on the night when...,但介词 on 及关系副词 when 已省略,故定冠词 the 加上时间名词可视为连词。

The day On the day when	he visited Dr. Lee, it was raining hard.

他拜访李博士那天正下着大雨。

The minute I saw her, I fell in love with her.

我在看到她的那一刻就爱上她了。

英式 IPA 音标与美式 K.K. 音标对照表

序号	IPA	K.K.	Key Words
1	ɪ	ɪ	bit
2	e	ɛ	bed
3	æ	æ	cat
4	ɒ	ɑ	hot
5	ʌ	ʌ	cut
6	ʊ	ʊ	put
7	ə	ə	about
8	i	ɪ	happy
9	u	ʊ	actuality
10	iː	i	bee
11	ɑː	ɑ	father
12	ɔː	ɔ	law
13	uː	u	tool
14	ɜː	ɝ	bird
15	eɪ	e	name
16	aɪ	aɪ	lie
17	ɔɪ	ɔɪ	boy
18	əʊ	o	no
19	aʊ	aʊ	out
20	ɪə	ɪr	beer
21	eə	ɛr	hair
22	ʊə	ʊr	tour
23	uə	ʊə	actual
24	iə	jɚ	peculiar

Notes:

1. K.K.音标取自美国两位语言学家 John S. Kenyon 和 Thomas A. Knott 两人姓氏的第一个字母。其特点是按照一般的美国读法标音。

2. 本列表所用的 IPA 音标是英国 Jones 音标的最新修订形式。

3. K.K.音标除辅音中[n̩]、[l̩]与IPA音标[n]、[l]符号不同外, 其余基本一致。

4. 美式和英式发音的不同点之一是卷舌音。如果单词的字母组合含有 r，该组合一般会发卷舌音。例：four ［fɔː］（IPA）；［fɔr］（K.K.）。